A BLAKE MORETTI THRILLER

MISTY RIVER

SMALL TOWNS AREN'T WHAT
THEY APPEAR TO BE

DAVID FRANCESCHELLI

ISBN-hardback: 979-8-35093-859-3
ISBN-e-reader: 979-8-35093-015-3

IABN audiobook

First Hardback Edition 2023

Cover art design by Rachel Kelli

Published by: BookBaby

To order additional copies of this book, contact:
https://www.davidfranceschelli.com

To all those who invite storytellers into their lives,
if only for a moment. Without you, stories
would go untold and be lost forever. Thank you
for allowing me to share my story with you.

TABLE OF CONTENTS

MISTY RIVER

EPIGRAPH

"The world is dark, and light is precious.
Come closer, dear reader.
You must trust me.
I am telling you a story."

—*Kate DiCamillo*

PROLOGUE

There is something warm and welcoming about small towns, which are often associated with tranquility and safety. Yet they can be sinister, with danger lurking all around.

Every murder happens somewhere, and this one happened in the small town of Misty River, in Leigh County, New York, located on the banks of the great Misty River. The Misty River snakes around the outskirts of the town, dividing it into two vastly different places.

As the sun rises, light filters through solitary clouds reflecting off the water, while wisps of mist drift across the distant horizon. The splashing and honking of geese can be heard, and ducks waddle on the moving current, indifferent to the fishermen who gather on the banks. As the sun sets in the evening, the fishing boats return to shore, and the dark river becomes a mirror.

At night, the Misty River becomes a forbidden place, ghostly gray, surrounded by a dark forest that exudes a musty, pungent smell from the deadfall and leaves. A single misstep can swallow a person whole.

The murder that occurred there remained unsolved for two years until a brutal rape brought a warm twist to the cold case.

PART ONE

"I've just got to get a message to you.

Hold on, hold on.

One more hour and my life will be through.

Hold on, hold on."

—Bee Gees. "I've Gotta Get a Message to You."

Idea. Atco Records, 1968.

CHAPTER 1

Cold Blooded Murder

March 2, 1985, Saturday morning

The date was Saturday, March 2, 1985. The time was around seven o'clock in the morning. The sun was hiding, and heavy rain appeared hovering over the nearby Misty River. It was the perfect day for a murder.

The town's quaint Italian bakery customarily filled the morning air with the lingering scent of freshly baked bread and pastries. But today, that comforting aroma was tainted by the metallic tang of blood.

In the peaceful and serene town of Misty River, a merciless, cold-blooded murder stunned its residents. The news of this violent act quickly permeated the tight-knit community, spreading like wildfire and leaving its inhabitants in a state of profound disbelief. The tranquility they once cherished was shattered, replaced by an overwhelming sense of fear and confusion. They grappled to comprehend how such a heinous crime could have taken place within the confines of their seemingly idyllic small town.

Frank Amoia, the beloved owner of the town's Italian bakery, was found dead, lying in a pool of blood on the restroom floor. A man had raised his right hand, clutching a knife, and slashed Frank Amoia's throat from ear to ear.

$$\mathbb{Q}$$

In 1950, Frank and his wife, Mary, moved to Misty River from Brooklyn, New York, and opened an Italian bakery in the historic Crossman building. The bakery was, and still is, on Lansing Street, on the south side of downtown. The brick paver-laid street is lined with Federal and Queen Anne-style buildings. For thirty-five years, the bakery was a local treasure.

$$\mathbb{Q}$$

Frank routinely arrived at the bakery at five in the morning to prepare for the seven o'clock opening. That morning, he and his wife got up before dawn as usual. When he arrived downstairs, she had coffee ready, and breakfast was on the table.

"Mary, have you made a decision?"

"Are you referring to selling the bakery and moving to Florida?"

"You know darn well what I am referring to. You're stalling. We both know the bakery business is grueling. Besides, aren't you sick of the snow and freezing winters?"

"I get it. You sound like a broken record. I told you I need more time. I am concerned we don't have the money to make that move."

"I'll have the money. It won't be a problem. I talked to Sonny, and he agreed to buy our interest in the business."

"Frank, I realize Sonny Calo is your best friend and business partner, and you are godfather to his oldest son. But Sonny doesn't know a damn thing about running a bakery. Sonny is a mob boss. The business would fold the minute you and I walked out the door.

"You know how much I love you. But it scares me to think about selling the business and moving to Florida. We have it good here. Misty River is where all our friends live."

"I don't know how else to say it. I'll have the money. We will make new friends."

Frank talked a bit longer than usual. Realizing he was late, he hurried out the door. After hopping into his 1980 green Volkswagen Beetle, he headed to the bakery. At 4:30 in the morning, there was no traffic. He drove the empty streets in silence, his favorite part of the day.

The moment he unlocked the bakery door, Frank felt dread wash over him. He was unaware the time had run out to say goodbye to his loved ones and atone for his sins.

Shortly before seven, the bakery was ready for the day's customers. He flipped the "Closed" sign hanging in the window to "Open" and went to the back restroom to replenish the paper towels, leaving the front of the store unattended. Frank hummed a tune as he worked, unaware of the danger lurking outside.

Outside the bakery on Lansing Street, a man in a black leather jacket, saggy jeans, and worn cowboy boots concealed himself behind an ornamental lamppost, staring into the display window, watching every move Frank made, waiting for the right moment to strike. When he saw Frank enter the restroom, he slipped out from behind the lamppost and made his move.

The bell above the door jingled as he stepped into the cozy bakery. He locked the door behind him, flipped the sign from "Open" to "Closed," and scanned the shop, looking for his target. As the man approached the restroom in the back of the bakery, he peeked inside. He saw Frank's back, crept up behind him, and pulled a Buck hunting knife from a leather sheath hanging from his belt. Before Frank could move, the man wrapped his left arm around his body and arms.

Frank's instinct was to fight back, but he couldn't move. With his right hand still grasping the knife, the man reached around, pulled Frank's head back, and slit his throat in one swift motion. Blood sprayed everywhere. The wound deepened from one ear to the other, then faded. As Frank collapsed on the ground, covered in blood and unable to scream, he gasped for air. The man clutched the sharp knife in his right hand, leaned over Frank's twitching body, and whispered in his ear, "Sorry pal, nothing personal," plunging the instrument of death several times into Frank's chest for good measure.

He rolled Frank onto his side, leaning him against the door, removed a wad of cash from Frank's blood-stained pants pocket, then stood up and stuffed it into the right front pocket of his jeans.

Trying to rid himself of guilt, he began washing his bloody hands and murder weapon in the sink, but soon realized his clothes and boots were also stained. There was precious little time left before someone discovered him covered in blood, standing over Frank's lifeless body. The room was filled with an eerie silence, broken only by the killer's heavy breathing and the sound of his boots leaving bloody bootprints as he began his escape. As he pulled the door closed, Frank's dead body rolled from his side to his back, barricading the closed door.

Desperate for money, before fleeing the murder scene, he made one more stop. It was worth the risk of being caught red-handed. As he made a mad dash to the pantry, bloody bootprints followed. There were thousands of dollars in the pantry waiting to be stolen. The money mattered, and he wasn't leaving without it. He ransacked the pantry, looking for the stash, but all he found was flour and sugar.

With anger coursing through his veins, he stormed out of the pantry, hastily unlocked the front door, and wiped his fingerprints from the door handle, leaving behind a dead baker, a scene of horror, bloody bootprints, and the one clue that would, over time, identify him as the killer.

Unbeknownst to the killer, hidden in the shadows of the alley across the street, a lone figure watched the man covered in blood exit the bakery. His heart pounded in his chest, and fear gripped him, knowing that he had become an unintended witness to what could only be a heinous crime. He knew he had to remain silent to evade the killer's notice. He had no desire to become involved. But deep down, he also knew that he held a crucial piece of information that could eventually lead to the identification of the killer.

CHAPTER 2

A Suspicious Death

March 2, 1985, Saturday morning

At 7:35 a.m., when Robby Benton stopped by the bakery, he was surprised the glass door displayed the "Closed" sign. Frank always opened it at seven, so when Robby tried the handle, he was surprised the door wasn't locked. Frank never left the door unlocked when the bakery was closed. Robby curiously peered through the glass window, but there was no sign of Frank. So, Robby entered the store, calling Frank's name. No one responded. He searched for Frank and saw a trail of bloody bootprints leading from the front door to the restroom.

Blood was oozing beneath the closed restroom door. Panicked, he called "Frank? Frank!" His brain couldn't keep up with what his eyes were seeing. His hands trembled, and his knees buckled. He decided to call the sheriff.

At 7:45 a.m., Officer Harvey Gates, a seven-year Leigh County Sheriff's Office veteran, was driving Lansing Street on routine patrol. He planned to stop and grab a coffee and, hopefully, a free Italian pastry at Amoia's Bakery when his radio phone lit up.

Gates routinely stopped at the bakery under the pretense of checking on Mr. Amoia. He was a sucker for the homemade cannoli, and Amoia never charged him for it, throwing in a complimentary cup of coffee. Half-heartedly, he refused, but Amoia always insisted.

Now Gates flicked on his blue lights and siren, turned around, and sped towards the bakery.

Robby was standing outside, visibly shaken.

"Sir, take a deep breath and tell me what happened."

"I stopped by for my usual coffee and a pastry. Mr. Amoia always displayed the "Open" sign when he unlocked the door. But the "Closed" sign was displayed this morning, and the door unlocked.

"I went inside, but no one was in sight, so I called Frank's name. He didn't answer and I couldn't see him anywhere, so I started to look for him. That's when I noticed a trail of blood leading to the restroom. The restroom door was closed, and blood was seeping out. I panicked because I thought Mr. Amoia might be in there, so I used the bakery phone to call you guys."

Gates's educated guess was that Amoia was in the restroom. "Would you mind waiting in my cruiser and writing everything you just told me? I'm gonna take a look around. I'll have another officer follow up with you."

Gates got on the radio. Deputies and rescue units were at the scene in minutes.

At 7:48 a.m., homicide Detective Bob Massey of the Leigh County Sheriff's Office shoveled four teaspoons of sugar into his black coffee.

Two hundred and fifty thousand people live in Leigh County. Massey joked he would never be out of a job in law enforcement. Without skipping a beat, his number was called.

Sergeant Cain interrupted his first sip. "I just got a call about a "suspicious death" at Amoia's bakery. I'm assigning you the investigation, and I need you out there now."

"Any details?"

"A customer saw blood on the floor, but no one was around."

"It never fails. The first call always comes before I've had my coffee."

"Take your coffee with you and bring the new camcorder. The sheriff insists we use it. He doesn't want any flak from the city council for spending all that money on the damn thing."

Massey had been investigating homicide scenes for two decades, but no matter how hard-boiled an investigator got, there was always one murder scene that would be too brutal to forget. It is common for homicide investigators to try and convince themselves that the next crime scene couldn't be worse than the one they're working on. But that is nothing more than wishful thinking. Inevitably, it gets worse. That day had arrived for Massey.

With his coffee in one hand and the camcorder in the other, he headed to the crime scene that would haunt him for years to come.

A short time later, Massey met Gates at the closed restroom door.

"So, whatcha got?"

"The witness is a frequent bakery customer," he said, reporting Robby's statement.

"Did he say if he noticed anyone else in or around the store?"

"Not really, but after he called the sheriff's office, he saw a home-less-looking guy sitting on the bench across the street. He told the deputies the guy walked off towards the alley."

"So, we're disqualifying the guy as a potential witness because he looks like he's homeless? Where's the guy now?"

"He's gone."

Massey shook his head. As usual, half the sheriff's department had arrived at the crime scene, but no one thought it was necessary to interview a guy who could have been the perpetrator or, at the very least, an eyewitness.

Outside the bakery, a bunch of recent Sheriff Academy graduates were socializing. "Nice day for a murder," Massey said.

"Gosh, Detective, do you think that's what happened?"

"I wouldn't know, since none of you jokers bothered to open the restroom door."

"We tried, sir," an eager young recruit said, "but something is blocking it. We didn't want to mess up the crime scene. So, we're awaiting instructions on how to proceed."

"And you never thought of getting your toolbox and removing the door and frame?"

"Sir, that's a great idea."

Massey turned to Gates, who had come up behind him. "The department paid a fortune for this new video camcorder. Does anybody know how to work it? I want the crime scene investigation recorded."

One of the young deputies grabbed the camcorder and started filming the technicians removing the door. He pointed the recorder into the restroom when the door was removed. Disturbed at what he saw, he almost dropped the camera. He had never seen anything so ghastly. A lifeless body was covered in blood on the floor, lying in a grotesque pose reminiscent of a slasher movie. It sent shivers down his spine.

Massey began to inspect the room. It was so small you couldn't swing a cat in it, with just enough room for a toilet, sink, paper dispenser, metal trash basket, and one dead man. Massey, a seasoned homicide detective who thought he'd seen everything, was rattled. The man's throat had been slit from ear to ear. His nearly severed head, body, and clothing were all soaked in blood. Massey turned away in disgust.

As Detective Massey surveyed the room, an unsettling feeling washed over him. The Detective meticulously observed every minute detail of the crime scene. It became evident that this was no ordinary murder, but rather a malevolent act driven by an evil, twisted mind. The room itself seemed to mirror the chaos of the crime.

The man's head was closest to the door, and his feet rested on the opened toilet. He wore a beige shirt, blue Levi pants, a brown belt, white socks, and brown lace-up shoes. Massey guessed the victim was about six feet five inches tall, an older, wiry-framed man, his graying hair stained blood red. His face was painted in blood, making it difficult to discern his features. But when he bent down to make a closer inspection, Massey recognized Frank Amoia's dark eyes, long nose, razor-sharp cheekbones, and jutting chin. The body was still flaccid and warm to the touch. Mr. Amoia hadn't been dead for long.

Massey straightened up and ran a chubby hand over his nearly bald head. "I swear, as God is my witness, I'll catch the bastard who did this."

He zeroed in on Frank's pants pocket. "Are you seeing what I'm seeing?"

His sergeant replied, "I'm looking at it now."

"His front pants pocket is inside out," said Massey.

"Well, if nothing else, we have a motive: greed," replied the Sergeant.

Massey's eyes were drawn to a dime floating in the blood. He sarcastically commented, "I guess money bags didn't need it. Call the medical examiner's office. That's a wrap on the suspicious death call. We now have a verified murder, the likes of which I have never witnessed before."

The Leigh County Medical Examiner, Dr. Daniel Smith, arrived at thirty minutes past eight with his investigators. The doctor's external examination of the victim's body revealed that Amoia had been repeatedly stabbed in the torso, in addition to the sharp-force trauma to the throat. The cause of death, pending a complete autopsy, appeared to have been the severing of the carotid arteries.

"Here's something you might find interesting," the doctor pointed out. "It appears the victim was still alive when the assailant stabbed him in his stomach and chest. The angles of the stab wounds suggest they were inflicted after the victim's throat was cut as he lay dying on the floor. I suspect the killer wanted to be sure the victim was dead before he left."

Massey quipped, "There's nothing like a goal-oriented killer on the loose. Can you estimate the time of death?"

"Yes. But I need time to take the victim's body temperature."

Doctor Smith made a small incision in the upper right abdomen and passed the thermometer into Amoia's liver tissue. Forensic doctors use the standard cooling curve: hours since death=98.6-corpse core temperature/1.5, to estimate the time of death.

He said, "Considering this victim's body temperature, lack of rigor mortis and livor mortis, I estimate the time of death between seven and seven thirty."

"Thanks, Doctor."

"Unless you need anything further, we'll take the body to the morgue."

Now it was left to Massey to inform the widow. God, how he hated that part of the job.

Deputy Gates shouted, "Detective, you better check this out before you leave."

Massey walked behind the service counter through a hallway to the storage area and into a pantry filled with baking supplies. Gates and an evidence technician were both pointing to an object.

"What are you looking at?" asked Massey.

"You won't believe it, but a crockpot is hidden behind sacks of flour and sugar, stuffed with fifty thousand dollars wrapped in money straps," replied Gates.

"In this business, nothing surprises me." Massey shrugged and said, "I should have been a baker."

Gates asked, "Why would Mr. Amoia hide money?"

"Either he hated banks or taxes, or perhaps both. Let me ask you a question."

Gates answered, "Sure."

"Why are you two jokers walking on bloody bootprints that I assume belong to the murderer?"

Gates glared at his shoes' blood-stained soles, and blurted out, "Oh, shit!"

"Take a video of the pantry and seize the crockpot and money. This room is a fucking mess. It appears the murderer missed out on the fifty thousand dollars. The question is why the killer picked the pantry to search for the money in the flour and sugar sacks."

Gates asked, "I wonder who knew about the money?"

Massey responded, "When we figure that out, we will have our killer. I'm on my way to inform Mrs. Amoia that her husband has been murdered. I'll ask her who knew about the money. Perhaps she can tell us who murdered her husband."

Massey was determined to find justice for Frank and bring his killer to account. The rain continued to pour outside, mirroring the storm of emotions brewing within Massey as he delved deeper into the investigation.

CHAPTER 3

Cannoli

March 4, 1985, Monday morning

A man sat at the oversized conference table in the office library, studying his trial notebook. His sharkskin, charcoal-colored suit coat was draped on the back of his chair, his white poplin dress shirtsleeves were rolled up, the button at his neck was undone, and the knot in his handmade Italian tie lay loosened at his throat. He had a look on his face like he wore when he played chess.

Movie star good looking, he stands tall enough, is dark, and solid. His chiseled features are accentuated by a strong jawline and piercing, intelligent hazel eyes that seem to hold a hint of mystery. With his perfectly styled black hair parted on the right, he eludes an air of sophistication, confidence, and quick wit. His name happens to be Moretti. Blake Moretti.

Blake's family had immigrated from the southern province of Calabria. Like most southern Italians, they valued loyalty, a strong work ethic, and respect for elders, traits that helped them become successful. Calabrians are strong, rugged, and hard-headed—*testa tosta*, as they were called in Italy. Their stubbornness wasn't malicious. It was a part of their character that made them tenacious. They didn't give up. Blake Moretti and his parents are no exception.

Blake grew up in a working-class Italian American neighborhood. In Blake's view, the things we cannot control define life. We are shaped by the values we learn from our parents, the neighborhood we grow up in, the people we interact with, and the religious and philosophical views we are taught. This was also true for Moretti.

The most prominent case of his young career was just a week away. He sued a surgeon whose negligent conduct led to the tragic death of a patient during a routine surgical procedure.

There was a knock on the library door. Blake's legal secretary, Susan, entered the room and said, "Blake, the Sheriff, has issued an update regarding the 'suspicious death' report at Amoia's bakery."

Gripping a Montblanc fountain pen in his right hand between his fingers, resting his other hand on a hardbound copy of *Black's Law Dictionary*, he looked up at Susan. He asked, "What's the latest?"

My boyfriend, a crime beat reporter for the Misty River News, told me that the Sheriff was keeping a tight lid on the situation and that the "suspicious death" was actually a robbery gone wrong.

"Are you fucking kidding? Does the Sheriff know who murdered Mr. Amoia?"

"Apparently not. The Sheriff offered a twenty-five thousand dollar reward during his press conference for information leading to the arrest and conviction of the killer."

It's hard to believe Frankie, the baker, was murdered. Blake gave Italians nicknames. It was what Italians did growing up in New York.

Blake referred to his barber, Joe Vito, as "Joey, the barber." Likewise, he called Anthony Netti, who owned the neighborhood meat market, "Tony, the butcher." The nicknaming expressed respect.

All he could think about was Frank Amoia. He thought about the times he'd swung by to grab a loaf of Italian bread because he wouldn't eat the imitation Italian bread sold at the local supermarket. Sometimes, he'd order a shot of espresso or a Campari soda, along with one of Frank's cannoli. If Frank wasn't too busy, he'd sit with Blake and share stories about growing up in Brooklyn.

Blake listened to Amoia's stories reminding him of his grandfather, who often sat on the porch after Sunday mass, biting on a dead cigar while sharing stories about life in Italy and what it was like coming from the 'Old Country' and living in America.

Blake hadn't forgotten his grandfather's stories about prejudice. Those stories, and the bullying he'd endured, had made him a fighter. Blake often listened to his grandfather tell stories about labor struggles, nativist hostility, and virulent prejudice commonplace in the late nineteenth century.

By the late nineteenth century in America, growing numbers of Italians had been brought in to replace other labor groups. Thousands of Italians arrived in New Orleans each year. Many settled in the French Quarter, which by the twentieth century had a section known as "Little Sicily."

During that time, racist theories circulated in the press that "Mediterranean" types were inferior to northern Europeans. Anti-immigrant groups sprang up across the county. The Ku Klux Klan membership increased. Catholic churches were vandalized and burned, and Italians were attacked by mobs.

The bloodiest attack on Italians occurred before Blake was born, but he'd heard about it. It was one of his grandfather's often told stories, a lesson he wanted to be sure the boy learned.

In 1890, the New Orleans police chief was shot to death. Mass arrests of local Italian Americans and Italian immigrants quickly followed the murder. The mayor ordered the police to scour the entire neighborhood and arrest every Italian they encountered. More than one hundred Italian Americans were arrested and falsely blamed for the murder, most of whom had to be released for lack of evidence.

Ultimately, nineteen Italian Americans and immigrants were charged with murder or as accessories and held without bail. Nine of the accused Italians were tried in 1891. There were six not guilty verdicts and three mistrials, because the jurors could not agree on a verdict. The remaining ten accused Italians never had their day in court. Just one day later, before any of them were freed, a mob of ten thousand people, including prominent citizens, broke into the jail, dragged eleven Italian Americans and Italian immigrants out of their cells, and lynched them. The eight remaining Italians escaped the lynching by hiding inside the prison. It was the largest mass lynching in American history.

Moretti wasn't born yet. But that prejudice became a part of American culture. While the lynching by mobs of bullies has stopped, discrimination against ethnic and racial groups still lingers.

Blake grew up surrounded by the same ignorant prejudices that afflicted Italians in the 1890s. It was common for Blake to be referred to as "Guinea" or "Wop," contemptuous terms for a person of Italian descent. Then there were the occasions bullies physically attacked him just for being Italian. When bullies picked a fight with Blake or his friends, he rarely avoided them.

He never forgot his grandfather's stories about prejudice and hatred directed against Italians or his own experiences. It was Moretti's experiences that inspired him to become a prosecutor.

Blake was raised Catholic, believing God had a plan for everyone. Amoia devoted his life to raising his family and serving customers. Suddenly, Frank Amoia was brutally murdered. It made Blake wonder, *What kind of plan was that? Why would a benevolent God allow such a heinous act to occur?*

Blake does not know what fate has in store for him. Over time, he realized his question about God's plan was misguided. Blake would become a prosecutor and pursue justice for his friend in two years. Justice would become his primary focus, overshadowing any contemplation of divine intervention. At the end of the day, it was Blake's plan that would matter, not God's.

CHAPTER 4

Money, It's A Crime

March 2, 1985, Saturday afternoon

Homicide Detectives Bob Massey and Ann Wilson arrived around noon at the home of the murdered victim, Frank Amoia. Feeling a heavy weight on his shoulders, Massey took a deep breath as he approached the front door and rang the bell. The door creaked open, revealing an older woman.

"Mrs. Amoia?" Detective Massey asked gently. His voice filled with empathy. "I'm Detective Bob Massey with the Leigh County Sheriff's Office, and this is my partner, Detective Ann Wilson. May we come in?"

Mary observed the grim faces of the detectives. She sensed something terrible had happened to Frank. She nodded, "Please come in," her voice barely above a whisper. "Is Frank okay? Did something bad happen to him?" She began to search his face for answers.

She led them into the living room and gestured to a worn-out brown leather recliner. Detective Massey was unaware the recliner was

Frank's favorite chair. The chair wasn't anything to brag about. But all Frank cared about was that it was comfortable, and it was the place he would often relax after standing on his feet all day, watching his favorite evening show, *Gunsmoke*.

Detective Massey accepted her invitation and lowered himself onto the chair. Instantly, he felt a sinking sensation as the seat cushion gave way beneath him, as if he had unknowingly stepped into the void left by the victim's absence. The realization hit him like a punch in the gut, intensifying his quest to find justice for Mrs. Amoia and her husband.

As Detective Massey informed Mrs. Amoia of her husband's murder, Detective Wilson sat beside her on the sofa opposite Detective Massey, ready to comfort her. Mrs. Amoia could sense that they cared for her and were trustworthy.

"This is never easy for me, Mrs. Amoia. After being called out this morning to investigate a "suspicious death" at the bakery, we found Frank dead."

The tragic news visibly shook Mrs. Amoia. Her eyes filled with tears, and her lip began to tremble. Detective Wilson held her hand, consoling her.

"My God. It feels like I have been struck by a freight train. I don't understand why anyone would want to harm Frank. Everyone loved him."

"Mrs. Amoia, I know it is not a good time to talk about this, but it appears your husband's murderer was after his money. We must learn as much as possible about business operations. It may help us solve the murder."

"I'll do my best. Frank carried two hundred dollars in his pocket every morning to set up the cash register. He would have given the money to whoever robbed him if asked. It is incomprehensible anyone would murder him. My God."

"I figured as much. We found the pantry ransacked. Sugar and flour sacks were broken open and dumped on the floor. A deputy searched the room and found fifty thousand dollars stuffed in a crock-pot, wrapped in currency straps, tucked behind the flour and sugar sacks. We believe whoever murdered Frank suspected the money was hidden in flour and sugar sacks. I was hoping you could identify the person or persons who may have had that knowledge."

"I don't know anything about fifty thousand dollars."

"I understand. But here's the thing: Frank's killer knew he had a lot of cash hidden in the bakery. Did you know your husband hid money?"

"No. Frank managed the money matters. Frank and Sonny Calo were business partners. They kept me in the dark when it came to finances. I find it strange that you asked me that question. Frank repeatedly told me he was tired of the bakery business in the past few months and wanted to sell and move to Florida. He told me Sonny was willing to buy our interest in the bakery."

"When was the last time Frank discussed the buyout?"

"Frank discussed it with me before leaving for work this morning. He was more determined than ever to sell the business and move. I sensed Frank was under a lot of pressure to sell."

"That's interesting. Can you tell me what was said?"

"I told him I was worried about finances and leaving our friends."

"What was Frank's response to your concern?"

"That's what's strange. The buyout money Sonny promised to pay was substantial, and Frank assured me we would be financially sound."

"Was the bakery business that lucrative?"

"I certainly wasn't complaining. After Sonny became a business partner, we expanded operations and sustained an excellent cash flow."

Detective Wilson asked, "Do you know anyone who would want to kill Frank?"

"No, as I already mentioned, everyone loved him."

"Sonny Calo, the mob boss? Do you think Calo had anything to do with murdering Frank?" Wilson asked.

"No. They were very close."

"Do you know anyone else, including employees, who knew Frank stashed money in the bakery?" asked Wilson.

"Frank and I employed several people. Frank did the baking. He left for work at four-thirty in the morning. By five, he started to bake and set up shop. Frank worked the counter until the two women employees arrived at nine. Another young man, Joey Fleming, did much of the grunt work, unloading delivery trucks and stocking the bakery supplies. There is no reason to believe anyone other than Frank and Joey Fleming knew about the money. The pantry is out of sight and off-limits to customers. Only Frank and Joey had permission to enter the supply room. On one occasion, I recall, Joey mentioned he was surprised the bakery business made so much money. He suggested he should become a baker. I never gave that comment any thought at the time. Looking back, perhaps I should have."

Detective Massey said, "I guess hindsight is a great tool. What do you know about Joey Fleming?"

"Not a lot. I know he dropped out of high school and lived near the bakery with his mother and her boyfriend for a while. The mother's name is Valerie. I don't recall the boyfriend's name.

"He began working for us a couple of years ago. The few times I was around Joey Fleming, he was polite. He was sometimes strapped for cash, and Frank would advance him money whenever the kid asked."

"Joey didn't like his mother's boyfriend. According to him, the boyfriend mooched off his mother and was abusive. I heard stories the boyfriend was an alcoholic. Joey didn't get along with the guy and moved in with his girlfriend."

The Detectives gave Mrs. Amoia their business cards and promised to stay in touch.

Wilson drove, and she didn't hesitate to prematurely solve the case. "So, aside from Frank, Joey Fleming was the only person with access to the pantry. Looks like we found our killer, Joey Fleming."

Massey rolled his eyes and said, "Let's head back to the bakery. I want to take another look around."

Detective Wilson's comment about Joey Fleming knowing about the hidden money seemed like a breakthrough in the murder investigation. However, Massey, the astute Detective, wasn't entirely convinced that Joey Fleming was the killer.

Tension hung in the air, while the two Detectives stood in the dimly lit bakery, surrounded by an absence of evidence and clues. The case was perplexing from the start. Massey couldn't shake off the feeling that there was more to this puzzle than met the eye.

Wilson said, "Massey, I'm disappointed you haven't congratulated me."

With a thoughtful expression, Massey turned to Detective Wilson and replied, "I guess time will tell." His words were laced with uncertainty, hinting at a deeper understanding of the situation. He knew that rushing to conclusions could lead them astray and potentially allow the real killer to slip through their fingers.

Meanwhile, back at the precinct, evidence technician Gomez was diligently creating piles of paperwork related to the case. He methodically packaged, labeled, and sealed the evidence collected from the murder scene.

A new academy graduate assisting asked, "Hey Gomez, what do you want to do with this?" holding up the video recorder.

Gomez responded, "I almost forgot. Hand me the recorder." Gomez removed the crime scene video, sealed it in a yellow evidence envelope, and marked it: *The Misty River Bakery Murder-Crime Scene Video*.

Before retiring for the day, Gomez placed the marked video on the property shelf and said, "Hey, kid, thanks for reminding me about the video. If I hadn't removed the video from the recorder, someone would have played over it the next time they used it."

Gomez was unaware he stumbled upon a crucial piece of information that could turn everything upside down: the crime scene video.

CHAPTER 5

Pointing The Finger

March 2, 1985, Saturday early evening

"Detective Massey, you have a call on line two."

"Who is it?"

"Just another kook trying to collect the Amoia reward money. She won't tell me her name. She says she knows who killed Frank Amoia. Phones have been ringing off the hook with nuts trying to get their hands on the reward money. I'll forward her call to you."

"Massey here. Can I help you?"

"I'm trying to reach someone in homicide. I know who killed the baker."

"I'm in homicide." Massey put her on speaker and signaled Detective Wilson to listen in. "Who are you?"

"I'm not saying, but I have information that can put the killer behind bars forever. Is there a reward for information leading to the killer's arrest?"

"There is a reward of twenty-five thousand dollars. I need to know your name first."

"That's not important. Capturing the killer before he harms someone else is what matters. "Buck" Owens is the man who murdered Frank Amoia. Can you tell me when I'll get my reward money? "

"You need to tell us your name, and the information you provide must be instrumental in leading to the arrest and conviction of the murderer."

"Owens will kill me if he finds out I snitched on him. Please promise me you won't reveal my identity."

"I can't make that promise."

"Then, at least promise me you will protect me."

"If you help us, we'll help you."

The caller paused a moment before saying, "Meet me at midnight in the McCarthy shoe factory parking lot. I'll be driving a beat-up army green Dodge station wagon. Once we meet, I'll decide what to do."

After hanging up, Massey asked Wilson, "So what do you think?"

"I suspect that was Joey Fleming's mother. Joey Fleming killed Frank Amoia, and she is framing Owens to save her son's ass."

"You are jumping the gun. We both need to wait until midnight to learn who killed Amoia. In the meantime, find out what you can about Owens."

Detectives Massey and Wilson waited behind the abandoned McCarthy shoe factory in an unmarked sheriff's car for the anonymous caller that night.

Damn, it's pitch black outside. Wilson said, "This would be a great place to kill someone."

He said, "Jesus, Wilson. I'm trying to solve a murder and you're planning one. Our caller is fifteen minutes late. I'm leaving if she doesn't get here soon."

Wilson spotted headlights approaching as they were getting ready to leave. A beat-up army-green Dodge station wagon spewing black smoke pulled into the lot and was parked.

"Hold on, there she is," Wilson said.

She exited her car and cautiously walked towards them. Observing the woman's hands, Massey and Wilson approached her.

"Keep your hands where I can see them and identify yourself," Massey instructed. Then he asked, "What's your name? "

"Do you promise not to include my name in the sheriff's report?" the woman asked in a shaky voice. "I'm as good as dead if Owens finds out I snitched on him."

Wilson asked, "Why don't you tell us how you know Owens?"

"He is my boyfriend. We live together."

She told Wilson, "We know you're afraid. You're trying to do the right thing. We can help you, but you must help us find Mr. Amoia's killer. Mrs. Amoia is suffering. She needs to know that whoever murdered Frank will be punished. You will have to trust us not to harm you. Massey and I have been around for a while without losing any witnesses. Let us know your name."

"You promise to protect my son?"

"We will do everything we can to protect you and your son."

"My name is Valerie Fleming."

Massey asked, "What is your son's name, age, and appearance?"

"Why do you need my son's information?"

"So we can protect him," Massey replied.

"I see. His name is Joey Fleming. He is twenty years old, six feet tall, skinny, and weighs a hundred and forty pounds, soaking wet. He has long, black, shoulder-length hair, and his arms and hands are tattooed.

"Joey has had a few run-ins with the law, but nothing major. He is addicted to painkillers. In high school, he was injured while wrestling. Joey dropped out of school after his coach kicked him off the team. Joey does odd jobs, mostly cutting grass. I suspect he blows what little money he makes on pain pills.

"Joey's father is gone to the world. When Joey was born, he abandoned us both. Joey never cared much for Owens, who functioned as his father figure.

"He usually stays at his girlfriend Ashley Fox's house. Occasionally, Joey stays with Owens and me."

Mrs. Fleming intentionally did not mention that her son worked for Mr. Amoia. Massey avoided asking Ms. Fleming questions about Joey working for Amoia and the money hidden in the bakery. He feared she would become upset and clam up. Instead, he asked, "Where does Joey like to hang out?"

"Kool's Pool Hall."

Kool's Pool Hall, owned by the ruggedly handsome and charismatic John Kowalski, was a dimly lit, smoke-filled haven for those seeking refuge from the mundane routines of daily life adorned with vintage pin-up girls and the smell of stale beer and chlorine lingering in the air.

Massey asked, "We'd like to know more about you and Owens."

"I work in a nail salon. I work hard to make ends meet. Occasionally, Owens works odd jobs to help pay the rent. It's no secret that he's an alcoholic.

"Owens is abusive when he's drunk, but he treats me well when he's not drinking. I fight with him a lot, but he isn't always to blame. Sometimes I can be a bitch."

"Tell us what you know about the murder of Frank Amoia," Massey asked.

"I learned about the murder of Amoia from the news. It didn't take long to put two and two together. Owens was out carousing the night before the murder. He returned home between eight and eight-thirty Saturday morning. His clothes were covered in blood. When he removed his bloody clothes, I saw his Buck hunting knife hidden inside a wad of blood-stained bills."

"He told me a story about stabbing a man who attempted to rob him. I knew he was lying, but I feared he'd beat me if I questioned him. Hell, he wouldn't think twice about killing me."

With the help of persuasion, Massey managed to convince the killer's girlfriend to disclose the location where Owens forced her to accompany him to bury the incriminating evidence.

"Essentially, he made me an accomplice by forcing me to go with him to bury his bloody clothing, boots, and knife in a secluded wooded area near the Misty River."

Massey said, "I see. We'll pick you up first thing in the morning, and you can take us to the burial site. In the meantime, tell us where Owens is tonight."

"He can be found at Last Call Saloon most nights. "He's always the last drunk to leave."

Massey looked at Ms. Fleming and asked, "By chance, do you have a photo of Joey and Owens we can use?"

"Yes, I do. The photo was of all of us taken last summer. Will that work?"

"It's perfect. Thanks. I'll return it in the morning."

As Wilson drove and Massey was deep in thought, she peppered him with questions about Ms. Fleming's interview.

"Massey, did you catch Ms. Fleming never mentioned her son worked for Amoia? She probably fingered Owens to cover for her son. Fleming was strapped for cash. It is a sure bet Joey Fleming robbed Mr. Amoia to sustain his addiction. He couldn't afford to allow Frank Amoia to be left around as a witness. What do you think of my theory, Massey?"

"As far as I'm concerned, it's just a theory. Take this turn. It's a shortcut to Last Call Saloon. Let's visit Owens. It's going to be a long night."

As they entered the dimly lit bar, the homicide detectives scanned the room for signs of their suspect. At first glance, they observed a few shady characters visible, whispering among themselves in dark corners.

The Last Call Saloon was the kind of beer joint you don't forget. Wilson elbowed Massey and whispered, "Jesus, this place stinks. I can't see a fucking thing in here. When was the last time they paid the light bill?"

"What are you talking about? This dump has it all. Great ambiance. It's romantically dimly lit, with the smell of stale beer, sticky wood floors, thick cigarette smoke, and the sound of pool balls clacking in the background, harmonizing perfectly with the lousy cowboy music playing on the jukebox. What more can you ask for? This beer joint is a great place for you to bring a date. I'm sure she'd like it."

"Screw you, Massey."

As they made their way through the crowd, catching Massey's eye was a face sitting at the opposite end of the bar that matched Owens' picture. Owens was talking to a woman with no teeth, who looked even more fucked up than Owens.

Owens, tall and imposing, with broad shoulders and a thick build, gave him a husky and burly appearance. His long, unkempt black hair fell in disarray around his face, partially obscuring his features. Massey could see Owens had a weathered and worn look about him, as if he had seen his fair share of troubles. His eyes, bloodshot and weary, betrayed a life filled with hardship and perhaps even regret. Owens sat hunched over the bar, nursing a drink in his calloused hands.

Massey could tell that he had been drinking heavily, as evidenced by the empty glasses scattered around him. Despite his disheveled appearance, an air of muted intensity about him made it clear he was not to be underestimated.

The second Massey flashed his badge, the woman with no teeth and everyone else at the bar disappeared. Massey told Owens he needed to speak to him and invited him to his unmarked car, where it would be much quieter. Owens asked why they wanted to talk to him, and Massey told him he would explain everything in his vehicle.

Detective Massey sat in the front seat with Owens, while Detective Wilson sat in the back. When Detective Massey questioned Owens about his involvement in the murder, Owens brushed it off.

"I didn't fucking kill old man Amoia. I've got an alibi. The morning Amoia was murdered, I was at home with my girlfriend, Valerie Fleming. Check it out. She'll tell you I'm telling the truth."

Owens then fingered Joey Fleming. "Look, I love Valerie, but I'm not taking the fall for Amoia's murder. Valerie's son, Joey Fleming, worked for Amoia. Joey constantly ran his big mouth about catching Amoia hiding a lot of money in the bakery and how easy it would be to steal it."

"Hell, he even had the motive to steal Amoia's money. Joey was addicted to painkillers because of a back injury he sustained while wrestling for his high school team. His coach kicked him off the team because of his addiction. The kid needed money to buy painkillers. Don't take my word for it. Go fucking interview the coach. I desperately tried to get counseling for Joey to get him off the painkillers, but he wouldn't listen.

"I wasn't planning on telling you guys, but I discovered my expensive Buck hunting knife went missing the morning of the murder. I don't know who stole it, but Joey Fleming stayed with us occasionally, and he knew where I kept the knife."

It caught Massey's attention that a sheriff's deputy found fifty thousand dollars in the pantry, hidden in a crockpot. The fact that Owens knew money was hidden in the bakery didn't go unnoticed.

The detectives weren't getting anywhere with Owens, and it was clear Owens knew the investigators didn't have a shred of evidence on him. Massey pulled the plug on the interview and told Owens, "Don't leave town."

"If you're out of questions, I'd like to finish my cocktail with that good-looking dame begging to get into my pants."

Wilson climbed into the driver's seat and started the car. As Massey slipped into the passenger seat, he commented, "Good looking dame? What the hell is he smoking? That woman's face could stop Attila the Hun."

"Massey, can't you say something nice once in your life?"

"Sure. I bet that lady with no teeth can blow your mind."

"Yeah, among other things."

Wilson said, "It appears Joey Fleming was not only aware of the money Mr. Amoia hid in the bakery but was also motivated to steal it to maintain his addiction. I will contact Joey Fleming's high school wrestling coach and ask him if what Owens told us is true."

"You do that and let me know what he says."

Unlike Wilson, Massey was not convinced that Joey Fleming murdered Amoia. Before Massey made his decision, there was more investigation to be done. First, there was the matter of interviewing Joey Fleming. Tonight was as good as any to catch up with him.

Second, there was the matter of escorting Ms. Fleming to the burial site in the morning to excavate the bloody evidence that could reveal the killer's identity.

"Wilson, turn the car around."

"Why, I thought we were headed back to headquarters."

Massey replied, "It's time for a talk with Joey Fleming. We're going to Joey Fleming's girlfriend's house. Get ready for a long night. I suspect he knows who murdered Frank Amoia."

The dilapidated exterior of the house mirrored the neglect and disregard that permeated its surroundings. Paint peeled off the weathered walls, revealing patches of decaying wood underneath.

As the detectives approached the run-down rental house looking for Joey Fleming, they were immediately greeted by the blaring sound of loud music emanating from inside.

The front yard was overgrown with weeds, obscuring any semblance of a pathway to the entrance. Massey quipped, "Welcome to *The Addams Family* residence. It appears Uncle Fester missed some spots when he cut the lawn. Wilson, watch where you step. There's a chance a dead body or two are hidden in the weeds."

Undeterred by the disheartening sight, the Detectives made their way to the front door, which appeared to have seen better days.

Massey pounded on the front door with forceful urgency. The knocks reverberated through the thin walls of the house. It took several rounds of pounding before Massey's persistence finally caught their attention. The door creaked open slowly, revealing a twenty-one-year-old woman, Ashley Fox, standing there, her disheveled appearance mirroring the state of the house. Her clothes were haphazardly thrown on, barely covering her petite frame. Her hair was unkempt and tangled like she had just awakened from a restless sleep. Dark circles under her eyes hinted at sleepless nights and a life filled with partying and cheap booze.

"Ashley Fox?" Massey queried.

"Yeah. Who's asking?"

Massey wasted no time in explaining their purpose to her. He flashed his badge and said, "I'm homicide Detective Massey, and this is my partner, Detective Wilson. We need to speak to your boyfriend, Joey Fleming. Where is he?"

"Upstairs. Joey has been sleeping all day."

"Yeah, right. Tell Sleeping Beauty I need to speak to him."

"Who?"

"Just go get your boyfriend and turn off the music. It's so loud you're waking the dead in the front yard."

"What dead people?"

"Jesus, lady. We're the ones who get to ask all the questions. Just get him."

"What's this about?"

"Murder."

"No shit. Who was murdered?"

"Look, do me a favor. Stop asking questions, turn off the fucking music, and go get Fleming."

Stepping aside reluctantly, she allowed them entry into the dimly lit interior of the house. As they made their way through the house, the detectives couldn't help but feel a sense of unease. The stench was suffocating, as if the walls were closing in. The air was thick with a musty odor, a combination of stale cigarette smoke and neglect. The furniture was worn and tattered, bearing the marks of countless years of use and abuse. Empty beer bottles and discarded pill bottles littered every available surface, evidence of a life spiraling out of control.

Massey slid a tube of Vicks out of his sports coat pocket, removed the cap, and rubbed a dash on his upper lip to kill the stench. Passing the tube to Wilson, he said, "Here, you'll need this. We're going to be here for a while."

As Wilson rubbed a dash of Vicks on her upper lip, she said, "Since we're going to be here a while, I think I'll take a load off my feet and have a seat."

"If I were you, I wouldn't do that. You may be taking a few unwanted guests home."

"Jesus," she said as she jumped from the couch.

A tall and emaciated figure emerged in the dimly lit room, his haggard appearance belying his young age of twenty, with long, unkempt black hair cascading down to his shoulders. and tattoos on his arms and hands. His face bore the marks of a troubled existence. The telltale signs of a life marred by reliance on painkillers were evident in his sunken eyes and trembling hands. As he stepped forward, the detectives could sense the aura of despair surrounding him, knowing that this man's troubled past may have made him a prime suspect in the murder investigation.

Massey asked, "Are you Joey Fleming, Valerie Fleming's son?"

"Yes, sir. I understand you want to talk to me. What's this about?"

"I'm Detective Massey, and this is Detective Wilson from the sheriff's office. We need to speak to you and your girlfriend about the Amoia murder."

"Why do you want to talk to me? I can't help you."

Massey replied, "That's not what Billy Owens told us. In fact, he fingered you as the murderer. He says you killed Frank Amoia with his stolen Buck knife."

"I've never killed anyone."

"I heard you had a good long sleep," Massey said. You should be prepared to answer some questions."

"Sure, no problem. I'll do whatever I can."

"Detective Wilson, how about escorting Morticia outside? I'll interview Joey in the living room?"

"I want to know how you knew Mr. Amoia and where you were when he was murdered."

Joey said, "Yes, sir. Ashley, my girlfriend, and I were together. We drank and partied Friday night until the early hours of Saturday morning. When Mr. Amoia was murdered, we were sleeping in."

"You didn't tell me how you knew Mr. Amoia."

"I worked at the bakery."

"That's it. That's everything?"

"Yes, sir."

"Joey, you are in a lot of trouble. I know you know more than what you told us. I have enough evidence to lock you up for the murder of Frank Amoia. "I'm giving you one last chance to come clean and tell me everything you know. You can start with the money. Owens said you told him you saw Mr. Amoia hiding money in the bakery and how easy it would be to steal it. Your mother and Owens both told us you are addicted to painkillers because of a high school sports injury. When Detective Wilson meets with your wrestling coach tomorrow, I suspect he will confirm that story. As we both know, you needed the money to maintain a supply of painkillers. It doesn't look good for you. You had both the motive and opportunity to kill Frank Amoia. It's time to tell me the truth."

"What if I saw Mr. Amoia hiding money in a crockpot? I didn't steal it. Why would I? Hell, all I had to do was ask for money, and he gave it to me. I told Owens I saw Frank hide money in the pantry. Owens offered me money if I told him exactly where it was hidden. To get him off my back, I lied and told him the money was stashed in the sacks of sugar and flour in the pantry. Owens must have gone to the bakery Saturday morning to steal Mr. Amoia's money and ends up killing him."

"So, you do know about the crockpot stuffed with money."

"Yes. But I didn't steal it."

"Let's go outside and hear what your girlfriend told Detective Wilson."

Wilson and Ashley Fox were standing on the front porch when Massey said, "Joey Fleming told me after partying all night, he was here with Ashley asleep the morning Amoia was murdered. What did Ashley tell you?"

Detective Wilson replied, "The same thing."

"Well, Joey, the good news is your alibi is confirmed. The bad news is it is corroborated by your brain fried on drugs, girlfriend."

"If her brain is fried on drugs, as you say, Ashley couldn't remember a made-up story that matches mine."

"Thanks, Columbo."

"Listen, I'm done talking. If you think you have a case, arrest me. But I am telling you the truth: I didn't rob or kill Mr. Amoia. I told you I was here asleep with Ashley at the time of the murder. God can strike me dead if that's not the truth."

Wilson anxiously glanced at the sky, expecting a lightning bolt to strike Joey dead in his tracks, suspecting Joey Fleming had killed Amoia.

Massey said, "Joey, you are off the hook for now. But don't leave town."

Ashley asked, "Joey, does that mean you didn't kill Mr. Amoia?"

Massey shook his head in disbelief and said, "Jesus, let's get out of here before I catch whatever it is she has."

Wilson pondered the next step, her fingers gripping the steering wheel as she ignited the engine. "Where do we go from here?"

Massey replied, "To get a stiff drink. Let's get out of here. I'm getting worn out with all the finger-pointing. Tomorrow morning, we are going to know who murdered Frank Amoia."

The following day, trusting Valerie Fleming's cooperation, Detectives Massey and Wilson and an excavation crew escorted her to a remote wooded area near the banks of the Misty River, where she claims Owens buried the murder weapon, his bloody clothes, and boots.

As they ventured deeper into the woods, the atmosphere grew increasingly eerie, with dense foliage blocking out much of the sunlight. Fallen leaves covered the ground beneath their feet, making each step treacherous.

Much to Detective Massey's astonishment, nothing is found after an extensive search and excavation. The unexpected event raised suspicions and caused Massey to question whether Ms. Fleming had lied to protect her son, who was increasingly becoming a prime suspect in the murder case. Gradually, doubts crept into Massey's mind about Ms. Fleming's initial statement that her boyfriend killed Frank Amoia.

Perplexed, Massey confronted Ms. Fleming about the murder weapon and bloody clothing not being buried as claimed. He also questioned her about her claim that Owens killed Mr. Amoia. Ms. Fleming refused to provide further information, leaving the Detectives with more questions than answers.

"Ms. Fleming, the excavation crew has been digging holes to China for hours looking for the evidence you claim Owens buried. I trusted you when you told me we would find the buried incriminating evidence. You can see that evidence does not exist. Tell me why I shouldn't believe Owens' story that your son murdered Mr. Amoia, and you helped him bury evidence that would incriminate him."

Ms. Fleming stood baffled, staring at the ground. Her pupils became dilated, making her eyes appear larger than usual. Her eyebrows were drawn together, causing the skin between them to wrinkle. Then she raised her head and whispered, "That son of a gun moved everything."

The meeting went sideways. Ms. Fleming recanted her accusation and refused to cooperate further with the investigation. She walks away, upset, and says, "Massey, go fuck yourself."

Massey and Wilson stood there, not saying a word. Massey's first thought was *Jesus, maybe Detective Wilson was right. Joey Fleming killed Frank Amoia.* After recalling Joey Fleming's crockpot comment, he quickly discarded her theory.

With a trail of cryptic messages and suspicious alibis leading them down a convoluted path, the case of the murdered baker became more unclear by the hour.

CHAPTER 6

Rejection

April 9, 1985, Tuesday morning

I n the district attorney's conference room, the atmosphere was tense as homicide Detectives Bob Massey, the seasoned investigator known for his cool and calm, meticulous approach, often making him the lead in high-profile cases, and Ann Wilson, known for her no-nonsense demeanor, often providing fresh perspectives, gathered with veteran prosecutors to present their case and persuade them to accept charges against Billy Owens for the murder and robbery of Frank Amoia.

The room was dimly lit, with a long wooden conference table surrounded by high-backed leather chairs at the center.

The Detectives exuded an air of determination and professionalism. Their faces were etched with lines of experience. Massey and Wilson sat at the long wooden conference table closest to the room's bank of windows, which offered a captivating view of the town's historic downtown business district. The eerie Misty River flowed silently in the background, its fog and mist adding an air of mystery and intrigue to the already tense atmosphere.

Sitting across from them were three prosecutors, each with their own distinct appearance and demeanor. The first prosecutor, Mr. Johnson, was middle-aged, with white hair and a stern expression. He leaned forward in his chair, holding his hands clasped tightly together as he listened intently to the detective's presentation.

Next to him sat Ms. Ramirez, a young and ambitious prosecutor known for her sharp wit and unwavering dedication to justice. She had a commanding presence, her dark eyes scanning the room as she absorbed every detail of the case being presented.

The third prosecutor, Mr. Thompson, was an older gentleman with a gentle demeanor that belied his years of experience in the courtroom. He leaned back in his chair, observing the Detectives and occasionally jotting down notes on his legal pad.

As the Detectives laid out their evidence, tensions rose in the room. The prosecutors questioned the validity of certain pieces of evidence and raised concerns about the potential gaps in the investigation. Massey and Wilson defended their work, providing explanations and justifications for each decision they had made.

The dialogue between them became increasingly heated as both sides stood firm in their positions. Voices grew louder, gestures more animated, and arguments more intense. Each party was determined to convince the others of their perspective and secure a favorable outcome for justice.

Amidst the heated exchange of ideas and opinions, this case would not be resolved. The Detectives were frustrated by what they perceived as a lack of trust in their abilities, while the prosecutors were adamant about not pursuing charges with no likelihood of conviction.

Johnson said, "Your department wants us to charge Owens with first-degree murder and robbery based on your gut instinct that he is the murderer. There are no eyewitnesses. No fingerprints. No murder weapon was recovered. Your entire case proving Owens is the murderer rests on your gut instincts and the recanted testimony of Valerie Fleming, whose son, Joey Fleming, has also been fingered as the killer. Detective Massey, did I get that right?"

"Yes. But if you agree to charge Owens, we can arrest and jail him. We can then persuade Fleming to testify against Owens since he won't be able to kill her."

"I understand, Detective. However, our office will not charge Owens simply because there is a chance Ms. Fleming will do what's right. The fact remains she recanted her story, fingering Owens. There is no way a jury will believe her."

As they returned to the office, Wilson asked, "Now, what do we do?"

"The only thing we can do is continue to look for new leads. Mr. Hardy will need to light a lot of candles and pray that Owens doesn't strike again."

On March 17, 1987, Saint Patrick's Day night, schoolteacher Valerie Spencer made a trip to the supermarket that changed her life forever. The murderer struck again.

PART TWO

"It's hard to wake up from a nightmare when you're not even asleep."

— *The Mind Journal – J.S.*

CHAPTER 7

Rape

March 17, 1987, Tuesday night

It was Saint Patrick's Day, but Olivia Spencer wasn't in the mood to celebrate. She'd returned home late after an exhausting day of teaching and parent conferences, and she and Dean had fallen out again. Quarrels were becoming more frequent and bitter. He took her for granted. Sex was becoming boring and mechanical. Unless his behavior changed, their relationship was doomed.

When she tried to express her feelings, he became defensive and demeaning. She didn't fight back because she wasn't good at confrontation. She wasn't wired that way.

She'd been looking forward to a solitary evening, fixing dinner for herself, relaxing on the couch in front of the TV with a bottle of wine, and watching her favorite movie, *Dirty Dancing*, on VHS. But when she opened the fridge, she realized she hadn't had time for the supermarket all week. So she grabbed her keys and switched off the lights. It was precisely seven p.m. when she left her safe haven for the grocery store.

Twenty minutes later, she pulled her white Chevy Citation into the supermarket parking lot, rushed inside, grabbed everything she needed, and waited impatiently in the long checkout line.

As darkness settled over the small town of Misty River, a sense of foreboding lingers in the air. The flickering parking lot lights cast long shadows, making it seem like the walls were closing in.

At exactly fifteen minutes after eight, Olivia left the supermarket, located her car, and began loading the grocery bags into the back seat.

A drunkard with a penchant for violence lay in wait. His eyes fixed intently on his next victim. His rough, calloused right hand gripped the handle of his thirty-eight caliber revolver. His clothes are stained with the remnants of last night's binge. Despite his unkempt appearance, there's a sense of calculated precision about him, as if he's been waiting for this moment for a long time.

Suddenly, he emerged from the shadows, his massive frame looming ominously. He stood at least six feet tall, a burly man with a menacing glare in his bloodshot eyes. His body odor, a pungent mix of sweat and body spray, wafts through the air, leaving a lingering stench that makes your stomach turn.

The assailant tightly gripped a thirty-eight caliber Long Colt revolver in his right hand. The gun was sleek and polished, with a black matte finish that added to its menacing aura. Its barrel was long and slender, extending outwards with a sense of purpose. The cylinder housing the ammunition rotated smoothly as the assailant prepared to carry out his sinister plan.

As he approached Olivia, the fluorescent beams illuminated the revolver's details, highlighting its intricate engravings and emphasizing its presence in the darkness. The gleam of metal caught glimpses of nearby objects, creating fleeting reflections that danced across its surface. The gun exuded an air of menace and danger. Its appearance conveyed a lethal intent, while the interplay of light and shadow heightened the atmosphere of suspense.

His clothes were stained with the remnants of his latest binge. Despite his unkempt appearance, there's a sense of calculated precision about him, as if he's been waiting for this moment for a long time.

He grabbed her from behind and shoved the barrel of his gun into her back. When she screamed, he covered her mouth with his hand, forced her into the front seat, ordered her to slide over to the driver's side, and climbed into the passenger seat beside her.

With his finger on the trigger, he directed her to a dark, secluded wooded area near the Misty River. "This is as good a place as any," he said. "Park and turn off the lights."

He became preoccupied with surveying the surroundings, giving her seconds to decide whether to try to escape. Finally, she threw open the car door and ran aimlessly into the woods, knowing he would pursue her. Her only hope was maybe, just maybe, she could outrun him.

He shot out of the car and hunted her like an animal, screamed, "Stop!" and fired in her direction, but she kept running until her legs gave out, and she fell to the damp ground.

He was on her in seconds, pinning her down with a foot on her chest.

"Take off your clothes!"

"Please, don't hurt me! Why are you doing this? What have I done to you?"

She was powerless, at the mercy of this stranger, and felt as though fire was raging through her body. A train rumbled into a nearby station, but she knew she was alone, and no one could hear her.

"I told you to take off your fucking clothes!" He lifted his foot from her chest but kept his gun trained at her head.

Fearful he would kill her, she obeyed, stripping off her sneakers, her jeans, her sweater, her blouse, and her bra, and stood in just her socks, her arms wrapped around her chest to conceal her breasts.

He looked her up and down, from head to toe. "I like that. Now give me that ring!"

She sobbed as she removed her engagement ring from her finger and clutched it tightly in her hand.

"If you don't shut up, I'll shut you up!" He shoved the gun into her stomach, and she winced in pain. "Want me to pull the trigger? No? Then be a good girl and give me the ring!"

He yanked the ring from her hand, stashed it in the front pocket of his jeans, pushed her to the ground, then lowered his trousers and forced himself on her. When she resisted, he slapped her face with one hand while pressing his gun hard to her head with the other. The air was heavy with tension. The assailant's menacing presence loomed over his victim, and his eyes were filled with malice.

She fought, flailed, and screamed.

"If you don't stop your whining, I'll fuck you hard, then blow your brains out."

The victim, trembling with fear and anguish, felt her heart race while he unleashed a torrent of vile words designed to degrade and demoralize her. The weight of the assailant's words bore down on her, leaving an indelible mark on her psyche.

He raped her, then forced himself into her again from behind as she lay naked and helpless in the mud and decaying leaves. She could smell his body odor and the alcohol on his breath, and knew that stench would haunt her forever.

She began screaming for help, but the deafening sound of a train speeding down the nearby tracks made it impossible for anyone to hear her. Finally, her assailant stood up and left her lying face down on the cold, damp ground, then leaned over her and hissed, "If you tell anyone what happened, I know where you live, and I will kill you and your boyfriend."

As he started gathering his clothes, Olivia laboriously managed to stand, pushed her attacker aside, and ran naked toward the end of the woodland, struggling to breathe. Having no energy to chase her, the rapist fired a shot in her direction. His only concern was getting out of there before someone saw him. He returned to her car, jumped into the driver's seat, maneuvered out of the brush, and drove off.

Olivia ran as far as her legs would allow, and when she thought she'd left the rapist behind, she stopped and bent over, her hands on her knees, trying to take deep breaths. Her vision was blurry, and her heart was racing. Panting, she dashed across the lawn toward what appeared to be a farmhouse. She pounded on the door with her fists as if she feared being taken captive again by the monster lurking outside. The older woman who opened the door found her naked, covered in dirt, and sobbing.

"Oh my god! Dear, are you okay?"

Olivia had no idea where she was or who the woman was. She had escaped the clutches of an evil, violent man, and that was all that mattered.

The house belonged to Zelene Elliot, who had run the farm single-handedly since the death of her husband, Charlie, several years earlier. She was a feisty woman, not to be messed with.

"I need to contact the sheriff, please," Olivia begged.

Zelene told her she'd better come inside, covered her with a blanket, and dialed 911. The deputy sheriff was at the farmhouse within fifteen minutes.

The deputy wrote down every detail of Olivia's tearful story. She described her assailant as tall, almost six foot four inches, muscular, with a scar above his right eye. She said he'd stolen her engagement ring and suspected he'd stolen her car.

The deputy took her to the nearest hospital, phoned in her license plate number, and broadcasted an all-points bulletin to alert law enforcement officers to be on the lookout for an armed rapist driving a stolen car.

The following morning, the sheriff reported the incident to the press and provided a sketch of the assailant based on Olivia's description.

An anonymous caller who'd seen the news reported that Billy "Buck" Owens was hiding at his girlfriend's rental house. Her car was discovered two houses away.

When the deputy sheriffs arrived at the rundown rental, a middle-aged woman answered the door.

Valerie Fleming wasn't surprised to see them. She'd been sickened when she recognized Buck from the sketch on the news and made the anonymous call. Now she was afraid Buck would kill her.

"Where is he?" the deputies asked.

Valerie pointed her chin in the direction of the attic. They drew their guns and cautiously approached.

"Owens, this is the sheriff. We know you're there. I'm telling you only once, come out slowly with your hands in the air where I can see them. Don't make us come in to get you."

Owens emerged, hands over his head. "What's up with you? What are you doing here?"

"You're under arrest."

"For what? I haven't done anything wrong!"

"You'll have time to tell your story downtown. Now, put your hands behind your head, stand facing the wall, and spread your legs so I can search you for weapons. If you move a muscle, my partner won't hesitate to end your life right here. Is there anything I just told you that you don't understand?"

"I don't have a gun or any other weapon on me."

"Great, so long as you don't make a wrong move, you'll get a ride to the county jail instead of the morgue."

"Where's your firearm?"

"I told you I don't have a gun."

"Okay, slowly put your hands behind your back so I can hand-cuff you. You're under arrest for the rape of Olivia Spencer."

The Misty River residents rejoiced at the assailant's arrest, bringing a sense of relief and justice to their community.

Olivia was strangely numb and indifferent to the news of Owens's arrest. She hated the attention and wished she could make herself invisible. She couldn't accept that her abduction and rape had irrevocably changed her life. How could she? The nightmare didn't end when she woke up the next morning. The godforsaken place along the Misty River was forever etched into her heart.

Little did she know this arrest would unravel a much larger mystery. Rumors rapidly spread that Ms. Spencer's assailant had committed a heinous crime two years prior, the cold case murder of Frank Amoia that had haunted the town for far too long.

Ms. Spencer's indifference towards her assailant's arrest deepened as she learned about his previous crime. Her depression intensified as she grappled with her own trauma and realized that she had narrowly escaped becoming another victim of his murderous tendencies. The weight of this knowledge threatened to consume her completely, leaving her teetering on the edge of despair.

With the newfound attention brought upon the sexual predator because of the rape case, the murderer's past actions were thrust into the spotlight.

As news of this revelation spread throughout the town, whispers filled every corner. The once dormant murder case was now reignited with fervor, capturing the attention of both law enforcement and curious residents alike. The community found themselves torn between relief at having caught one criminal and unease at realizing there may be more darkness lurking within their midst.

Questions loomed over the small town. Would justice finally be served for the cold case murder? Could they trust this arrest would bring an end to their collective fear? And would the young schoolteacher ever find healing and reclaim her life from the clutches of darkness?

PART THREE

"The little details are by far the most

important for any case."

—Sherlock Holmes

CHAPTER 8

The Prosecutor

March 18, 1987, Wednesday morning

B lake Moretti was running late. He'd spent the night at the veterinary hospital with his cat, who was recovering on his bed after being drugged into oblivion.

He usually took his time to shower in the morning. His hair was consistently meticulously styled, and he was always impeccably dressed. He was known for his sharp sense of style and attention to detail. His immaculately tailored suits showed off his trim physique and were carefully chosen to enhance his captivating appearance. His wardrobe comprises various colors and textures, reflecting his physical demeanor and personal taste. Blake's clean-shaven face adds to his polished, refined look.

But he didn't have time for that today. He grabbed a clean shirt from his walk-in closet, tore off the cellophane laundry wrapper, and began to button it, examining his face in the mirror, hoping he could get away without shaving, just this once.

At thirty-two, Blake is strikingly handsome, possessing the kind of looks that could easily belong to a movie star. His life was organized around his work, and he preferred to live alone, spending solitary evenings playing the piano, or kicking back with a glass of wine and spinning vintage vinyls of John Lee Hooker, B.B. King, and Muddy Waters.

His suit jacket was still on the bed where he'd thrown it when he got home. He shrugged it on and rushed out the door. He threw his Mont Blanc leather backpack onto the passenger seat of his Porsche 944, backed out, and sped away.

The district attorney, Graham Hardy, had been Blake's professor of criminal trial practice at Syracuse University College of Law. Blake's potential became apparent when he entered private practice and developed a reputation as a tough and effective trial lawyer. Despite Blake's stunning appearance, he remained down to earth, never using his looks as an advantage; instead, he relied on his intelligence and intuition.

Blake is well-educated and self-reliant. Equally important, he has a sixth sense of reading people and situations, which is essential in his line of work.

In the summer of 1985, when Hardy offered Blake a position as an assistant district attorney, the timing couldn't have been better. Blake knew he'd take a significant cut, but money wasn't a factor for him. He'd recently won a multi-million-dollar verdict in a medical malpractice suit and was set for life. His reward for accepting the position was knowing he could put a stake in the hearts of cold-blooded killers.

At an early age, he'd dreamed of becoming a prosecutor. The timing was perfect, and he accepted Hardy's offer and joined the Leigh County District Attorney's Office.

He still hadn't made it to the murder trial team, though Leigh County had no shortage of murders. So he'd volunteered to sit second chair on several successful high-profile murder trials, earning Hardy's confidence.

John Barnes, the detective overseeing the rape investigation, called Hardy to notify him that the sheriff had arrested a man in connection with the Saint Patrick's Day rape.

"The press is going to crucify you," he said.

"Why would that be?"

"Because the man we arrested goes by the name Billy "Buck" Owens."

"And?"

"Graham, don't you remember? Owens is the same man Detective Massey believed murdered Frank Amoia two years ago. Massey begged your assistant district attorneys to file murder charges against him on three occasions, and they flat out refused to do it!"

"Oh yeah, I remember. I think there were one, if not two, more suspects in the case. The only alleged witness was Owens's scorned girlfriend, and she recanted her statement."

"That's true, but Massey always believed she recanted because she was scared Owens would kill her for snitching."

"Listen, I'm assigning Blake Moretti to prosecute the rape case. You need to set an appointment with Jennifer to present the case to a two-prosecutor panel this afternoon. I'll have Moretti take care of the press."

Blake Moretti's disregard for office policy had held him back, but this time, Hardy chose to overlook it. He knew he could count on him to accept complex cases; the more experienced prosecutors refused, and Blake would be adept at controlling the negative press.

"By the way, did someone from your department feed this story to the media?"

"Not that I'm aware of."

"I hope that isn't the case. If your sheriff needs to respond to the media, have him contact Blake so they can hold a joint press conference."

"I'll pass him your message."

Graham Hardy got off the call and shouted to his secretary, "Carol, find Moretti and get him in my office ASAP, and if anyone from the media calls, tell them I'm in a conference. Tell Moretti to manage the media. Before you call Moretti, turn on WLCNY so I can listen to their spin."

Hardy was taking a beating in the press. The 1987 Saint Patrick's Day rape and the 1985 Frank Amoia murder were all over the news. Billy "Buck" Owens, the arrested suspect in the rape case, had been a suspect in the Frank Amoia murder case. A commentator blamed Hardy for the Saint Patrick's Day rape because he'd consistently refused the sheriff's request to prosecute Owens for the murder. Calls from irate residents flooded the sheriff's and district attorney's offices.

As he watched the morning news, Hardy couldn't believe his ears. "Carol, please bring me another bottle of Maalox!"

"Gosh, Mr. Hardy, you don't look good. Are you okay?"

"Jesus, Carol, I'm being crucified on the news. How do you expect me to look?"

She watched him gulp the antacid.

"You should be careful not to drink too much Maalox. You can get an overdose of calcium, and we all know what can happen."

"No, Carol, I don't. What the heck can happen?"

"Constipation and diarrhea."

"Thank you, nurse Houlihan. I don't know what I'd do without you."

Hardy had trouble reaching Blake, so he called his legal assistant, Jennifer Anders.

"Where in the world is he?"

She was used to covering for her boss. "He's investigating another case and preparing for trial."

"Yeah, right. Tell Blake he's got a new assignment. It's all over the news that the sheriff is looking for a filing regarding the woman who was raped last night. The suspected perpetrator may be the same guy who killed Frank Amoia. I don't care what you must do but find him."

The Amoia case had been Leigh County's most high-profile murder case in recent memory, but no arrest had been made. Massey was convinced that Owens murdered Amoia, and he had the evidence to prove it. Massey met with three senior prosecutors in Leigh County and requested a murder on Owens. He was told that suspecting Owens murdered Amoia was not the same as having evidence to support his suspicions. He tried again twice, but the prosecutors were concerned they didn't have enough proof to guarantee a guilty verdict.

Hardy speculated that someone in the sheriff's office leaked the story to the press that his office had refused to charge Owens with the murder of Frank Amoia. Should his suspicions prove true, Hardy was prepared to call a press conference and announce murder and robbery charges were rejected because the sheriff's investigators had more than one plausible suspect, and they spent all their time only investigating Owens, ignoring the other suspects.

Blake arrived at the office, uncharacteristically disheveled. His hair was rumpled, and his Hugo Boss suit looked like it could use a pressing.

"Too much green beer last night?" Jennifer asked.

"I wish. I was at the vet all night with Roxanne."

"Sure, you were."

Blake ignored the cynical comment because he had earned it from his well-established nightlife behavior.

"That coffee smells great. May I have a cup?"

"I'll pour you one if you wash the coffee pot."

"I can manage that."

In middle age, Jennifer Anders was still beautiful, her luxurious blonde hair piled in a chignon, her green eyes flashing behind stylish, black-framed glasses. Blake never thought of her as anything but a reliable, smart assistant. They'd worked together for the past year without confiding in each other or inquiring about their personal lives.

Jennifer set the mug of black coffee on his desk.

"Thanks. But what's up with you?"

"A young woman was brutally raped last night. It's all over the news."

Blake took a sip of the scalding coffee and grimaced. "Yeah, I heard it on the radio on my way in."

Jennifer slipped her hands into the pockets of her tweed skirt. "*The Wizard of Oz* wants you on this case." It was her nickname for Hardy, whom she considered nothing more than a wannabe prosecutor. The governor appointed him district attorney when his predecessor, Michael Dornan, left to become a Leigh County court judge. "He's worried about the negative press and wants you to take charge and control it. You need to assemble a three-prosecutor panel to determine if criminal charges are warranted. And he wants it done this afternoon. The file is on your desk." She pointed to a blue folder.

"Okay. Sorry, I was late this morning. Thanks for covering for me. I owe you."

"You'll be owing me for the rest of your life."

"Why is the office getting bad press?"

"We're under fire because someone leaked information that the suspect may be a rapist-slash-murderer."

"What are you talking about?"

"The sheriff believes he's the same man who murdered Frank Amoia two years ago."

"I remember that murder. What's the status of that case?"

"There is no status. The violent crime team panel denied criminal charges three times, claiming they didn't have the evidence to prosecute."

"Well was that true?"

"It depends on who you choose to believe."

"So, what connects the rape and murder cases?"

"Hardy says the rapist's girlfriend informed the sheriff that she had information proving he was the murderer, but she recanted the story almost immediately. That same woman informed the sheriff's office that she had information that Owens was the rapist."

Blake tapped his fingers on his desk, nodding. "So, some disgruntled person in the sheriff's department, off the record, blamed the rape on Hardy."

"It is reassuring that I'm not the only person who figured that out," Jennifer said. "By the way, you'll also need to review the red file on your desk."

"Red files are used for murder cases. Why is this one on my desk? I was assigned the rape case."

"Because Detectives Massey and Wilson, who investigated the Amoia murder case, will be accompanying Detective Barnes, the rape investigator, to present their cases to the three-prosecutor panel this afternoon. Massey has information related to the rape investigation that connects Owens to the Amoia murder. Don't be surprised if he requests a murder charge in the Amoia case."

"That's fine with me. But I need you to do something."

"All right. What is it?"

"When you're assigning prosecutors to the panel, select rookies who've never overseen a murder case."

"You've got to be kidding me."

"No, I'm not. I have a plan."

"Blake, that's not a good plan. When Hardy hears about it, he'll blow a gasket, and we'll both be in trouble."

"The Wizard will get over it. Besides, you came with the furniture; he can't get rid of you."

As Jennifer exited Blake's office, she thought, "I could feel it in my bones. Whatever the hell Blake's plan is, it is doomed to fail, and I'll be lucky to end up flipping greasy burgers at Big Daddy's Burger Joint."

CHAPTER 9

Just The Facts

March 18, 1987, Wednesday afternoon

B lake subscribed to the time-honored principle that when a crime is committed, it's the duty and responsibility of the prosecutor, not the sheriff, to decide who should be arrested and charged. The prosecutor's authority would be usurped if those decisions were entrusted to the sheriff.

Prosecutors sometimes shied away from that responsibility, leaving it up to law enforcement agencies to determine who to charge and what to charge, causing wrongful arrests and convictions. As a precaution, Leigh County's District Attorney's Office established a panel of three senior prosecutors to review and approve all violent crime charges.

Blake was acutely aware that if the prosecutors who had previously refused a murder charge in the Amoia murder case were to be present on the afternoon's panel, there would undoubtedly be a recurrence of their refusal to pursue a murder charge for the fourth time. Determined to avoid repeating past failures, Blake strategically assembled a team of fresh-faced rookie prosecutors who had yet to tackle the daunting challenge of a murder case.

Despite the potential weakness of the evidence, Blake willingly embraced the daunting task of ensuring that Amoia's murderer would face justice. In his relentless pursuit of justice, Blake understood that murderers often inadvertently leave behind a trail of breadcrumbs, whether a fingerprint, a strand of hair, a drop of blood, or even an overlooked personal item. These seemingly insignificant remnants can serve as invaluable leads for an astute prosecutor like Blake. By meticulously examining every minute detail at the crime scene, Blake aimed to uncover that one elusive piece of evidence that would ultimately unravel the mystery and expose the identity of Frank Amoia's killer.

In preparation for the upcoming panel, Blake invited Detectives Massey, Wilson, and Barnes to convene in his office. Their meeting aimed to establish a potential connection between the Spencer rape and the Amoia murder. Massey, actively pursuing charges in the cold-case murder, possessed valuable information that could benefit both investigations. Recognizing the significance of linking these two cases, Blake urged the detectives to collaborate and uncover any possible correlations. Eager to contribute, Massey took the lead and began sharing his insights.

Massey unbuttoned his brown jacket and took a deep breath.

"My investigation last year revealed that Owens murdered Amoia, but at the time, your office refused to prosecute him."

Blake, playing the devil's advocate, said, "I reviewed your file, and it appears that, in addition to the suspect Owens, you found equally damning evidence pointing the finger at Joey Fleming."

"You are correct. Vickie Fleming, who has had an on-and-off-again relationship with Owens, serves as the common denominator in both the Amoia murder case and the Spencer rape case. Ms. Fleming fingered Owens as the perpetrator in both cases. As you know, because she'd recanted her story that Owens murdered Mr. Amoia and that her son Joey Fleming was a possible murder suspect, your office refused to charge Owens with murder. I promised I could get Valerie to testify against him once he was in jail. They said it made no difference because she wouldn't have credibility with a jury. With her son a potential suspect, the case couldn't be proven beyond a reasonable doubt."

"I've read your reports. Is there anything else you want to add?"

"No. That's it in a nutshell."

"Thank you. Detective Barnes tell me about the rape case investigation."

"A woman contacted Massey with information about the Spencer rape. It turned out that the caller was Valerie Fleming. Massey relayed the news to me, and I interviewed her at the sheriff's office. Again, Fleming fingered Owens, this time for rape.

"During the interview, Fleming provided a detailed account of the events leading up to the rape. She told us that Owens had given her an engagement ring the night of the assault. The information was powerful evidence linking him to the crime because the ring was later found to be the same one that had been stolen from the victim. The discovery of the engagement ring was also significant because it corroborated Ms. Spencer's story and provided concrete evidence of Owens' involvement in the rape. The information provided by Fleming was instrumental in leading to the arrest of Owens for the rape of Ms. Spencer.

"Ms. Fleming considered herself as guilty of the rape as Owens and said she couldn't live with herself if she didn't make things right. She wanted me to promise I'd keep the call confidential because she was frightened Owens would kill her. I told her she would have to testify. Because Owens would be incarcerated on the rape charge, I assured her he would have no chance to harm her physically.

"After Owens' arrest, I interviewed him. He told me he had never raped anyone. I placed a photograph of the victim's engagement ring on the table and asked him if he recognized it. I watched his nonchalant attitude change to anger. He wanted to know how I got the ring.

"I said, 'So you recognize it?' He told me a woman had seduced him and then gave it to him. He added the sex was consensual."

Blake scribbled notes on a yellow legal pad, leaned back in his desk chair, and said, "Gentlemen, I have everything I need. It's time to make your sales pitch to the panel."

Massey said, "Blake, I've been turned down three times. Why should this time be any different?"

"Let's just say I think you'll like this panel."

Blake phoned Jennifer and told her to notify the panel that he was ready to proceed.

The two assistant prosecutors were reviewing copies of the case files at the conference table when Blake entered the law library with

Detectives Massey, Wilson, and Barnes. It was their first day on the job. Jennifer had outdone herself.

"Afternoon. Thanks for agreeing to be on the panel. It's an excellent opportunity," he said.

They looked up. A blonde guy wearing a new suit and a fresh shave said, "We were supposed to go to HR and fill out a bunch of paperwork, but when Jennifer told us this would be the opportunity of a lifetime, we jumped. She also told us to ask if we could try those cases with you."

"No, that's not going to happen," Blake replied, annoyed at her suggestion.

Detectives Massey, Wilson, and Barnes made case presentations and fielded questions. Then, they were excused from the room to allow the prosecutors to express their views.

Blake told the panel members that, based on the detectives' presentations, a grand jury would indict Owens because he was likely to be convicted. They had concerns, but they followed his lead, and Owens was charged with first-degree murder, rape, and related criminal charges.

After the panel reached its conclusion, Blake stopped by Hardy's office to inform him, but found the door locked. Blake returned to his office and asked Jennifer why Hardy's office was closed.

"Hardy and his staff are attending an award luncheon."

"Listen, the office is closing in thirty minutes. I'm meeting Ralph for a drink to plan our next moves."

Ralph Morgan was Blake's investigator.

"What do you want me to tell Hardy?"

"Tell him I hope he had a pleasant lunch and congrats for whatever award he received. I'll talk to him in the morning."

"Oh, that's just great. You know he'll be pissed off when he hears what you did. I don't think you'll be getting any office awards."

"That's okay. My mantel is already crowded with New York Yankees memorabilia. I'll catch you in the morning."

When Graham Hardy returned from the luncheon, he peered into Blake's office, looking annoyed. "Jennifer, where are Blake and his sidekick?"

"They're out trying to locate a witness."

"I need to see Blake as soon as possible. The violent crime team is irate. They think Blake charged Owens with murder to make them look bad for turning down the case three times."

"He would never do that. I'm sure he must have new evidence that Owens murdered Mr. Amoia."

Hardy shook his head. "Am I the only sane person in this office?"

Jennifer remembered that Blake had said they were meeting for drinks and knew how to find them.

"The Exchange at 36th, Andrea speaking."

"This is Blake Moretti's legal assistant, Jennifer Anders. Might either Blake or Ralph be at the bar?"

"Hold while I get their attention."

Morgan, sixty, was thin but powerfully built, quick-tempered, and a brilliant investigator with a tough reputation. His son had been robbed and murdered at the age of twenty-five, and the sheriff's precinct where he'd worked for a quarter century hadn't solved the case.

After his son's death, he'd gone into a depression and left law enforcement until Graham Hardy convinced him to join the District Attorney's Office.

At the bar, Ralph turned to Blake. "I've got this."

"Jennifer, Ralph here. What's up?"

"Hardy is looking for you two. He's pissed that Blake charged Owens for the Amoia murder and wants him in his office ASAP."

"Hang on a minute, Jennifer." He went back to Blake and leaned over. "I knew this was coming."

"Blake said to tell Hardy he was tied up and that he would catch up with him in the morning. Oh, he also said don't forget to tell him congrats on his award."

"Ralph, you're both going to be the death of me!"

District Attorney Graham Hardy was a small man with a big ego. He considered himself a legal genius, but he was a legend only in his own mind. He sat back in his leather chair and folded his hands in his lap, a smirk on his lips. "That was quite a stunt, Moretti, picking two of the most inexperienced lawyers in the office to sit on the murder panel."

"Mr. Hardy, I assume you only hire the best prosecutors. Unfortunately, the homicide team lawyers weren't available when the meeting was scheduled."

"Damn it, you're one of the brightest lawyers I have. How is it that you can never follow office policy? You could have scheduled the meeting for another day."

"Great question. I don't have an answer. I guess it is just one of life's unsolvable mysteries."

"Moretti, you don't have any fucking evidence."

"Mr. Hardy, as you know, murderers always leave incriminating evidence at crime scenes. I'll find it soon enough."

"You'd better pray you don't lose the murder case, or you'll be packing your bags."

"Nothing lasts forever."

"Listen Blake, I need you to get the press off my back."

"I've already taken care of your public relations problem with the media, at least for the time being."

"Oh yeah, how's that?"

"Since word got out that Owens was charged with murder, they've moved on from castigating your failure to act."

"You'd better be right. You're gambling away my future."

"It's worth taking a gamble if it means doing the right thing."

Hardy's well-kept receptionist sat behind a cheaply made particleboard single pedestal desk. Inscribed on the desk plaque was Carol Applegate's name.

Her matching jacket was paired with a navy pleated skirt and a white blouse. The edges of her curly blonde hair covered her pale white neckline. A gold cross hung from her petite necklace, complementing her solid gold hallmark clasp cable chain bracelet and emerald double heart birthstone ring on her right little finger.

No one could ever accuse Carol of having common sense, but her outgoing personality and attractive looks make up for it. All the eligible men in the office and some of the not-so-eligible men hit on her. Unfortunately for them, she was only attracted to Blake and didn't hide her feelings. Sadly for her, Blake wasn't interested.

She was painting her nails when Blake walked by. "Hi, Mr. Moretti. From the smile on your face, it appears the meeting with Mr. Hardy went well."

"I guess you could say Mr. Hardy was at a loss for words."

"Oh, that's great. Sometimes he worries too much."

"Gee, you think? By the way, don't stop painting your nails on my account. I love how the purple nail color matches your eyeglass frames."

Blake returned to his office and carefully reviewed the Owens files. Getting all the details right was crucial to building a successful case. He'd been educated by Catholic priests, nuns, and monks who didn't tolerate errors or mental weakness, so from a very early age, he'd hated losing more than he'd loved winning.

Owens intentionally caused his victims' pain and suffering. They had a right to be remembered, and he needed to pay for his crimes. No one had put a gun to Owens's head and made him kill Amoia or rape Olivia Spencer. Owens had written his ledger. His ship had sailed, and there was no turning back. The reckoning was coming, and Blake would make damn sure of it.

CHAPTER 10

Hear My Voice

March 24, 1987, Tuesday morning

Olivia Spencer nervously entered the prosecutor's conference room, her heart pounding. She had never been involved in a criminal case, let alone be the victim of a brutal rape. Olivia couldn't help but feel intimidated by the gravity of the situation. She'd had to force herself to meet with the prosecutor.

Jennifer, Blake's efficient and empathetic legal assistant, greeted Olivia. "Thank you for coming in today, Olivia," she said warmly. I am Jennifer Anders, Mr. Moretti's legal assistant, and this is investigator Ralph Morgan."

"We understand this process can feel intimidating, but we are here to support you." Jennifer motioned for Olivia to take a seat at the conference table.

Olivia nodded, her voice barely above a whisper. "I appreciate your help."

Jennifer offered Olivia a glass of water. "Mr. Moretti is running late. Judge Croghan had a matter to discuss with him. "He will be here any minute."

On cue, there was a sudden knock on the door. When the door opened, Olivia shuddered at the sight of the tall, well-dressed man who entered, Blake Moretti, the seasoned prosecutor known for his unwavering dedication to justice.

"Ms. Spencer, good morning, I'm Blake Moretti, the prosecutor assigned to your case." He extended his hand, but she hesitated, and he awkwardly withdrew it. He didn't take it personally.

"I see you've met my legal assistant, Jennifer Anders, and my investigator, Ralph Morgan."

They both nodded.

It had been a week since the attack. Olivia Spencer's ordeal had crippled her emotionally. She was so frightened she couldn't step outside her house. At twenty-seven, she felt her life had become a nightmare.

Her engagement was in shambles, and her heart was beyond repair. Although she'd done nothing to deserve her fiancé's indifference, she felt culpable. He'd promised to love her, no matter what, but he'd changed so much that she no longer recognized him and felt she was being punished for having been the victim of a crime. Dean didn't want a rape victim for his wife. That was the explanation he gave her when he phoned her. She kept thinking, *Hell, I'm the victim here. This is insane.* She was livid, but she was also scared and tired.

"Mr. Moretti. I want your assurance the man who did this to me is held accountable."

Blake's eyes softened as he listened intently to Olivia's words. He had seen countless victims walk through his door, each with a unique pain and suffering story. But he never grew desensitized to their pain; instead, it fueled his determination to fight for justice. Blake genuinely cares for victims and their families, going above and beyond to ensure justice is served. Using his disarming smile during interviews, he is adept at building rapport with witnesses because of his charisma and charm. In the world of crime fighting, his charismatic personality makes him stand out.

"I assure you, Ms. Spencer, your voice will be heard," Blake replied firmly. "We will do everything in our power to bring your assailant to justice."

As the meeting progressed, Blake carefully guided Olivia through the legal process, explaining each step and ensuring she understood her rights as a victim. He patiently answered her questions and addressed her concerns with empathy and compassion.

Jennifer diligently took notes throughout the meeting, capturing every detail that could aid the investigation. The seasoned investigator, Ralph, listened intently.

"I know this won't be easy for you, but I can assure you my team will try to make the process as smooth as possible. Would you mind telling me a bit about yourself?"

Blake knew he was walking on eggshells. One mistake could scare her off. He'd have to make her feel comfortable with him, and he wanted her to know he understood her situation. He needed to convince her they would do everything legally possible to see that the defendant received the maximum sentence.

"Look, Mr. Moretti, please understand this is very difficult for me emotionally. There's no way I can handle a trial."

"I understand. It's not my first time hearing a victim express that feeling. Before you make any trial decisions, let me share some thoughts. People who know me will tell you I don't sugarcoat anything. Let's make a deal. Indulge me for five minutes. We can pretend we never met if you aren't ready to help after that."

Olivia asked, "Before I decide, may I ask you a question?"

"Fire away."

"I hope you don't take offense, but I read in the papers that the monster who raped me may be the same man who killed Mr. Amoia two years ago, and the prosecutor's office refused to charge him. Is that true? Because if it's true that your office could have charged him with murder and prosecuted him, this nightmare would never have happened."

"That's a fair question, and I'll answer it, but I warn you that you won't like everything I say. Should I go on?"

"Of course."

"When I inquired about it, I learned that three of our most senior violent crime prosecutors decided there was insufficient evidence to arrest and charge Mr. Owens with murder. Prosecutors sometimes disagree about whether there's enough evidence to charge someone with a crime. I can't get into the details with you, but I can tell you that the prosecutors who reviewed the case all agreed that, in all likelihood, if they had gone forward, the suspect would have been acquitted.

"After reexamining the case, we determined that the likelihood of Owens being convicted for the murder has changed. On the 18th of

March, he was charged with the murder of Frank Amoia. I'll personally prosecute the case, and I've asked Ralph to collaborate with me on both cases, which is why he's attending this meeting.

"Nothing I said may change your position, but you have my word, Owens will be held accountable. I'm sure you would be the first to agree that no one in this room wants to see Owens inflict harm on anyone else. With your help, Owens will spend the rest of his life in a six-by-eight-foot cell.

"One last thought. Olivia, I know you want this nightmare to end. The first step in that process is acknowledging your fears and working with us to prosecute Owens."

"Yes, you're right," she said. "I'll tell you everything from the beginning." She had been staring at her hands, tightly clasped in her lap. Now she looked up and met his eyes. The gesture told him she was ready to talk.

Olivia stared at Blake for a moment, then bent a bit forward, her arms still crossed, she said, "My name is Olivia Spencer. I am twenty-seven years old and an elementary school teacher in the Leigh County School District. I'm an only child, and until recently, I was engaged to marry Dean Neely."

By the end of the meeting, Olivia felt a glimmer of hope. She knew she had a dedicated team on her side, fighting for her and seeking justice on her behalf. As she left the conference room, she couldn't help but feel a sense of gratitude for Blake and his team.

This meeting was just the beginning of a long and arduous journey towards justice. But with Blake leading the charge, she knew she had an unwavering advocate by her side.

Blake was more committed than ever to getting justice for her. "I want you to know that you're far stronger than you think. You are one of the bravest women I've ever met."

"I appreciate your honesty."

"So, can we count on you to help us put Owens away for the rest of his life?"

"How can I say no? I'll do my best."

Blake extended his hand, and this time, she shook it.

"If you have questions, please call. I recommend you contact Jennifer; somehow, she always finds me."

When Olivia left, Blake asked Jennifer and Ralph to stay. "I'm sick to my stomach," he said. "Her life is in shambles. Jennifer, a penny for your thoughts."

Jennifer pushed an errant blonde strand away from her face and leaned toward Blake. "I have a couple of thoughts," she said. "Olivia Spencer seems like a wonderful woman. Owens needs to pay the price for the pain and suffering he inflicted, and I firmly believe that Mr. Amoia's murder must be avenged.

"One thing I know about you, Blake, is that you've never shunned a challenging case. You're a brilliant trial lawyer. Ralph is a successful investigator. Between the two of you, there is no question you will successfully prosecute and convict this son of a bitch for rape and murder."

"Ditto," Ralph said.

"Well, I guess that answers my question and more," Blake said. "That's what I like about you, Jennifer. You speak your mind. So, Ralph, I think it's time to visit Owens's ex-girlfriend. Considering how persuasive you are, I suspect Ms. Fleming will share everything she knows about the Amoia murder."

"Yeah, I hope so," Ralph said.

Jennifer says, "Blake, don't forget we're meeting with Mrs. Amoia this afternoon at two. She is visiting family in Florida and will arrive at noon. Ralph will pick her up at the airport and transport her to our meeting. Make sure you arrive on time for the meeting, Blake."

"Thank you for the motherly reminder. By the way, how is she?"

"The murder of her husband has taken a toll on her, but she's a strong woman."

"I'm not surprised; she's Italian. I've spoken to her several times on the phone. She reminds me of my Aunt Josephine. Despite being soft-spoken, she is not afraid to speak her mind."

Ralph asked, "Are you going to ask her why Mr. Amoia hid money?"

"No. I don't need to. I already know the answer to that question. Instead, I am going to ask her about Sonny Calo."

"Why?"

"Don't you see, Sonny Calo is why Frank Amoia is dead?"

"What?!"

CHAPTER 11

Survivor

March 24, 1987, Tuesday afternoon

Two weeks after her seventieth birthday, Mary Amoia slouched into a wooden chair at the conference table. She shifted her weight several times to get comfortable while she waited for Blake to arrive.

"Thank you for your patience. Mr. Moretti will be here shortly," Jennifer said.

"I've waited two years for this day to come. What's a few more minutes?"

At ten minutes past two, Blake appeared. "Afternoon, Mrs. Amoia," he said, shaking her hand. This was his first chance to meet her in person, and she was just as he had imagined.

She smiled faintly and softly said, "Thank you for taking an interest in my husband's case. I thought I was the only one thinking about Frank's death and wondered if his killer would ever be caught and punished. Your call informing me that an arrest had been made was a great relief. Do you have a good case against Owens?"

Ralph and Jennifer fixed their eyes on Blake.

"Mrs. Amoia, let's just say that cases are like treasure hunts. One minute there's no gold in the chest; the next thing you know, you're a millionaire."

Mrs. Amoia responded, "Well, I pray you hit gold soon."

"Yeah. Me too," said Ralph.

She and Blake had talked about Frank's Brooklyn childhood, and why they'd moved to Leigh County. The more she described the baker and his family, the more Blake was reminded of his Italian grandparents, and he wondered if that was why he'd taken a particular interest in the case.

"By the way, Mrs. Amoia, Detective Massey asked you about the money your husband hid in the bakery. I must ask, do you know where it came from?"

"Like I already told Detective Massey, I don't know."

"That's what I thought you would say, but I had to ask because I suspect it will come up at trial."

"I understand. You're doing your due diligence; I am not concerned since I won't be testifying."

"Well, the thing is, I plan on asking you to testify."

"What could I possibly testify about? I wasn't there when Frank was murdered."

"That is true, but I want you to describe the events leading up to Frank's murder and how it affected you. Would you do that for me?"

"Mr. Moretti, I'm a devout Catholic. It is my belief that both God and Satan exist, as do heaven and hell. People say things to me like, 'Frank's death was God's plan,' or 'Frank's time had come.' But I believe that everyone has free will. So, I choose not to listen to that rubbish. The man who murdered Frank chose to kill my husband. That wasn't God's decision.

"I choose not to forgive him and to do whatever it takes to be sure he rots in prison and someday in hell. If my testimony will help convict him, count me in. I hope you don't think ill of me for feeling that way."

Blake answered, "Mrs. Amoia, some survivors find it in their hearts to forgive. Some seek an eye for an eye. It's not my place to judge who is right. You are a survivor, and you have that right."

"I was wondering if Frank knew Sonny Calo?"

"Who doesn't know Sonny? He's constantly in the news. Why do you ask?"

"I'll get to that in a moment."

"Yes, Frank was godfather to Sonny's son, Anthony."

"Do you know if your husband was doing business with Sonny?"

"That was Frank's business partner. Frank knew I didn't care for Sonny coming around, but that was Frank's friend. Frank and Sonny knew each other from the old neighborhood. Nothing I said would stop Frank and Sonny from hanging out together.

"Frank had been pushing to sell the bakery, retire, and move to Florida, seeking my approval. But I worried we didn't save enough money to retire, and I procrastinated giving him an answer. The morning he was murdered, Frank was pressuring me to provide him with an answer before he left for work and reassured me he had the money. I couldn't figure out where he got enough money to retire until I learned about the fifty thousand dollars the sheriff found in the crockpot. I figured Frank and Sonny had something cooked up. Of course, fifty thousand wasn't enough to retire on, so I assumed there was more money the sheriff never found or the killer stole."

"I see. We can talk about this another time."

Blake thanked Mrs. Amoia for her time, and the meeting ended. Blake sensed that Sonny Calo and the hidden money dilemma wasn't going away soon.

Ralph asked, "Blake, do you think Sonny Calo had anything to do with Frank's murder?"

"Time will tell. I suspect it won't be long before I hear from Sonny Calo."

That night, Blake found it impossible to sleep. His thoughts drifted to Olivia Spencer, her hands clenched and eyelids drooping. He promised himself he wouldn't let her down.

He was just as determined to solve the Amoia murder, and he knew that if he were to have any chance of convicting Owens, he'd need more evidence and time to mount a case against him.

He'd started dozing off in bed when his phone rang. Still half asleep, Blake rolled towards the nightstand, reached over, picked up the receiver, and answered, "Hello, this is Moretti."

"Moretti, this is Sal Marino. Do you know who I am?"

"As long as you know who you are, that's all that matters. What can I do for you this late in the evening?"

"I've been asked to inform you that Sonny Calo wants to speak with you. You'll find him at half past eight at the *City Club* tomorrow night. He'll be at the private table in the back of the bar lounge with a white carnation on his lapel. Don't bring anyone with you."

"Jesus, Sal, I know who Sonny Calo is."

"Great, Moretti. Thanks for taking my call. I'll let Sonny know you'll be there on time. Sleep fucking tight."

CHAPTER 12

Hardball

March 25, 1987, Wednesday morning

The following morning, Ralph picked Blake up at six-thirty to make a surprise visit to Owens's girlfriend. He slammed the door as he got out of the car.

"Jesus," Blake said, "I thought we'd surprise her. Hell, you could have just called and warned her we were coming."

"Calm down and keep your eye on the window in the upstairs bedroom," Ralph said.

The curtain moved. "Must be Valerie," Blake whispered.

"Way to go, Sherlock. Let's get her attention."

Ralph repeatedly knocked on the door but got no response, so he began pounding and announcing who they were and that they needed to speak with her. Still no response. He told Blake, "Stay here. I'll be right back."

"Where are you going?"

"To get my car. Just stay put."

Ralph started his vehicle, drove it rapidly over the curb and across the sidewalk, and pulled up inches from Valerie's front porch. He reached out the driver's window, attached his mobile emergency lights to the roof, and activated the lights and siren. Then he strolled up to the front porch.

"What the hell are you doing, Ralph?"

"Give me a minute. I guarantee Valerie will answer the door when she realizes we're not leaving. Her neighbors will threaten to drag her ass out of the house if she doesn't." He was enjoying his crazy plan.

"Ralph, why is that tow truck pulling up to the blue Buick?"

"I ran the plate. It belongs to Valerie Fleming."

"But it's legally parked. How in the world do you have the right to tow it?"

"I don't. Relax. I'm not a betting man. But if I were, I'd bet that when she sees her vehicle getting hooked up, she'll run her ass out the front door."

"Ralph, I have to give it to you. You play old school hardball better than anyone I've ever seen. Today's soft young investigators would have placed a calling card on the door and left after the first unresponsive knock."

They heard footsteps, and then Valerie walked out the door in a faded cotton robe and slippers, her dark curls in disarray, her blue eyes still clouded with sleep.

"Oh, hi Valerie. I didn't think you were home," Ralph said with a big smile.

"What the hell are you doing?" she yelled. "That's my car!"

"I'm simply giving you an opportunity to do the right thing and talk to me about Amoia's murder."

"What makes you think I know anything about it?"

"Perhaps we should all go inside. We can talk about what we know, and you can tell us what *you* know."

She looked at Ralph for a minute, and then she noticed Blake. Her expression registered his expensive suit and handsome face. "Your face looks familiar."

"Yeah. It's just one of those faces that gets around."

"Call off the tow truck first, then we'll talk."

The living room was shabby but clean. Valerie pulled her robe tighter around her neck and sat on an old rocker. Ralph and Blake took the sagging couch. "Look, Valerie," Ralph began, "We know your boyfriend, Owens, killed Frank Amoia."

"I told the sheriff two years ago; I don't know who killed that poor man." She reached into the pocket of her robe and took out a pack of cigarettes.

Ralph leaned forward and clasped his hands between his knees. "You and I both know that's not true. I know you feel you're between a rock and a hard place. Right now, as we sit here, you're not in any trouble. But if you continue to lie, you'll be charged with a felony and end up serving a long prison term. Do we understand each other?"

Valerie lit her cigarette and took a puff without taking her eyes off Ralph. "Yeah, I get it."

"Good. I know you initially told the sheriff that when you saw Owens after the murder, his clothes and boots had blood on them. Then you turned around and recanted that story. You said you didn't know anything about it, but that was a lie, wasn't it? We both know you know who murdered Frank Amoia. So now's the time to tell the whole truth. You're aware that aiding and abetting a murder, even after the fact, is a felony."

Valerie put her head in her hands. For a few minutes nobody said a word. When she looked up again, her eyes were teary. Ralph and Blake glanced at each other. They could see that her conscience was bothering her.

"Look," she said softly, "I need some time to think. I want to be sure Buck won't get off on the rape case. I want to talk to a lawyer before I say anything more."

Blake nodded. " I'll give you to the end of business today. Have your lawyer call me." He stood up to leave, then turned to Valerie, "Oh, I forgot to tell you about my conversation with Detective Massey. Owens informed him that your son Joey stole his Buck knife and used it to murder Mr. Amoia. He also said that Owens told him you helped your son dispose of the murder weapon and bloody clothes. Maybe that explains why you and Detectives Massey and Wilson couldn't find the bloody murder weapon you claim Owens disposed of."

"That's fucking bullshit!"

"Maybe, maybe not. Listen carefully to my words. There will be a price to pay for the murder of Frank Amoia. I promised Mary Amoia that her husband's murder would not go unpunished. Someone will be held accountable for his death and spend the rest of their life in prison.

"Here's the best part. I never make promises I can't keep. It doesn't matter to me if Billy "Buck" Owens, Joey, or you get locked up for Frank Amoia's murder. Hopefully, what I said has clicked with you, and you'll do what's right by telling us who killed Frank Amoia. You'll hear from me soon. Enjoy your day."

Driving back to the office, Ralph asked, "Why did you give her more time? I had her on the ropes?"

"I want her to decide it's time to tell us everything she knows on her own terms. Besides, she is not going to call a lawyer. Let her sleep on it tonight. Ralph, you taught me that a reluctant witness won't cooperate unless they feel more heat from us than the perpetrator. First thing in the morning, make her another visit and turn up the heat.

"Don't fool yourself into thinking she doesn't know how much hot water she's in. She confessed to aiding and abetting Owens when she went with him to ditch the bloody murder weapon and clothes. Hell, she could get as much time in prison as Owens. As we speak, her asshole is puckering, because she's gravely concerned that if Owens walks, her son may end up the fall guy.

"She's finally feeling more heat from us than from her loudmouth boyfriend, Owens, who's stuck in jail getting fatter by the day on turkey bologna. He won't be going anywhere anytime soon. She understands how the system works. If she doesn't cooperate and tell us the truth, she knows her son could go to prison for a crime he may not have committed, and she'll be right behind him."

"I get it," Ralph said, "Everyone has a breaking point. She just needs a little more time to realize she's reached hers."

"I'm not a gambler, but I'd bet my entire blues vinyl collection that Ms. Fleming is having a 'Come to Jesus' moment. By morning, she'll be prepared to nail Owens to the cross. By the way, I need you to locate Joey Fleming. I must determine if he has a legitimate alibi for the morning of the murder. I also want to question him about his knowledge of the money stashed in the bakery and his conversations with Owens about it."

"I've got you covered,"

The following morning at six, Ralph knocked on Valerie Fleming's door and announced his presence.

"Valerie, I know you're home. Your vehicle is in the driveway. I can have a tow truck here within five minutes if that's how you want to roll. It's your choice. By now, you know I'm not playing."

The front door slowly opened and out walked Valerie. "Why the fuck do you keep harassing me? Do you want me to call the sheriff?"

"Be my guest. While you're at it, why don't you call your boyfriend Buck? Oh, I forgot his fat ass is in jail. And that's where you will wind up if you keep up your 'leave me alone, I'm just a poor victim caught up in this mess' attitude. I've seen that bullshit act done better. You need to understand you're not the victim here. Olivia Spencer and Frank Amoia are the victims. You're a witness in a murder and a rape case, a material witness. If you choose not to cooperate, that's fine. In fact, I hope you do so that I can bring you before a judge on a material witness warrant, and you can explain why they shouldn't lock your sorry ass up. Hell, I should just arrest you now."

Valerie leaned against the open door, her hands in the pockets of her robe. "What the hell for?"

"How about obstruction of justice, harboring a fugitive, or just being a pain in the ass."

"I get it already. Give me five minutes to throw on some clothes and get my purse."

Ralph and Jennifer sat on either side of Valerie in the prosecutor's small conference room. Blake walked in with Detectives Massey and Barnes and laid what appeared to be a law book and some paperwork on the conference table, making sure Valerie noticed.

He took a seat, and as he pulled his chair closer to the table, he held Valerie's eyes. "Thank you for agreeing to talk with me. Ralph told me how eager you are to do what's right, but you'll have to do three things this time. First, you'll have to admit you lied to Detective Massey when you recanted your statement that Owens killed Amoia. Second, you'll have to take the lie back. And third, you'll have to tell the truth and nothing but the truth. Do you understand?"

"That's cute. But yes, I'm ready."

"Please state your full name and date of birth."

"Valerie Joan Fleming. July 16, 1947."

"And are you currently employed?"

"I do manicures at the Luxury Nail Spa on Brown Street."

"Please understand that if you lie to me, I'll charge you as an accomplice after the fact to murder. You've told Detective Massey that Buck set you up to be charged as an accessory, so you recanted your story. You were also afraid Buck would kill you if you snitched on him. Isn't that true?"

"Yes, sir."

Blake was fully attentive, leaning forward, his elbows on the table. "Tell us what you know about the murder of Frank Amoia and the rape of Olivia Spencer."

"I know Buck killed Mr. Amoia. He said he would kill me if I told on him. That day, he came home around eight in the morning after being out all night drinking."

"Are you referring to the morning of Saturday, March 2, 1985?"

"Yes, I vividly remember the day because when he came in, he was out of breath, acting weird, with fresh blood on his jacket, pants, and boots. Then he reached into the front pocket of his jeans and pulled out a wad of money covered in blood. When I asked him where it came from, he told me some half-baked story about a man robbing him. He said he'd fought the guy off, stabbed him, and took his money. I didn't know what to think at first. Then he wanted to watch the news, which wasn't like him. That's when I learned Mr. Amoia had been found dead in the bakery and realized the robbery story was bullshit. Buck figured I'd put two and two together, so he said he'd kill me if I told on him. Then he made me go with him to ditch his bloody clothes, and I saw him wrap his bloody Buck knife and the sheath in the clothes. He told me I was an accessory to murder and would go to prison for the rest of my life if I told on him. That's the God's honest fucking truth."

Detective Massey, who had been bent over his notebook, looked up. "Thank you, Ms. Fleming. We just want the truth so that we can hold Mr. Amoia's killer accountable and bring closure to his family."

Blake said, "Now tell us about the rape."

Valerie choked up, and Jennifer handed her a tissue box and a glass of water. "Relax," she whispered, "take a breath and drink water. You're doing fine."

"It was nighttime," Valerie said, wiping her eyes. "I guess around midnight. I was in bed when I heard Buck come into the house. So, I got up to see what was going on, and he was sitting in his chair in the living room with his eyes wide open, just staring at the ceiling like his mind was elsewhere. His clothes and hair were messy, and he was all sweaty.

"I asked him what was going on, but he didn't answer me. He just stood up, reached into his coat pocket, pulled out a ring, and stared at it. I asked him why he had the ring and where he got it, and he said, 'Baby, I got it for you. I want you to marry me.'"

"I didn't know what to say. Before I could answer, he approached me, took my hand, and tried to put the ring on my finger, but it didn't fit.

"The next day, he turned the television on to watch the news. I said to myself, 'This isn't going to be good.' Channel Seven was reporting about a woman raped in the woods near the Misty River. I thought, 'Please don't tell me Buck did this.' A sheriff sketch of the suspect came on for what seemed like forever, and I knew Buck raped that woman. Buck saw the expression on my face, and said he'd kill me if I told on him.

"The first thought in my head was, *It's my fault the lady was raped.* Then I went to the bathroom and threw up."

"Thank you." Blake asked, "How does it feel to tell the truth finally?"

"Like the world's weight has finally been lifted off my shoulders."

"Valerie, we will do everything we can to ensure Owens spends the rest of his life in prison."

"Moretti, that's great. But you'd better watch out. Owens is a sociopath. Never underestimate Owens's cunning and manipulative nature. It's a sure bet he has a plan to escape justice."

CHAPTER 13

Do Me A Favor

March 25, 1987, Wednesday Late night

Sonny Calo exuded an air of sophistication as he occupied the seat directly opposite the intricately carved cherry wood bar. Adorned with his trademark white carnation, elegantly pinned to the lapel of his impeccably tailored Brioni suit worth a staggering six thousand dollars, he commanded attention in the upscale establishment. The smooth jazz melodies gracefully wafting through the background further enhanced the ambiance. As he sipped on bourbon and anxiously awaited, Blake's arrival, a young blonde woman in a too-short skirt cozied up beside him.

Blake knew Sonny, but he didn't have a clue who the young blonde woman was sitting beside him, wearing a skirt hiked up way too far. As Blake approached, the woman took a cigarette from a gold case and Sonny lit it.

"Moretti! Sit down. *Posso offrirti da bere?*"

"I'll pass. I'm driving."

Calo turned to his date. "Why don't you and Sal have a drink at the bar while I conduct business with my friend?"

"All right, but don't be long."

When she left, he leaned in and asked, "Moretti, is my lady friend hot or what?"

"Are all your *goomas* underage hookers?"

"I understand you dislike me, but please respect my lady friend. Listen, Mary Amoia has something that belongs to one of my friends, and he wants it back. She's unaware of the problem."

"Like what?"

"Like two hundred thousand smackers. I need your help to get it back for my friend."

"Sonny, the police recovered fifty thousand dollars stuffed in a crockpot. I don't know anything about the two hundred thousand dollars. What do you know about the fifty thousand dollars?"

"Let's just say Frank and my friend had a deal. It is Frank's money. Frank hated banks, so I suspect he hid his money. I can't say that I blame him. Bankers are pigs."

"How did Frank Amoia get his hands on two hundred thousand dollars from your friend without Mrs. Amoia knowing?"

"Let's just say my friend left it there without her knowledge."

"I don't understand. What makes you think I can help you?"

"I heard you're meeting with Mary to discuss Frank's case. I need you to convince her to let my friend collect his money. She doesn't need to know why."

"How can you be sure the murderer didn't steal your friend's money?"

"Moretti, two years have passed. Don't think I haven't made inquiries. Trust me, I know the money is still in the bakery. I put Sal, my best guy, on it. Sal met with a person of interest familiar with the money and was satisfied no one had stolen it. It's hidden somewhere in the bakery."

"I can't help you."

"Moretti, I'd hate to see what my friend would do if he doesn't get his property back. You feel me?"

"Why don't you ask your friend to call the sheriff and ask for his money? And I'm sure the Feds would be thrilled to discuss tax planning."

"Moretti, I'm done being nice. I want my fucking money!"

"You mean your friend's money. I can't help you. You need to talk to Mary."

"Look, I was Frank's friend. Mary didn't like me coming around. Considering how much I gave back to my community, I'm not sure why."

"Mother Teresa would be proud of you."

"Fuck off. Look, what can we do to resolve our problem?"

"Don't make your problem mine. Listen to me. You know I don't take kindly to anyone's threats, including yours. If anything happens to Mrs. Amoia, Joey, or Valerie Fleming, I'm coming after you. That includes getting struck by lightning if you get my drift. Sonny, I guarantee should you have any interest in sex for the remainder of your life, you will be on the receiving end. You feel me?"

"Look, Frank is my son's godfather. Mary suffered enough misery dealing with his murder. I'd rather not involve her."

"Sonny, wait for the murder case to play itself out. There is no reason both Mary Amoia and you can't get everything you want. Look, Sonny, you said you knew my grandfather and trusted him. He once told me, 'If you do a favor for someone, one day they'll do the same for you.'"

"I understand. You won't hear from me again. How's that for a favor?"

"I always said my grandfather was an intelligent man. I'm late for a date with a lovely woman who, believe it or not, is legal, so this meeting is over. By the way, keep your messenger boy, Paul Revere, away from me. There are enough people in my life telling me the sky will fall if things don't go their way."

"Moretti, enjoy your evening with your lady friend. I can't imagine she'll be as much fun as my girl." Sonny looked over at the bar and called out, "Cinnamon, honey, my friend and I are done with business. Get your things, we have a busy night ahead."

It was a sizable crowd for a Monday night at the *Club Blue Note*. The band playing in the background had decided it was time for one of their countless breaks.

Rusty, the barrel-chested bartender, was leaning against the bar, talking to an attractive young woman in a black dress with a ruffled neckline and short red hair, cut in the current style. She was on the band side of the bar, swirling a red plastic swizzle stick to release the bubbles in her champagne glass.

The woman tapped her perfectly manicured nails on the bar counter, her foot tapping impatiently against the stool's metal leg. She glanced at her watch for what felt like the hundredth time, her brows furrowing in frustration. "I can't believe he's making me wait like this," she muttered under her breath, her eyes scanning the crowded night-club for any sign of her late date.

Rusty asked, "What name do you go by?"

"Kate," she answered.

Rusty says, "Kate, let me get you another glass of champagne. Moretti will be here soon."

"How did you know I am waiting on Blake?"

"When you bartend here for as long as I have, it's my business to know. Don't look now. Guess who just walked in?"

"Blake." A smile appeared on her face. Kate embraced him, kissing his lips while rubbing his back.

Blake whispered in Kate's ear, "You look like a million bucks."

"Good evening, Rusty," greeting his confidant. "I'll have my usual, make it a double. Kate don't move. I need to make a quick phone call. I promise I'll be right back."

"No worries. I wouldn't expect anything less."

"Ralph, this is Moretti. Listen, I just left a meeting with your buddy, Sonny Calo. Have you located Joey Fleming yet?"

"Calo is no friend of mine. Guess what? I'm sitting in my car, watching this ramshackle of a house, on the east side of town. Guess who showed up and knocked on the door? Joey Fleming and there is a woman letting him in."

"Where are you?"

"Seven Spring Street. Most of the houses don't have numbers on them, but you can't miss this one. It's the shabby deserted looking blue dump with the termite-infested front porch. I'm parked two doors down on the opposite side of the street. If you get here soon, you can ask him all the questions your little heart desires."

"Wait for me. I'll be there in twenty minutes."

Kate's barstool was abandoned when Blake returned.

"Don't ask me," Rusty said. "Your lady friend left."

"Did she say anything? I told her I'd be back. Why did she leave?"

"Seriously! She said something about turning into a pumpkin if she didn't make it home before midnight. She said to tell you she hopes you have a good life and don't call her again."

"Really."

"Moretti, I swear, you could fuck up a wet dream. Just think about it. This gorgeous, charming woman accepts your invitation for cocktails. Then you show up late, do some bullshit meet and greet, leave her stranded at the bar, wander off, and spend the rest of your time in a phone booth calling who knows who. What did you expect her to do? Why should she hang around waiting for you when she can have any guy she wants?"

"You're right, Rusty. I'm such a schmuck."

"Your problem is all you care about is your work. It's admirable that you care about everyone else's problems. You need to take time for yourself. Keep it up; one day, you'll wake up, and except for your cat, there won't be anyone around. Trust me, I've been there."

"Thanks for the Sigmund Freud advice." Blake emptied his glass, tossed a twenty-dollar bill on the bar, and left. It was time to catch the killer.

CHAPTER 14

Do I Look Like
A Murderer

March 25, 1987, Wednesday Later that night

B lake had just raised his fist to knock on the door when a squirre-ly-looking young man with long stringy hair and tattoos up and down his arms opened it. While Blake made his introductions, he detected Joey's name tattooed on the fingers. Luckily for Joey, the letters in his name matched the four fingers on his right hand.

"Let me guess, you're Joey Fleming?"

"Yeah. How'd you know?"

"Oh, just a lucky guess."

"Mr. Moretti, it's so wonderful to meet you. I've seen you on TV. You have a great reputation as a trial lawyer."

Blake pretended he didn't hear the accolade and said, "Ralph and I have a few questions. Is this a good time?"

"Sir, any time late in the day is fine with me. Early mornings are the only time that's a problem."

"Is it because of your work schedule?"

"No, sir. I don't work. I party all night and sleep in."

"Well, it's late, so I presume this is as good a time as any?"

"Absolutely. Shoot."

"I have a few questions for you, but first, I must know if you are sober."

"Yes, sir, I'm sober. I just got home from Bobby Kool's Pool Hall. I play pool for money and take the game seriously. I would never drink alcohol or take pills before I shoot pool. Afterward, well, that's a different story. I'm up all night partying. I just got home, and the next thing I know, you all are knocking on my door before I can do any serious drinking."

"Great. Then you won't mind if we come in and chat?"

"Sir, no problem. Make yourselves at home and ask away."

"We have to ask you some questions about Frank Amoia."

"That's strange you want to ask me questions about Mr. Amoia."

"Why is that?"

"Recently, everyone has been asking me about Mr. Amoia. Fire away."

"Besides Detective Massey, who else asked you about Mr. Amoia."

"Last week around 9:30 p.m., a mobster-type looking guy and his two goons wearing expensive-looking suits and sunglasses visited me. They asked me about Mr. Amoia and whether I knew he hid money in the bakery. I know people are spreading rumors that I robbed Mr. Amoia and knocked him off for his money."

"Well, did you?" Ralph asked.

"Do I look like a murderer?"

"Don't ask."

"I'll tell you the same thing I told those goons. I never killed anyone, and I certainly didn't kill Mr. Amoia. I'm not like that psycho Owens. He'd kill his own mother for a dollar and enjoy every dying minute."

"At first, I lied and told them I didn't know what they were talking about. Then the fat guy pulled a meat cleaver from inside his topcoat and told me he'd see to it that I would never be able to dial my rotary phone if I didn't tell him the truth.

"When I asked him what he meant, he said he'd cut off my fingers one at a time until I talked."

"That's fucking crazy," responded Ralph.

"So, what did you tell "Fingers?" Moretti asked.

"What do you think? I told him everything. I told him I saw Mr. Amoia stash money away in a crockpot hidden in the pantry and that the cops confiscated it. Then the guy with the cleaver started waving it around, screaming like a banshee. I was so scared I thought I would piss my pants. That's when I blurted out the money is in the duct vent."

Blake asked, "Is that everything?"

"Yes, sir, that's everything."

"Then what happened?"

"The fat guy waved the cleaver in my face and said he knew where I lived, and if he found out I was lying, he would return and finish the job. Do you guys really think he would cut off all my fingers?"

Ralph replied, "Absolutely. He is one crazy motherfucker. But that's not a big deal. Just get yourself one of those new push-button phones."

"Just great. That's the best advice you can come up with?"

"What do you want for free?"

Then Ralph asked, "Did you ever steal money from Mr. Amoia?"

"No, sir. What would be the point of doing that? If I needed money, he'd give it to me. That's the kind of person he was. I liked Mr. Amoia. He was the only one who was nice to me. He knew I was having problems and never threw me under the bus. Can you feel me?"

"Yeah," Ralph replied.

Blake asked, "Did you tell Owens about the money?"

"Yes, sir. But when Owens pressed me about it, I lied and told him Frank hid the money in the sugar and flour sacks in the pantry. He told me he'd split the money with me if I went with him. I said that wasn't going to happen, to go screw himself and to leave the old man alone."

"What did you tell Massey about the money?" Blake asked.

"I told him I saw Mr. Amoia hide money in the crockpot. I didn't say anything about the duct vents."

Blake asked, "Why not?"

"Because the cops would confiscate the money, and I didn't need the fat guy with the cleaver back in my life."

"Smart move. Are you willing to testify in court about everything you told us?" Blake asked.

"Testify against that psycho Owens? You bet. That man deserves to rot in hell. Mr. Amoia would still be alive if I hadn't told Owens about the money. But that crazy cleaver shit, no way."

Blake said, " I'll take care of that problem. Is this where I can find you if I have more questions?"

"You can find me here or at Kool's."

On the way back to the office, Ralph asked. "What do you think about Eddie Haskell?" Eddie was a character on the *Leave It To Beaver* sitcom TV series in the late fifties and early sixties, known for stirring up trouble, mischievous behavior, and hiding his sneaky character. He would greet his friends' parents with fake overdone manners and hand out disingenuous compliments.

"He's an edgy character, but I believe him. Ralph, think about it. The fat guy is Sal, and his thug friends are Sonny Calo's henchmen. You know as well as I do that Sal and his goons believed Joey Fleming's story. Sal was convinced Joey wasn't the killer or the thief. That's the only reason Joey can still count to ten on his fingers today.

"Sonny Calo wants my help to get his money back. He knows the police didn't locate all the money. Either the killer has the money or it is still hidden in the bakery."

"Ralph, you can't honestly believe Joey would bother to kill Frank and leave fifty thousand dollars sitting in the crockpot? Besides, with little effort, Joey could have stolen Frank's money without killing him. And why kill Frank and cut off Joey's only source of money? No way Joey's the killer. I think the money is still hidden in the duct vent."

Ralph asked, "How do we know Owens didn't find Calo's hidden money?"

"Well, for starters, Owens thought the money was in the flour and sugar sacks because that's what Joey told him. Joey was the only person besides Frank who knew the money was in the crockpot. Reason tells me that if Owens knew the money was in the crockpot, he wouldn't have spent time searching in the flour and sugar sacks."

Ralph asked, "So, what are you going to do about Calo's money?"

"Ralph, you know better than to ask me that question. Why don't you ask Sonny Calo?"

CHAPTER 15

Indictment

March 26, 1987, Thursday morning

W hen Blake arrived at his office, he was greeted with a stack of sheriff reports relating to the rape and murder cases. He called for Jennifer.

"I could use a cup of coffee, please."

She stood still for a minute, her lips pressed together and her hands on her narrow hips. She was a trained paralegal, not a waitress. Then she snapped, "One cup of coffee coming up." She strutted towards the machine in the back room and returned with Blake's usual mug.

"Thanks," he said, leafing through the files. His plan was to convince Owens's court-appointed attorney, Robert Sweeney, that his client would certainly be convicted of rape, and make a bargain that if he pled guilty, he'd downgrade the murder charge from first to second degree and run the sentences simultaneously so he could avoid a life sentence. He'd given the defending attorney a week to respond. Now the day of reckoning had arrived, but Sweeney hadn't responded.

Blake's gamble had failed, so he had no choice but to present the rape and murder cases to the grand jury.

Blake finished his presentation to the grand jury at four-thirty. He took the back stairs instead of the elevator to his office to avoid bumping into the press.

When he arrived, Jennifer and Ralph were waiting to find out how the grand jury had gone. He sat down, twirling his pen, playing dumb. "So, what are the two of you up to?"

"You know exactly what's going on," Jennifer said.

"Grand jury went well. I'm sure they believed the witnesses. I expect to hear something soon. I'm just waiting for Claire to call when she receives the voting sheet."

His desk phone rang. "Has the grand jury voted?"

"The grand jury returned true bills of formal charges for murder and rape and all other related charges you requested. Blake, I could hear them arguing during their deliberations. The murder vote was close."

"I'm not surprised. Thank you, Claire." Blake grinned and hung up.

Not saying a word, Jennifer asked, "Blake, when are you planning on telling us the result?"

"Owens was indicted for rape and murder by the grand jury. I appreciate your concern. Would one of you close the door on the way out? I need to make a private call. I'll catch up with you both later."

A sliver of light streaming through his office window caught his attention. He peered at it and began to formulate his next move.

CHAPTER 16

Arraignment

March 30, 1987, Monday morning

"All rise," the bailiff announced, and Judge Richard Carpenter took the bench and said, "We will begin the court proceedings now."

Blake came forward and called Owens's cases, reading out the criminal charges in open court in the presence of the defendant and his attorney.

The judge asked, "Mr. Owens, do you understand the charges against you?"

"Yes, Your Honor."

"How do you plead, guilty or not guilty?"

Typically, the defense attorney would answer the judge's inquiry. But before Sweeney could open his mouth, Owens blurted, "I didn't do nothin'. I'm bein' framed. I demand a meeting with the persecutor to explain my innocence."

"Mr. Owens," Judge Carpenter said, "do you see the young woman seated here? She is the court reporter, taking down every word of this proceeding. I advise you that before you put your foot in your mouth and say something Mr. Moretti can use against you, you should consider keeping it shut. God gave you two ears and only one mouth. He did that for a reason. Lucky for you, I appointed a great lawyer to represent you and protect your constitutional rights. Mr. Sweeney is one of the best, and he's not cheap, so why don't you let him earn his money and speak on your behalf? Now, for the last time, how does the defendant plead?"

Ignoring every word the judge said, Owens began to respond, but Sweeney interrupted him. "Your Honor, my client, pleads not guilty and demands a speedy trial."

Judge Carpenter responded, "Mr. Sweeney, I am more than happy to grant your request for a speedy trial. Be careful what you wish for. If no one has additional words of wisdom to share with the court, this hearing is adjourned."

The judge left the bench, and Owens was escorted from the room in handcuffs and leg irons.

Owens's appeal for a meeting with the prosecutor was too good for Blake to pass up. He'd needed a Plan B, a careful strategy for conviction, and Owens had given it to him on a silver platter. He just had to get him to talk, and that was precisely what he was demanding.

That night as Blake drove home, his mind raced with ideas about how to trick Owens into admitting his guilt. Sweeney was a civil practice trial attorney who lacked criminal law experience. It was time to give him a call.

CHAPTER 17

Plan B

April 1, 1987, Wednesday morning

Billy "Buck" Owens hoped that with the help of his super lawyer, he could strike a deal. The hearing for the motion to suppress was scheduled for March fifth, giving them only two days to convince the prosecutor that the defendant had no connection with the case, and that the charges against him were without merit.

Owens had gotten away with devious, evil acts all his life, simply by lying. He'd survived that way, persuaded Valerie Fleming to take him in and kept her from kicking him out with his lies. The jeopardy he faced was nothing new, and he was confident that his usual tactics would get him off this time.

He was brought into the jail's small, bland private room, where Sweeney was looking through his file.

"I'm not going to waste anyone's time," Owens said as he sat on the folding chair opposite his lawyer, "I will only say this one more time. I'm not guilty and won't plead guilty. Do you think I'm guilty?"

"Mr. Owens, it doesn't matter what I think," Sweeney said. "My job is to convince a jury you're not guilty."

"That sounds like a cop-out. I'll tell you the same thing I told Detective Massey. That punk Joey Fleming murdered that baker with the knife he stole from me, which is still missing. The Fleming kid had a drug problem and needed money to support his habit. He used to work for the guy and knew the old man hid his money in the bakery to avoid paying taxes. As far as the rape case is concerned, I didn't rape that woman. She seduced me. Who was I to turn her down? I told Detective Barnes that story and he obviously blew me off. I want you to get me out of here as soon as possible."

"Yes, I understand. But it's not that easy. I need more time to investigate your story and build a strong enough case to convince the prosecutor to dismiss the charges."

"You're not listening. I don't want to stay in this dump a minute longer. Prove to me you're a good lawyer," Owens said, standing up. He looked into the lawyer's eyes with rage and called for the officer to take him back to his cell.

Sweeney remained seated, wondering what he'd gotten into. The wealthy, demanding clients he customarily dealt with were intelligent and followed his advice. But Owens was a different animal. He trusted no one, including his attorney, and was used to doing things his way. Why stand in the way if his client wanted to meet with the prosecutor?

No sooner had Sweeney returned to his office when his secretary notified him that Moretti was on line one.

"I believe your client has something he wants to tell me," Blake said. "I can make that happen. Maybe he'll convince me he's innocent. What do you have to lose?"

Sweeney leaned both elbows on his desk. "Man, I'm not sure. I'll check with my client, but I won't advise him to discuss his case with you."

"But you'll talk to him, right?"

Sweeney hesitated, not out of indecision but to make Blake nervous. "Yes, I guess I will."

"Good. Let me know what your client decides."

"I'll get back to you this afternoon."

Owens was convinced that Moretti would drop all charges and agreed to the meeting against Sweeney's advice. When Sweeney returned to his office, he notified Blake that the interview was a go. Because he was incarcerated, they'd have to meet in the jail's interview room.

"Plan B is a go," Blake told Jennifer. "Set it up."

"Maybe there really is a god," she said.

Blake was out on a limb by himself. He knew he had one shot at saving himself and proving Owens murdered Frank Amoia.

That night, Blake locked himself in the media room with a pot of hot coffee and a handful of *Snickers Bars,* loaded the VHS tape of the murder scene investigation into the player, and intently began looking and praying for the smoking gun.

CHAPTER 18

Crime Scenes Tell A Story

April 2, 1987, Thursday Night

In the realm of murder investigations, it is not uncommon for cases to remain unsolved for extended periods of time. These unresolved cases, commonly referred to as cold cases, often rely on a single, undeniable clue that, once unveiled, serves as the crucial link between the perpetrator and the crime. In the case of Frank Amoia's murder, Blake was relentless in his belief that this particular investigation fell into the category of cold cases with a definitive clue waiting to be discovered.

The absence of the usual evidence that Blake relied upon to establish the identity of Frank Amoia's killer left him at a loss. There were no eyewitnesses, no murder weapon, no bloody clothes, and no fingerprints.

Blake would only have one chance to interview Owens, who was eager to speak. Still, anything he said would be useless without a smoking gun. Two years later, the crime scene was long gone, but the crime scene video still existed. Blake was convinced that the video was key to tripping up Owens.

Blake methodically reviewed the video, starting with the pattern of bloodstains, searching for the one clue that would reveal the killer.

The pattern of bloodstains can help investigators recreate the crime scene. When a bloodstain hits a flat surface, the tail points in the direction of travel. The blood splatter pattern provides a map determining the direction blood traveled. Blood splatter patterns covered the walls, ceiling, floor, and door.

The video revealed that on the northwest wall, a white bucket containing hair was found next to a toilet-paper dispenser and a toilet, which were also covered in blood. Blood spatter on the northwest wall started approximately five feet from the floor and trailed downward, then continued clockwise along the north and east walls. A small sink and a hand-paper dispenser on the east wall were covered in blood spatter, evidencing the angle of impact and the point of origin of the blood, supporting the manner of death.

"Ralph, do you agree the blood spatter patterns demonstrate that Mr. Amoia was standing in the restroom facing the back wall when the killer attacked him from behind as he slashed his throat?"

"Yes, absolutely."

"Do you also agree there is only one set of bloody bootprints beginning inside the restroom, leading to the pantry, and eventually out the front door?"

"No question about it."

Blake looked at Ralph, "There has to be something I am missing in this video proving who killed Frank Amoia."

Ralph replied, "Yeah, but we still haven't found anything. We've watched this video so many damn times, I'll see it in my sleep for the next month."

"It's probably more entertaining than the other things you dream about."

Sarcastically, Ralph replied, "You're a funny guy."

Blake rewound the videotape for what seemed like the hundredth time. Blake then focused on the evidence technicians who had removed the restroom door.

"Jesus, Ralph, that's it! There's the smoking gun."

"Where?"

It's right there in front of you. You can't miss it.

"I don't see it."

"Look, it's late. Let's call it a night and catch some sleep. I'll explain later. We both have a busy day tomorrow."

It was almost midnight.

Blake lay in bed, his mind consumed by the weight of the impending interview. The room was shrouded in darkness, except for a faint glow from the streetlights outside, casting eerie shadows on the ceiling above. Sleep eluded him like a fleeting dream.

Restless and anxious, Blake's eyes remained fixated on the blank expanse above him. Thoughts raced through his mind, each one a puzzle piece waiting to be fitted together. He knew that tomorrow's interview with the accused murderer was his last chance to unravel the truth and bring justice to the victim's grieving family.

Blake's determination burned like a flickering flame as he stared into the abyss of his thoughts. He replayed every detail of the case in his mind, meticulously examining each shred of evidence he had gathered over countless hours of investigation. The weight of responsibility pressed upon his chest, making it difficult to breathe.

In this moment of solitude, Blake's mind became a battlefield of strategies and tactics. He knew he needed to devise a plan to coax the accused into revealing something incriminating during their conversation. It was a delicate dance between manipulation and truth-seeking, a high-stakes game where every word mattered.

The room seemed to close in around him as he grappled with the enormity of the task. The silence amplified his racing heartbeat, echoing through his ears like a relentless drumbeat. Time ticked away mercilessly, reminding him that failure was not an option.

With furrowed brows and clenched fists, Blake mentally rehearsed every possible scenario that could unfold during the interview. He analyzed the accused's demeanor, searching for any cracks in his facade that could be exploited. Every word and every gesture became a potential clue that could lead him closer to the truth.

Blake's determination solidified into a steely resolve as he lay there in the stillness of the night. He knew the accused's freedom hung in the balance, and he couldn't afford to let them slip through his fingers. The weight of the victim's memory bore down on him, fueling his relentless pursuit of justice.

In the depths of that sleepless night, Blake vowed to leave no stone unturned. He would enter the interview room with unwavering confidence, armed with a plan meticulously crafted to extract the truth from the accused's lips. Failure was not an option; Blake would fight tooth and nail to ensure justice prevailed. If Blake could find a way to get Owens to admit he was in Amoia's bakery the morning of the murder, the video would take care of the rest.

Blake glanced at the clock on his nightstand. It was now two in the morning,

The following morning, Ralph was waiting in Blake's office, leaning back in Blake's executive navy leather high-back desk chair, both hands and fingers wrapped behind his neck. His feet kicked up on the antique wooden desk. When Blake entered his office, Ralph was grinning ear to ear, obviously proud of himself.

"No one told me Hardy fired me. Please tell me Hardy replaced me with you. If he did, he needs to have his head examined. If he didn't, and you don't have a fucking great reason to be sitting with your feet on my desk, you better move your butt somewhere else before I relocate you."

"So, Moretti, take a load off your feet, sit, and listen up. I just saved your ass. My snitch, Blood, called me after you left last night," Ralph said, grinning.

"I'd asked him to check around to see if anyone was talking about the Amoia murder because of all the recent news coverage on the rape case. Blood stumbled on a guy at one of the State Street run beer joints, aptly named the Dive Bar."

"Ok, I'm listening. This better be good. By the way, who is Blood?"

"You know Blood. Remember, Blood was the first guy I introduced you to when we first met and drove you around town, showing you the ropes."

"How could I forget? I thought you would get me disbarred with all your shenanigans that day. I remember you pulled your undercover car over the curb onto the sidewalk, almost striking a young Black man."

"That's him."

Blood is in his late twenties or early thirties, but he looks like he is fifty-something. He is a tall, lean man, at least taller than Ralph, who is every bit six-five. He has short, dark hair and piercing brown eyes. He wears a scar above his right eyebrow and a silver hoop earring in his right ear. Blood often wears black jeans, a black leather jacket, and a white T-shirt, giving off an edgy, intimidating vibe.

He is street-smart and learned to survive with his wits and his ability to keep his mouth shut. He is loyal to those he considers friends. But he has no qualms about betraying others if it serves his interests. He is cunning and manipulative, continually seeking ways to gain power and control over those around him. Despite his tough exterior, Blood has a soft spot for vulnerable individuals and is known to go out of his way to help those in need.

Blood grew up on the streets, struggling to make ends meet and avoid the attention of law enforcement. He quickly learned how to navigate the criminal underworld, connecting with various gangs and drug dealers. He became a valuable asset to Ralph Morgan, providing him with information on the streets and helping him solve cases.

Blake never was told the man's real name, nor did he want to know why his nickname was Blood.

State Street is peppered with two kinds of bars: cheap and cheaper, bars where the local drunks were willing to turn over their pay and welfare checks to surly bartenders who never lost a moment of sleep serving watered-down drinks.

The Dive Bar is in a seedy part of town, with rundown buildings and sketchy characters lurking around every corner. Despite the rough surroundings, the bar is always bustling with activity, with customers coming and going all hours of the day and night. The neighborhood is a bit rough around the edges, but it's home to a tight-knit community of regulars who all gather at the dive bar to drink, laugh, and forget their troubles for a little while.

It was at one of those bars Blood found a man claiming to have information regarding the Amoia murder.

"Blood overheard a conversation between a bartender and a customer. They were discussing a television report about the Misty River rape case and how the man who raped her may have been involved in the murder of Frank Amoia. A customer claimed to have seen a man outside the bakery the morning of the murder."

"Are you kidding me?"

"I'm not joking. It's amazing what you can learn hanging out, drinking after hours, and listening to drunks. You should try it sometime."

"So, who is the witness?"

"He goes by the name Chris Stewart. He'd been hanging around the bakery since he came to town just a couple of weeks before the murder. Blood told me he would keep an eye on him until I arrived."

"Well, what happened?"

"I squeezed in next to Blood, who was sitting closest to the juke-box at the far end of the bar, and asked him which one was Stewart.

"He pointed to a man sitting at the opposite end of the bar, eyes closed, leaning back in his chair passed out. I did a double-take when I saw him. I'll be honest with you, he's no Paul Newman. His hair was overgrown and knotted, and his eyes were sad and worn. Besides look-ing weird, his clothes smelled musty, like old wet socks. I heard that the townies nicknamed him 'Rags'. I told Blood I was concerned about this witness, and he said, 'Don't worry, he'll be fine. Don't let the rough edges bother you. You can fix him up later.'"

I said, "So, what you're telling me is a guy named Rags is my star witness?"

"Blood said, 'Not to worry. He's just been drinking a little.'"

"So, I said, 'If that's what a little drinking looks like, I'd hate to see him drunk.' I asked the bartender what's up with this guy, and he told me the guy spends his entire military pension check on cheap booze. He said Rags was a quiet guy who didn't bother anyone except when he cursed at himself. He'd experienced some horrific things in Vietnam. Sounds like PTSD."

"Jesus, Ralph, this story gets worse by the minute. It doesn't feel good relying on a drunk with PTSD who goes by the name Rags to save my case."

"It'll be fine. We can put him up in a hotel and clean and sober him up before his testimony. I'm sure he'll be a great witness. He won't look the same after I'm done with him."

"Whatever. Were you able to interview him?"

"Well, yeah, that's the reason I went there."

"Is there anything good you can share with me?"

"There's no need to worry, Blake. My snitch, Blood, helped me pour him in my car, and we drove to the office where I forced black coffee down his throat."

"How the hell can that be good?"

"Listen, Perry Mason, stop cross-examining me and let me finish. As soon as he sobered up, I introduced myself and explained that I wanted to speak with him about information he had regarding Frank Amoia's murder. He asked if he could have a drink first. I gave him another cup of coffee, but he pushed it away.

"I asked him why he was hanging out in front of the bakery on the morning of the murder. He asked me if I thought he looked like a murderer. Rather than piss him off by saying he did, I lied and said of course not. Then he told me what he saw that morning.

"He was in the alley across the street from the bakery and saw a man with long, greasy black hair standing behind the lamppost, acting nervous and looking around like something was coming down. He said the man was wearing a leather jacket, dirty blue jeans, and worn-looking cowboy boots. With ... are you ready? ... a scar above his right eye."

"Jesus, Ralph, great work!"

"That's not all. Because the man was acting like something was about to come down, he kept an eye on him and watched him slowly enter the bakery, then rush out and take off running."

"Did Rags ever talk to any of the deputies?"

"I asked him that question. He said he was sitting on the bus stop bench the whole time the deputies were at the scene, but not one of them interviewed him. I asked him why he didn't approach the sheriff, and he said they have a habit of arresting him for loitering. A home-less-looking guy isn't a good look for the business district."

Blake clapped Ralph on the back.

"Well, was that good enough to sit in your desk chair?"

"Yes, Ralph. But it's time to head to the jail and interview Owens."

As Blake made his way to the jail, he couldn't help but feel a sense of anticipation. The defendant had requested this meeting, confident that he could convince Blake to drop the murder case against him. Little did the defendant know, in the last twelve hours, Moretti had stumbled upon damning evidence that would seal his guilt.

With each step towards the jail, Moretti's mind raced with thoughts of how he would confront the defendant. He knew present-ing the new evidence was crucial to breaking through the defendant's facade of innocence. The evidence he discovered was irrefutable, a piece of the puzzle that had been missing all along.

CHAPTER 19

The Man Who Talked Too Much

April 3, 1987, Friday morning

As Blake entered the dimly lit interrogation room, Sweeney was already sitting there.

"Good morning," Blake began, his voice steady but filled with an underlying determination.

"Sorry, we're a little late," Blake said. "An emergency needed my attention. I suspect you've dealt with that yourself."

Sweeney looked up and nodded. "I understand."

"Are we ready for your client?"

"Let's do it," Sweeney replied, signaling the officer.

A buzzer sounded, and Owens shuffled in dressed in an orange prison jumpsuit, white socks, and blue plastic sandals. His wrists were handcuffed, his ankles shackled. Ralph recorded the meeting as agreed.

Blake knew that when faced with a tricky situation, Owens could be counted on to lie. He wasn't sure the interview would be fruitful, but he had nothing to lose.

Sweeney began by explaining the interview process to his client, who looked around the room without paying much attention to him. From Owens's facial expressions and body language, Blake concluded that he lacked empathy, exhibiting neither remorse nor guilt. It was clear he hadn't thought twice about taking the life of Frank Amoia or the harm he'd done to Olivia Spencer. Women were a dime a dozen to him. He sat grinning from ear to ear while Ralph explained his Miranda rights. He'd convinced himself he'd escape this mess as he'd always done. His attitude motivated Blake to hold him accountable.

As he studied Owens, he thought of the most egregious crimes he'd prosecuted. Despite the passage of time, he couldn't erase the memories of those crimes. The names and faces of the victims changed, but the evil of the perpetrators' hearts and the darkness in their souls remained the same. Meeting with the victims was a priority for him. The scenario never varied. At first, the surviving family stood so quietly you could hear a pin drop as they waited to discover why someone they cared about had been violently attacked or murdered. When they spoke, anguish filled their voices, and Blake's heart cried out for them.

His head was filled with Olivia's gut-wrenching questions: "Why did he do this to me? What had I ever done to him? What did I do to deserve this?" He understood why victims always asked these questions, and his response was always the same. Prosecutors aren't obligated to prove motive, but jurors want to know "why".

So, he explained that people kill and commit violent crimes for many reasons, some of which can be explained, like greed, jealousy, and the heat of the moment. While those motives may be understandable, they're of little solace to those left grieving.

The worst perpetrators are twisted-minded criminals who kill or harm victims in cold blood with premeditation and malice without any plausible explanation. They are "tin men" who lack empathy and have no heart. For them, life is meaningless. Their behavior is impulsive, and their cruel actions thrill and excite them. Simply put, it's in their nature.

Billy "Buck" Owens was the poster child for the twisted-minded criminal.

Blake opened the interview. "Let me introduce myself. I'm Blake Moretti, the assistant prosecutor, or, as you call me, the 'persecutor' assigned to prosecute you for the rape of Olivia Spencer and the murder and Frank Amoia. This is my investigator, Ralph Morgan."

"I didn't kill or fucking rape anyone," Owens said. "The sheriff is framing me."

"That's what you've claimed, which is why I granted your request to meet with me. I wanted to give you a chance to explain why you insist I'm prosecuting an innocent man, but as Mr. Sweeney just pointed out, whatever you've been dying to say to me better be the whole truth and nothing but the truth."

"Yeah, sure," Owens replied. "But what will you do for me if I talk to you?"

"Mr. Owens, I am here only because your attorney told me that you requested a chance to prove your innocence. I already have enough guilty defendants to prosecute without adding innocent ones to my caseload. As you know, declaring you are innocent proves nothing. If you want your criminal charges dismissed, you'll have to provide me with independent evidence that proves your innocence. As an example, if you proved you were not present at the scene of the crime, that would serve as your alibi. But your assertion alone would not do a damned thing for you. You would have to present irrefutable evidence. Do I make myself clear?"

Owens crossed his arms and looked defiant. "Yeah."

"Let's begin with the rape case. You're welcome to explain what happened."

"I didn't rape that woman. I was going to the grocery store to buy a six-pack. As I was entering the store, she came out with her groceries. When she saw me, she must have liked what she saw 'cause she approached me and started flirting, and before I knew it, she asked me if I wanted to fuck her. I thought, what the hell? She was good-looking in a tight skirt, and I didn't have anything better to do. So, I said, 'Sure. I'll fuck you.' She said we could use her car and knew about some secluded spot by the river. We got in her car, and she drove me to a wooded place, parked, took off her clothes while I removed mine, and jumped on top of me. God's truth."

Blake glanced at Sweeney, who wore a poker face but probably wanted to vomit. "You have a very imaginative mind, Mr. Owens. I probably shouldn't ask, but do you have anything else you'd like to share about that encounter?"

Owens was hitting his stride. "No, that's how it happened. I can't believe she ran off crying rape. She must have some mental problems. Maybe she fucked me to get even with her boyfriend. She was having second thoughts about marrying the dude. She said they fought the very night she picked me up at the supermarket. She was pissed off because he wouldn't go out and party on Saint Patrick's Day night. So, she went out to look for a man to party with and have sex with. That man was me. She knew damn well that if her fiancé found out, he would dump her. To cover her tracks, she concocted this bullshit kidnapping and rape story."

"Is it true you gave Valerie Fleming a ring you stole from Olivia Spencer?"

"I didn't steal any ring. She gave me her engagement ring as a gift because she enjoyed the sex so much. That's what she told me. Looking back, I realize she set me up. Her plan was to make it look like I stole the ring."

"Do you admit you drove off in Olivia Spencer's vehicle after you had sex with her?"

"Yes. I borrowed her car to get home after that crazy bitch ran off butt naked. Since I did her a favor and fucked her, I figured she owed me that. She drove me out to the middle of nowhere. How the hell else was I supposed to get home?"

"Do you own or possess a firearm?"

"Doesn't everyone have a gun?"

"Did you own a firearm on March 17, 1987?"

"It's possible. I can't recall. To make money, I buy and sell them all the time."

"You appear to have a selective memory. Despite all the other events you described, you cannot remember possessing a firearm on that day."

"What if I did? So what?"

"So, you don't deny possessing a handgun on March 17, 1987, is that right?"

"Right."

Owens hadn't hesitated once. Blake thought he'd either carefully rehearsed his responses or was such a liar that he could make them up on the spot. He decided to switch to the real reason for the interview.

"Let's discuss Frank Amoia's murder. What can you tell us about that?"

"I didn't murder him or anyone else."

"Where were you at approximately seven the morning of March 2, 1985?"

Owens grinned. "I wondered the same thing about you. But, hell, that was so long ago, you probably can't remember."

"I can tell you, Mr. Owens, that I was nowhere near Mr. Amoia's bakery. So, I ask you again, were you anywhere near the bakery on March 2, 1985, at approximately seven in the morning? Weren't you inside the bakery when Mr. Amoia was murdered? Let me add that I already know the answer to every question I will ask you today."

"I heard of him, but I never went to his bakery on that day or any other day."

"Are you one hundred percent sure, Mr. Owens?"

"Yeah, sure." Owens sat back in the metal chair and sucked his teeth.

"It's my understanding that your nickname is Buck. Is that correct?"

"Sometimes people refer to me that way. Sure." He smiled.

"Isn't your nickname Buck because you always carry a Buck knife?"

"I suppose so."

"There's no need to suppose. It's a simple question. You are known as Buck because you always carry a buck knife. Yes, or no?"

"Yes, since you put it that way."

"Just where were you at seven in the morning on March 2, 1985?"

"I was at home sleeping with my girlfriend, Valerie Fleming. I wasn't anywhere near Amoia's bakery if that is what you're getting at."

"You claim that you were not at Amoia's bakery when Mr. Amoia's throat was slashed with a Buck hunting knife. Here's the problem: So how is it you are seen entering his bakery at seven in the morning on March 2, 1985?"

Owens's arrogant confidence evaporated, and he rose from the chair. "That's bullshit!" he yelled. "Someone's trying to frame me!"

The guard standing behind Owens instructed him to sit down.

Owens took a deep breath. "I'm being framed," he said more calmly. "Valerie and I were home when that man was killed."

Blake leaned forward in his chair and looked into Owens's eyes. "That's interesting. Valerie Fleming told the sheriff you were not with her when Amoia was killed.

"Additionally, she told the sheriff you had blood stains on your clothes and two hundred blood-stained dollars in your pocket. She provided the sheriff with a detailed description."

Owens pounded the metal table. "The woman is a fucking liar! She even told the sheriff she lied!

"I hadn't planned on telling you this, but Valerie has a twenty-year-old son named Joey Fleming who worked at Amoia's bakery.

"I've known Joey for a long time, and he was always up to no good," Owens said. "During his high school years, he was injured and got addicted to painkillers. He consumed them like candy. The more pain pills he ate, the meaner he got. And it was expensive. He was constantly conniving ways to make a fast dollar."

"Did you know Joey Fleming worked for old man Amoia? Joey told me that while he was at the bakery, he caught Amoia hiding thousands of dollars wrapped with currency straps. At first, I thought he was bullshitting me. I didn't know you could make that kind of money selling cookies.

"The kid stayed with us sometimes. The morning Amoia was killed, my Buck knife came up missing. I figured Joey took it."

"I'll look into it," Blake said.

"Look, Moretti, as God is my witness, I did not kill Amoia."

Blake didn't mention hearing the same story from Detective Massey. It seemed odd that Joey Fleming would steal only a couple hundred dollars from Frank's pocket when he could have taken fifty thousand dollars hidden in the crockpot.

"Yeah. You do that, Moretti. You'll discover I'm telling the truth. Joey Fleming should be in jail, not me."

Owens was getting under Blake's skin, not because of what he said, but because he knew he was lying. The more Owens talked, the more pieces of the puzzle began to fit. Valerie Fleming had fingered Owens as the killer. Then Owens fingered her son, Joey Fleming. The police fingered Owens but didn't eliminate Joey.

"Look, Buck," he said quietly, "You've got a bigger problem than Valerie. We have a witness who saw you enter the bakery the morning of the murder. Within ten minutes, the witness observed you run from the bakery toward the house where you were arrested for the Olivia Spencer rape. That witness appears to have confirmed what Ms. Fleming told Detective Massey you were wearing before she recanted. The reason she recanted is because you threatened her."

Owens leaned into Blake, who moved forward so they were within an arm's length of one another.

"Look, I was never at the bakery. Did you ever think maybe your so-called witness murdered the baker and fingered me to save his own ass?"

Blake reached into his briefcase, took out a folder, and passed it to Sweeney, who skimmed it and then returned it. Then Blake slid it to Owens. The defendant's confident demeanor wavered momentarily before he regained his composure.

"I'm here to prove my innocence," he replied defiantly. Blake leaned forward, placing a folder on the table between them. "You may want to reconsider that stance," he said cryptically. Curiosity and unease mingled in the air as the defendant hesitated before opening the folder. His eyes scanned over the pages, and with each passing moment, his expression transformed from defiance to shock. "This is the eyewitness's handwritten statement. His physical description of the perpetrator matches you, and he described a leather jacket, jeans, and cowboy boots. You'll see that he also noticed a scar above the man's right eye.

"The clothing he described matches Ms. Fleming's description of the bloody garments you wore when you returned home the morning Amoia was killed. If Valerie Fleming and the eyewitness were in the same room, they would not know each other. By the way, how did you get the scar above your right eye?"

"Fuck you, Moretti."

"Buck, I started this conversation by asking you to be honest. I can't help you unless you tell me the whole truth. Ralph and I know you tell a lie every time you open your mouth. I know you were in the bakery the morning of the murder. Now you know how I know."

Owens rested his head on the table long enough to invent his next lie. "Okay, this is what happened. When I opened the bathroom door, I saw him lying on his back on the floor. He was already dead. So, without moving him, I reached into his pocket and took a wad of cash. But I never killed him. I closed the restroom door when I left him."

Owens felt a sense of relief wash over him. He believed he had successfully covered his tracks and left no evidence behind. Little did Owens know the crime scene video would capture the one clue that proved he committed the murder. Only Blake had caught it. Now the most significant puzzle piece was in place. Blake knew everything Owens said was a lie. Blake had proof that Billy "Buck" Owens had murdered Frank Amoia.

Owens had trapped himself with his own words. He'd established an opportunity to commit the murder and a motive – greed. Blake had everything he needed; the crime scene video would be the nail in Owens's coffin.

Before he was led away, Owens asked, "Moretti, did you get what you needed to make things right?"

Blake looked at Owens and smiled. "Yes. Thanks to you, Mr. Owens, I did. If you hadn't talked so much, I don't know what I would have done."

"Oh, good to know. I told you, Sweeney. I was right to insist on this meeting."

"Right," Sweeney replied, looking down at his hands.

Ralph said, "Can you believe that guy? He thinks we bought his bullshit."

Blake took his eyes off the road and glanced at his investigator. "Yeah, he's not the sharpest knife in the drawer. It's a good thing most murderers aren't geniuses. Otherwise, murders would never be solved."

CHAPTER 20

Deal Or No Deal

April 6, 1987, Monday morning

"Look, Moretti," Sweeney said, "My client upheld his end of the bargain. Not only did he answer all your loaded questions, but he also solved the Frank Amoia murder case. Just because you didn't like his answers doesn't give you the right to withdraw your offer to dismiss all criminal charges in exchange for the interview. Granted, he admitted to stealing a couple hundred dollars from the dead guy after discovering the body. But that's only a misdemeanor. If all charges are dismissed, my client is willing to plead guilty to theft. So, what are you inclined to do?"

Blake sat quietly at his desk. Ralph was sitting behind Sweeney, serving as a witness to the settlement conference. Blake looked at him over Sweeney's shoulder and raised his eyebrows, silently asking Ralph if he'd gotten all that drivel. The detective nodded.

Blake had defense attorney Sweeney figured out. In law school, defense attorneys are taught to blow smoke when they don't have both the law and the facts on their side.

"Sweeney, I heard everything you said. Please don't interpret my silence to mean I agree to your offer because I don't. I'm not buying a word of it. I'll get back to you after I finish my review of the case file."

"When will I hear from you?"

"Soon."

"By the way, Moretti, I reviewed the discovery regarding the two hundred thousand dollars Sonny Calo stashed at Frank Amoia's bakery. That tidbit of evidence will likely delight the jury. Should you decide not to accept my offer, I'll be forced to present evidence that Joey Fleming murdered Amoia so he could steal two hundred thousand dollars that Amoia laundered for the Calo crime family and hid in his bakery.

"There's no doubt in my mind that the jury will find my client not guilty based on Joey Fleming's knowledge of the stash."

After Sweeney left, Ralph and Blake looked at each other, their eyes wide.

Blake said, "We have one item of business to take care of before I respond."

"Tell me you're not contemplating his offer."

"You know me better than that. Hell no. Sweeney can go fuck himself."

"Are you concerned about the laundered money? What will you do when Sweeney reveals Joey Fleming's financial motive for killing Mr. Amoia?"

"I'm not concerned. In fact, I would be thrilled to see Sweeney bring the issue up."

"Are you fucking serious?"

"Yes, I'm serious. You must know me by now, Ralph. I'll turn that issue around and drive it up Sweeney's ass sideways. Sweeney's threat is toothless. He's trying to frighten me into giving away the courthouse."

"Why do you believe that?"

"Because if Joey Fleming murdered Frank Amoia to steal two hundred thousand dollars, why doesn't he have it? Sweeney won't bring the issue up. And should he decide to make that move, I'll have a surprise for him he will haunt him the rest of his legal career."

"But Blake, the sheriff doesn't have the two hundred thousand dollars either."

Blake smiled and said, "Ralph, you're finally catching on; you just don't know it."

The following day, Sweeney came to Blake's office to discuss resolving the two cases.

"Morning, gentlemen. Have you thought about my offer?"

Blake leaned back in his desk chair. "I have no intention of doing a damned thing for your client. I found your offer insulting."

Sweeney was nonplussed. "I arranged for my client to speak with a psychologist, Dr. Eugene Berry. He discovered that Mr. Owens's past is a treasure trove of mitigating evidence, and I respectfully request that you consider that information before rejecting my offer. You may find the cases difficult to prosecute when the jury learns the extent of the abuse he endured as a child."

"I'm game," Blake said. "Have at it."

"Dr. Berry reported that Mr. Owens was fatherless, his birth the result of a one-night stand. His childhood was replete with problems and dysfunction. His mother was an alcoholic and a drug addict who began to abuse him sexually when he was just five years old. When he turned twelve, she convinced him to sell drugs to his friends at school and rewarded him with oral sex. He feared offending his mother and wanted her to be proud of him, so he did everything she told him to do. By the time my client was twenty, he was not only dabbling in drug dealing but also cheating people and was accused of making unwanted sexual advances towards women multiple times. Dr. Berry will testify that because of his mother's sexual abuse, my client developed a hatred for women and was aggressively violent in relationships. What do you think, Moretti? Can you cut my client some slack?"

Like a straight man, Blake asked Ralph, "Gee, what do you think?"

"I suspect Owens's father would have only made things worse. Living with Broome Hilda was enough."

"Have a heart," Sweeney said. "Didn't you hear me say his mother compelled my client to deal drugs in exchange for blow jobs?"

"Ralph replied, "Your client most likely turned out to be the salesman of the year."

"Excuse me, but I fail to see the humor in Mr. Owens' dysfunctional childhood," Sweeney said. "I came here to discuss the cases pending against him in good faith, and your response resembles a Martin and Lewis comedy routine."

"With all due respect," Blake said, "it's hard to imagine that Mr. Amoia would have felt more comfortable while his head was almost cut off if he'd known your client had a dysfunctional childhood. Owens isn't skating on some Mickey Mouse misdemeanor theft charge. Sweeney, your client is a regular Norman Bates!

"Then there is Ms. Spencer? Would she have felt better being sexually assaulted by your client while he held a gun to her head had she known his mother engaged in an incestuous relationship with her son? Perhaps your client should have directed his anger toward his mother and not some stranger who never caused him harm."

For the first time in his career, Sweeney had no response. He sat silently for a moment, then stood up to leave. "I guess I'll see you in court," he said.

"Have a good day." And the door closed behind him. "Ralph, what do you think about Sweeney's defense?"

"Well, I don't know what F. Lee Yahoo's defense is, but it sounds dysfunctional."

CHAPTER 21

Calm Before The Storm

July 6, 1987, Monday morning

The Leigh County grand jury indicted Owens on two counts of rape, kidnapping, and robbery with a deadly weapon. The People vs. Billy Owens, a.k.a. Buck Owens, would begin in seven days. Blake had decided to prosecute the rape case first for strategic reasons. From an evidentiary perspective, he believed it was the stronger case. There was no doubt in his mind that a jury would convict Owens on every charge. If Owens chose to testify in the murder case, Blake could present the rape convictions as evidence. He would bet the farm Owens would never keep his mouth shut and would testify despite his attorney's advice. The court would issue a jury instruction that the defendant's previous convictions could not be considered evidence. Still, Blake knew the rape, a crime of violence, would be impossible to ignore.

When he arrived at the courthouse with Ralph Morgan and Detective Barnes, the judge was already on the bench. Mary Croghan was the first female judge in Leigh County. Her father, Michael Croghan, former general counsel of Niagara Electric and Gas Company, just so happened to be a close friend of the governor who appointed her. She was an attractive older woman who wore her brown hair in a stylish bob. And she still had the solid, muscular physique that had helped her achieve fame as a member of the rowing team at Ohio State University.

Judge Croghan didn't mince words. She knew the rules of criminal procedure and evidence like the back of her hand, couldn't stand make-believe legal arguments, and hated continuances. Her philosophy was that if you had a case, bring it on. Otherwise, stay out of her courtroom.

That Friday, she summoned the lawyers to her chambers to discuss the pretrial motions.

"Gentlemen, good morning. To keep this trial moving, I set this meeting to hear arguments on any pretrial motions you may have. As you know, the trial begins on Monday morning at eight-thirty. At seven-thirty, the jury panel will meet to watch everyone's favorite video, *Jury Duty. What to Expect.*

"Before I address the pending pretrial motions, may I ask if you attempted to resolve this case as well as the murder case?"

Sweeney replied, "Your Honor, despite my best efforts, Mr. Moretti has rejected my offer to settle this case."

Judge Croghan said, "I've worked with Blake Moretti for several years and have never found him unreasonable. However, I suspect that we will see who is being unreasonable in due time. I see that the defense and the state have both submitted pretrial motions. Therefore, I intend to rule without argument.

"The state has requested that the jury view the alleged scene of the rape. That request is granted. A bus will be provided to transport jurors and lawyers following jury selection. If the defendant wishes to view the scene, he will be transported in a marked cruiser. However, he cannot leave the patrol car."

Sweeney said, "Your Honor, the defense objects."

"Of course you do. The jurors would be prejudiced by visualizing how terrifying it would have been to be hunted down in a secluded place where no one could hear her cries for help. Is that your argument, Mr. Sweeney?"

"Yes, Your Honor."

"Very good. It's what I expected. Overruled."

"But, Your Honor, the prejudice outweighs relevance in this case."

"Mr. Sweeney, I suspect Mr. Moretti's words are prejudicial every time he opens his mouth. Moretti, would that be your response? How'd I do?"

"As usual, you nailed it."

"Great. Mr. Sweeney, your objection is once again overruled. You also requested that Dr. Berry testify about your client's dysfunctional upbringing. Do I have that right?"

"Yes, Your Honor."

"Mr. Moretti, since the defendant has raised neither an insanity defense nor a competency issue, would you object if I allowed him to present that evidence?"

"Yes and no, Your Honor. The defendant has not claimed insanity, and competency has not been raised. However, I have no objection to Sweeney shooting himself in the foot by calling Dr. Berry to testify to the defendant's adventurous childhood. Anticipating your next question, the State will not call an expert witness to counter Dr. Berry."

"Well done, Mr. Moretti. All remaining motions from the defense are summarily overruled. I will issue a written order and cause it to be filed before Monday morning. I will allow time for either party to raise any further issues and rule on them before the court's business begins at eight-thirty."

Blake, Jennifer, and Ralph gathered in Blake's office to review the game plan before the start of the trial. Jennifer would be responsible for contacting the witnesses and coordinating their scheduled appearances. Ralph would locate and transport any less-than-cooperative witnesses to the court in a timely fashion.

Blake's role as the trial prosecutor would be to manage the case and bring it to a successful conclusion. There was no room for loose ends.

Blake approached the trial like a game of chess, which he'd mastered as a child. In the same way that chess was war on a board, Moretti believed that trial was war in a courtroom. With every legal move, he masterfully checked his opponent, the defense attorney. Blake recognized that criminal lawyers, like any other creatures of habit, tried their cases the same way every time. Defense attorneys often sat back and shot arrows at the prosecutor's case, hoping to convince at least one naive juror that all the evidence they'd witnessed during the trial had been an illusion.

A jury was selected and anxiously awaited the presentation of the evidence. Battle lines were drawn. So, with the fate of the trial hanging in suspense, Blake prepared himself for an intense battle of wits. The courtroom was in suspense, awaiting the next move in this high-stakes game of legal chess.

PART FOUR

"The only real lawyers are trial lawyers,
and trial lawyers try cases to juries."
—*Clarence Darrow*

CHAPTER 22

The Rape Trial

July 13, 1987, Trial commences

T he Sunday night before the trial commenced, Blake followed the same routine. For what felt like the hundredth time, he revised and fine-tuned his notes for the next day's session. Then he'd pour himself a glass of wine, sit back with Roxanne, his cat, and listen to a vinyl copy of *Somethin' Else*, featuring Cannonball Adderley and Miles Davis, recorded on March 9, 1958, for Blue Note Records.

He'd retire for the night feeling confident that having studied the case for countless hours, he was prepared to counter Sweeney's defense.

He never wavered from his commitment to ensuring Olivia Spencer's voice was heard. Any survivor of a violent sexual assault had the right to be sure their pain and suffering would not be forgotten and to be granted justice and closure.

At eight, Monday morning, Blake entered the courtroom with his team before Sweeney could claim the attorney's table closest to the jury box. The jury would be less likely to be exposed to the defense's whispered, tainted comments. And the defense wouldn't be able to display notes with false or inadmissible evidence.

The trial commenced with the selection of the jury. The jury selection process is crucial in shaping the case's outcome. The jury selection process begins with summoning potential jurors, whom both the prosecution and defense attorneys question to determine their suitability for jury service. This questioning process, known as voir dire, aims to identify any biases or prejudices that may affect a juror's ability to impartially evaluate the evidence presented during the trial.

Peremptory challenges are an essential tool used by attorneys during jury selection. These challenges allow attorneys to dismiss potential jurors without providing a specific reason or justification. However, there are certain limitations and guidelines surrounding the use of peremptory challenges.

Attorneys may employ peremptory challenges when they believe that a potential juror has biases or prejudices that could affect their ability to consider the evidence fairly. Attorneys may exercise peremptory challenges based on their intuition or observations made during voir dire. For example, if a potential juror expresses strong opinions or beliefs that align with one side of the case, an attorney may choose to exercise a peremptory challenge to remove them from the jury pool.

There are restrictions on using peremptory challenges to prevent discrimination or bias in jury selection. The Supreme Court has ruled that peremptory challenges cannot be used to exclude potential jurors based on race, gender, or other protected characteristics. According to Batson v. Kentucky (1986), striking jurors solely on the basis of their race violates the Equal Protection Clause of the Fourteenth Amendment.

During jury selection, Blake chose as many women as possible. He was masterful in exercising his peremptory challenges without appearing to be motivated by prejudgment or bias.

He used his preemptive challenges to exclude engineers, believing that they lacked the common sense necessary to determine guilt or innocence, relying instead on mathematical formulas.

He was a master of framing questions to identify prospective jurors with biases or prejudices that might prevent them from following the court's instructions.

He'd once prosecuted a man for raping a prostitute. The evidence had been overwhelming, but he'd weeded out prospective jurors with prejudice against prostitutes using only one question. "Do you believe a prostitute can be raped? Yes, or no?" Few lawyers would ask that question because they were afraid to ask it.

The only prospective jurors left standing were those who believed it was possible to rape a woman who earned a living by charging for sex. The defendant was found guilty as charged.

In Blake's experience, female jurors were harsher on defendants when the victims were women.

Because of Blake's masterful questioning of prospective jurors and his use of peremptory challenges, when the jury selection process ended, Owens learned his fate rested in the hands of a panel of nine women and three men.

Blake was confident that when the women jurors heard Owens brag that he was the best gift a woman could receive, there would be no question they would find him guilty as charged. His only question was how quickly the jury would reach a guilty verdict.

In the dimly lit courtroom, the first day of the highly antici-pated rape trial had finally arrived. The air was thick with tension as the defendant, Billy Buck Owens, sat anxiously at the defense table. Spectators, journalists, and curious onlookers packed the courtroom.

From the prosecution table, Blake could hear the clamor carry across the room. Olivia's family and closest friends occupied the front row of the spectator seats. Print, television, and radio reporters occu-pied the second row. Behind them sat the curious. Every day, the faces changed. Whatever their motivation for attending the trial, Blake could sense their desire to witness the defendant brought to justice.

Misty River Daily News photographer Scoop Brady was among the crowd, known for his keen eye for capturing pivotal moments of high-profile criminal trials. Scoop was masterful, positioning himself stra-tegically to get the best shots without disrupting the solemn atmosphere.

Scoop ditched his old noisy Nikon camera with the through-the-lens focusing and armed himself with the more expensive Leica range-finder camera with the much quieter shutter, allowing him to be discreet and unobtrusive. Scoop would move silently around the room with every click of his camera.

Focused on capturing key moments that would convey the gravity of the trial, Scoop was famous for capturing the raw emotions etched on the faces of those involved – from the determined prosecutor to the worried family members of the victim.

He zoomed in on Owens's face, capturing his nervous demeanor and searching for any signs of guilt or innocence. Before the trial was over, Scoop would snap hundreds of shots of Blake Moretti meticulously presenting evidence, ensuring that every detail was documented, as well as capturing the expressions and gestures of witnesses who would take their turns on the stand, knowing that their visual cues could hold crucial information for both sides of the case.

Throughout the day, Scoop's presence would go unnoticed by most as he blended seamlessly into the background. His photographs would later grace the pages of the local newspaper, providing a visual narrative of this high-stakes trial for readers who were unable to attend. Scoop knew his photographs would influence public perception. With each image, he would capture a piece of the truth, allowing the readers to form their own opinions about the case. Scoop couldn't help but feel a sense of satisfaction.

Judge Croghan's law clerks and staff sat in folding chairs along the wall opposite the jury box. Erring on the side of caution, the judge had requested two deputy sheriffs to be stationed at strategic locations inside the courtroom.

In the bustling courtroom on the first day of testimony, two deputy sheriffs stood watch, their presence ensuring the safety and security of everyone present. Each deputy had a distinct appearance. The first deputy sheriff stood tall and imposing, his trim physique suggesting years of experience in law enforcement. He was of average height but carried an air of confidence that commanded respect. His uniform was crisp and neatly pressed, emphasizing his professionalism. Beneath his dress shirt, a bulge hinted at the presence of a bulletproof vest, a necessary precaution in such high-stakes situations.

The second deputy sheriff stood apart from the other due to his physical build. He was noticeably overweight but compensated for it with an unwavering commitment to his role. His uniform fit snugly around his frame and bulletproof vest, emphasizing his dedication despite his physical limitations.

Both deputies wore a black belt that held various tools of the trade, including a revolver holstered securely at their side, ready to be drawn if needed. A leather cartridge case adorned their belt, housing extra ammunition for their firearms neatly arranged, providing quick access to additional ammunition if required. A pair of handcuffs dangled from another loop on their belt, a reminder of their authority to restrain those who posed a threat. Completing their ensemble was a sturdy baton, nestled snugly in its designated holder, its weight reassuringly familiar.

Each of the deputies was within easy reach, a symbol of their authority and readiness to act. Together, the deputy sheriffs formed a formidable presence in the courtroom, their appearance reflecting their commitment to maintaining order and safeguarding the proceedings. Their collective expertise and preparedness served as a reminder that justice would be upheld, no matter the challenges faced.

The gallery was populated with "court watchers," an interesting group, most of them retired people who regularly attended trials. For them, a trial was like a TV soap opera. At the end of the day's session, they'd share their opinions of the proceedings.

Early in Blake's career, he'd been curious and would take a moment while he packed his files and notes to hear their thoughts. But he soon realized that only one or two of these armchair quarterbacks were worth his time.

Judge Croghan's bailiff shouted, "ALL RISE." And the room filled with the sound of chairs being pushed back and shuffling feet. "Hear ye. Hear ye. The Superior Court for the County of Leigh is now in session, the Honorable Mary Croghan presiding."

The judge, wearing pearls at the neck of her black robe, took her place on the platform; the bailiff struck the gavel; everyone sat down, and the case of the People versus Billy "Buck" Owens began.

"Ladies and gentlemen of the jury, it is now time for each side to present their side of the story. You will first hear from the State, followed by the Defendant.

"Is the State ready to proceed with opening statements?" Judge Croghan asked.

Blake thought, *Hell, yes, I'm ready.* It was time for Owens to be held accountable, time for the reckoning, and he was prepared to battle. The jury expected the prosecutor to be fair but tenacious. Blake checked those boxes.

He'd developed a strategy to achieve justice for the victims and their survivors while holding the accused accountable for their crimes. And he recognized that the People's lawyers needed to display confidence.

Blake subscribed to what he called the Rule of Three, which meant the more times a person heard the same story, the more they believed it. He divided the trial into three phases.

First, he attracted the jury's attention with the opening statement by telling the story of the crime. Second, he reinforced his theory of the case during his presentation of the evidence proving the defendant's guilt. Third, during the closing argument, Blake would tell the story a third time, explaining what he'd proven and what the jury must do.

That morning, in a commanding voice, he responded to the judge's question, "Your Honor, I am prepared to begin with the opening statement on behalf of the People."

"You may begin. Ladies and gentlemen of the jury, please give Mr. Moretti your undivided attention."

Blake always started with the obligatory introduction, "May it please the court, ladies, gentlemen of the jury, Detective Barnes, and counsel for the defendant." There was nothing standard about the remainder of his opening statement. His goal was to compel the jury to focus on his case.

Blake had acquired a love of storytelling when he was a boy and was damn good at it. As a young man, he'd attended mass at Saint Francis Church every Sunday. To accommodate the neighborhood's ethnic makeup, the archbishop made sure the pastor was Italian and allowed mass to be said in Italian rather than Latin, for which he was rewarded monetarily. After mass, Blake would sit on his grandfather's front porch with his uncles and listen intently to the stories they told about the days when they were growing up.

Not only the nature of the stories piqued his attention, but also the tone and rhythm. A story that captured the jury by varying the pace, keeping them in the moment of the crime, brought them closer to a guilty verdict without ever saying, "the evidence shows".

Blake could listen all day long to the indelible voice of actor Morgan Freeman. Deep, reassuring, and authoritative, Freeman's passionate delivery commanded his audience's attention. Blake recognized he was no Morgan Freeman, but he knew his voice could make a jury sit up and listen. And he knew it was important to be himself, to speak sincerely from his heart as he sold his case.

To give the jury the impression that they were present at the time of the offense, he told the story in the present tense, an end run around the Golden Rule, which prohibits a lawyer from asking jurors to put themselves in the victim's shoes.

Blake approached the jury box without getting too close and began his story in a soft, slow cadence to avoid making the jury uncomfortable.

"East Lakeville Valley, here in Leigh County, is not the nicest part of town, but it's not the worst part, either. In the local village mall, there are a set of storefronts. You know, the kind, connected but not quite upscale. So, as you walk along the sidewalks of the shopping center, you can see the stores' lightweight curtains and panel façades running end to end.

"At one end of the mall sits Hanger's Market. That's where Olivia Spencer shopped for last-minute groceries on Monday night, Saint Patrick's Day, March 17, 1987. That fateful evening, Olivia was kidnapped at gunpoint in the parking lot, forced to drive to a secluded end of town, and brutally raped by this man, Billy "Buck" Owens."

Blake pointed to the defendant, an essential move because it evidenced confidence that the correct person had been charged with the crime. Owens displayed an uncaring look on his face and turned away.

"Olivia Spencer is a young, single, elementary school teacher who lives alone here in Leigh County. She was engaged to be married, but that's up in the air now.

"That evening, she arrives home exhausted after a long day of teaching and parent conferences, and finding nothing substantial in the refrigerator, she freshens up and leaves for the grocery store at approximately seven p.m."

Blake paused momentarily, allowing the jury to picture the scene, then continued. "Ms. Spencer arrives at the shopping center parking lot at approximately 7:22 p.m. The sun has already set.

"Less than an hour later, at approximately 8:15, she leaves the store with her cart full of groceries. We turn and look, watching her load her groceries into her car.

"Suddenly, from behind her, the defendant presses a gun into her ribs, pushes her into her vehicle, and forces her to slide across the front bench into the driver's seat. Reeking of alcohol, he asks her, 'Do you want to live or die? Drive!'

"As she drives, the defendant continuously barks directions, making her realize he has a destination in mind. But fearing he'll kill her if she disobeys him, she follows his instructions.

"The defendant orders her to drive along Misty River Road, cross the bridge, and turn left onto a dirt road that leads to a densely wooded area along the bank of the Misty River. The entire time she drives, the defendant keeps his gun pointed at her. It becomes apparent to her that after he finishes doing whatever he has in mind, he'll have to kill her. He hasn't bothered to mask his identity, so he'll have no choice.

"Olivia Spencer's life begins to flash by. First, she thinks about her parents and the toll her death will take on her mom and dad. Then her fiancé. Knowing his nature, she thinks he'll come looking for her, but will have no clue where to start. Then she thinks about her students, associates, and close friends and the sadness they'll carry in their hearts.

"And what is the defendant doing while Olivia Spencer's life flashes before her eyes? He's holding his gun to her head, screaming driving directions in her face, and riffling through her purse for money. She's scared to death. Who wouldn't be? But she doesn't panic. Instead, she replaces thoughts of the remainder of her life being stolen with thoughts of survival. Regardless of the risk, she decides that at the first opportunity, she'll attempt to escape. She'll have to get out of her vehicle. It's the only chance of survival she has.

"As she approaches the end of the dirt road, the defendant directs her to stop and park.

"Ladies and gentlemen, this is the place you visited on the jury view. The only difference is that you were there in broad daylight, and Olivia Spencer is there in the dark of night, the waxing crescent moon above providing little light. Eerily quiet.

"The defendant tells her, 'This is as good a place as any,' and with his gun still aimed squarely at her head, he orders her to take off her clothes.

"Olivia Spencer knows she's trapped. She sits quietly, contemplating her escape, and surveys the area, looking for the best escape route. She's hemmed in by the Misty River to the right and surrounded by dense woods. In the distance sits the R and X railroad. She sees no sign of anyone who could help. No houses are visible where she might run to seek assistance.

"Nonetheless, Olivia has to run. It's worth the risk.

"She toys with the buttons on her blue cotton sweater, pretending to unbutton them. Then, thinking he is in total control of his captive, the defendant takes his eyes from her, places his gun on the floorboard of the passenger seat, and begins to focus on removing his own clothes."

Blake paused for effect and surveyed the jury box. All eyes were fixed on him. No one fiddled or squirmed.

"The moment has arrived for her escape. While the defendant is unfastening his pants, she opens the driver's side door and vaults out of the car in a flash, running aimlessly into the woods, as fast as humanly possible. She prays that her assailant won't pursue her, but her prayer goes unanswered.

"In one motion, the defendant retrieves his firearm and jumps out of the car in pursuit of his prey, screaming at her and threatening to kill her if she doesn't stop running."

Blake sped up his delivery and raised his voice a couple of decibels.

"Olivia doesn't get far before her legs give out, and she stumbles and falls to the ground. She looks up to see the defendant standing over her. He drives his foot into her chest and pins her to the ground, grabs her arm with his left hand and pulls her towards him, then using his right hand, violently strikes her head with the gun. Dazed but conscious, Olivia falls to the cold, damp, muddy ground.

"The defendant yells, 'Get the fuck up! I'm going to teach you a lesson you'll never forget.' Olivia stands on unsteady legs, knowing this nightmare is about to get worse."

Blake moved from the lectern, drawing closer to the defendant's table. Then, catching him off-guard, he pointed at Owens's cowering face. This time, he had no opportunity to look away.

Blake turned to face the jurors and asked them to listen carefully to the orders the defendant barked at his victim.

"This defendant, while pointing his gun in Olivia's face, barks, 'Take off your clothes!'

"Olivia freezes. This defendant screams, 'I told you to take off your fucking clothes!'

"Trembling, she begins to strip off her clothes, one item at a time. She unbuttons and removes her blue cotton sweater, Converse sneakers, jeans, bra, and panties, sure he'll kill her if she fails to obey him. She's humiliated, embarrassed to be standing naked and instinctively wraps one hand over her breasts, and the other over her genitals.

"The defendant stares at her naked body, smirks, and says, 'I like that.' Then staring at her left hand. which is covering her breasts, he spots her engagement ring and orders her to give it to him.

"Olivia looks at her ring and begins to sob. The defendant has no sympathy and says, 'If you don't shut up, I'm going to use my gun and shut you up.'"

Blake lowered his head and slowly stepped towards the jury box, stopped, and raised his head to look into the eyes of the jurors. Then softly and in a slow cadence, he told the rest of the story.

"The defendant shoves his gun into Olivia's stomach, making her moan in pain. He issues her an ultimatum to give him her engagement ring, or he'll pull the trigger. Olivia doesn't comply, and the defendant grabs her hand, rips the ring from her finger, stuffs it in the pocket of his jeans, and shoves her to the ground.

"He removes his jeans, mounts her, and forces himself into her. When she valiantly resists, the defendant's cruel attack becomes more violent. He raises his left arm over her head, and with a closed fist, strikes her face as hard as he can. With his other hand, he jams the gun barrel into her head.

"Ladies and gentlemen, note well what I am about to say. The defendant did everything he could to terrify her and force her into submission. He beat her and threatened to kill her.

"It would be reasonable to think that Olivia Spencer gives up after everything she endures at the hands of this defendant. But hear me when I say to you that she does not. Olivia continues to fight the defendant. She begs him to stop.

"He doesn't.

"She asks, 'Why are you doing this? I never did anything to you?'

"He doesn't care.

"Olivia cries out for help, but no one hears her. The only response is the whistle of a passing train.

"The defendant overpowers her, and for the next hour, he rapes her repeatedly.

"When he decides he's satisfied, before rolling off her, he whispers that he knows where she lives, and if she snitches on him, he will find her and kill her. He begins to put his jeans back on, surveilling the surrounding area, most likely to be sure that no one witnessed his attack.

"Realizing this is her last chance to survive, Olivia stands and pretends to retrieve her clothes, then runs as fast as she can in the direction of the train whistle.

"Perhaps because he is too tired to chase her, the defendant repeatedly fires his gun at her. Thank God he's a lousy shot. He returns to Olivia's vehicle and flees the crime scene.

"Olivia disappears into the woods without looking back. She continues to run as far as her legs will allow, praying the monster won't pursue her. This time, her prayers are answered.

"Realizing that her assailant is not behind her, she stops to rest her legs and sits on the ground for a moment. She bends over, her head in her lap, and for the first time since this nightmare began, she tells herself that at least she's alive.

"When Olivia looks up, she spots what turns out to be the Elliot farmhouse off in the distance. Naked and out of breath, she makes it to the front porch, crying for help. Finally in a safe place, she encounters the widow, Zelene Elliot.

"Members of the jury, I am going to bring into this courtroom the exhibit bag utilized by the sheriff's evidence technician to preserve the soiled clothes recovered in the secluded area of the woods where this defendant repeatedly beat her and violated her. We're going to open it up, and you'll smell the stench of the dank, musty, decomposing leaves, vegetation, and mud, the same stench Olivia smelled while she was forced to lie on the ground while the defendant sexually abused her."

Blake pointed to the witness chair and said, "You'll see Olivia in that chair, and she will tell you what happened."

"At the close of this trial, you'll have no choice but to hold that man accountable for what he did to her." Blake pointed once more at Owens.

"The evidence, the law, and decency will demand that you convict him."

He paused, then said, "Thank you."

"Thank you, Mr. Moretti." The judge turned to the defense table. "Mr. Sweeney, you may deliver your opening statement."

Sweeney walked to the lectern, took a moment to peer at his notes, and began. "May it please the court, ladies, and gentlemen of the jury, Mr. Moretti and Detective Barnes. As he sits here today, my client, Billy Owens, is innocent of every charge he is falsely accused of committing. Simply put, Billy has been framed.

"I cannot emphasize enough that my client has no legal obligation to prove his innocence."

Pointing at Blake, he told the jury, "The judge will instruct you that the government has the burden of proving its case beyond a reasonable doubt, the highest duty of proof there is in our great country.

"I am here to tell you that the government's case has more holes than Swiss cheese. First, their entire case rests on the testimony of a troubled woman. Now, I do not take pleasure in pointing out the complaining witness's mental health issues, but my client's life is at stake, and we cannot sit back and allow the government to railroad him. It is unfair to my client and to you, whom the government is using to do their dirty work.

"Ladies and gentlemen, my client does not deny having a consensual sexual fling with his accuser. However, she engaged my client to have sex with her after staking him out in the supermarket parking lot.

"Although we do not have to offer any evidence, I will tell you now that my client is not going down without exposing the government's fraudulent case. Mr. Owens will take the stand, take his oath to speak the truth, and tell you what happened.

"The truth is that Ms. Spencer lured my client to leave in her vehicle and drive to a secluded area in the woods, which I must tell you she was very familiar with, to have sex with my client. When they finished making love, the woman gave her engagement ring to him as a gesture of thanks.

"As Mr. Owens was getting dressed, his companion abruptly dashed off into the dense woods, completely unclothed, leaving him in utter bewilderment and isolation.

"He didn't know then, but we now believe she was not on good terms with her boyfriend and desired to have sex with my client. She was concerned that somehow her boyfriend would hear about it, so she staged a fake rape, then ran into the woods to locate anyone she could to substantiate her fairytale story.

"At the time, my client was in a long-term relationship with Valerie Fleming. He was about to ask her to marry him when this phony rape occurred.

"Mr. Owens is a fantastic person. His father left him when he was a baby. His mother was a drug addict and consistently abused him growing up. Yet, despite coming from a dysfunctional family, he graduated from high school and made something of himself.

"Ladies and gentlemen, there are always two sides to a story. So, on behalf of Billy Owens, I respectfully ask you not to decide this case until all the evidence has been heard and seen.

"Thank you for your attention."

"Thank you, Mr. Sweeney," Judge Croghan said.

"The state may call its first witness." She looked expectantly at Blake.

CHAPTER 23

The Prosecutor's Case

The Rape Trial Continues

Witnesses for both sides are precluded from listening to the others' testimony, so they are held outside the courtroom until they are called.

"Thank you, Your Honor. The People call Olivia Spencer."

All heads turned as the bailiff led Olivia into the courtroom. Jennifer and Blake had spent countless hours preparing her to testify. She had one opportunity to be heard, and her testimony would determine whom the jury believed. There was no room for error.

Jennifer had discussed how to dress, her demeanor entering the courtroom, and her posture on the witness stand, while Blake explained the importance of looking the jurors in the eye and speaking up when she answered questions so everyone in the courtroom, including the people in the last row, could hear her.

During Blake's direct examination, she tried to remain calm, but choked up and had to pause several times to hold back the tears as she recounted her nightmare. Blake could see from the jurors' faces that Olivia had touched their hearts. Her story visibly shook everyone in the courtroom, and there was an eerie silence when she paused.

Blake saw that her testimony had left her mentally exhausted. He'd often seen that look on the faces of victims reliving their heinous attacks. So he paused in his direct examination to give her time to think about the reality of her assault. He knew what would come next. Olivia put her head in her hands and sobbed uncontrollably. He poured a glass of water from the pitcher on the counselor's table.

"Your Honor, may I approach the witness?"

"Yes, please do,"

The court reporter offered her a box of tissues.

Judge Croghan leaned toward the witness stand. "Ms. Spencer, we can take a break if you like."

Olivia shook her head. She knew Blake was nearing the end of his direct examination.

He left the lectern and positioned himself as close to the far end of the jury as possible to be sure that Olivia would be in their line of sight. He paused before asking his last questions, allowing Olivia and the jurors to make eye contact.

"Ms. Spencer, for the last hour, you have described in detail the horrific acts of violence you were forced to endure on the evening of March 17, 1985, at the hands of a man who pointed a gun at your head."

For the first time, Sweeney stood up to object. "Your Honor, does Mr. Moretti have a question he would like to ask this witness, or is this just another of his fairytale speeches?"

"Mr. Sweeney," Judge Croghan replied, "I suspect Mr. Moretti is laying the foundation for his next question. Accordingly, I grant him that latitude and overrule your objection. You may continue, Mr. Moretti."

Blake thought, *Jesus, if Sweeney was upset with my last comment, wait till he hears what I say next.* "Thank you, Your Honor," he said. Then slowly, softly, and methodically, he asked, "Ms. Spencer, you told us that on March 17, 1985, you were kidnapped and carjacked at gunpoint, then forced to drive to a secluded area along the Misty River. After attempting to escape, you were hunted down like an animal, your attacker threatened to shoot you, and you were stomped on after falling to the muddy ground. You were beaten, then forced to remove one item of clothing at a time: a blue cotton cardigan, jeans, sneakers, bra, and panties. Your engagement ring was ripped off your finger. You were verbally threatened, and when you fought to resist your assailant, he became more violent, slapped your face, threatened to blow your brains out, and I quote, 'fuck you hard after he killed you.' And after all that, you were brutally and repeatedly raped."

Sweeney was on his feet again. "Your Honor, is there a question coming any time soon?"

"I suspect you're going to get to it forthwith. Proceed, Mr. Moretti."

"Thank you, Your Honor. Ms. Spencer is the man who committed these heinous, cruel, and cold-hearted acts of kidnapping, robbery, and rape in this courtroom?"

"Yes, sir, he is."

"Please point to your assailant and, for the record, describe what he is wearing."

Strong now, her head held high, Olivia raised a steady hand and pointed. "That is the man who kidnapped, robbed, and raped me. He is wearing a white shirt, red tie, and blue suit and is seated next to his lawyer, Mr. Sweeney."

Blake turned to the judge, "Your Honor, let the record reflect that the witness has identified the defendant."

"Yes, the record shall reflect the witness identified the defendant as her assailant," Judge Croghan responded.

"Ms. Spencer, are you absolutely sure?"

"There is no doubt in my mind. I have relived the pain Mr. Owens caused me almost every waking moment. Mr. Moretti, some people have the kind of face you can't forget. Mr. Owens has one of those faces. I will never forget that man's face, the stench of his body, his filthy clothes, and the strong odor of alcohol on his breath."

"Thank you for your courage in coming here today and sharing your tragic story with us. No further questions."

Blake returned to the prosecutor's table.

Judge Croghan asked, "Mr. Sweeney, do you have questions for the witness?"

"Yes, Your Honor."

"Very well, proceed."

Sweeney stood, buttoned the jacket of his dark suit, and approached the witness box. "Ms. Spencer, on the night of March 17, 1987, first responding, Officer Barlow asked why you went shopping so late, and you replied, 'You needed to get out because something on your mind was troubling you.' Perhaps you were having second thoughts about getting married when you ran into my client in the supermarket parking lot. Isn't that true?"

"Yes, sir, I had some things on my mind that night."

Sweeney walked towards the jury box and asked, "Ms. Spencer. Oh, by the way, it is Ms., not Mrs., correct?"

"Yes, sir."

"You told the jury you were engaged to be married. When was your wedding to take place?"

"April 22, 1987, sir."

"I see. So you never did get married. Isn't that true?"

"Yes, sir?"

"Isn't it true that you were having second thoughts about marrying your fiancé on the night of March 17, 1987?" Sweeney turned to the jury, gauging their reactions.

Olivia replied, "Perhaps that was on my mind, as well as work-related issues."

"Ms. Spencer, isn't it true that on Saint Patrick's Day night, March 17. 1985, a night when thousands of folks are out partying and drinking green beer, you were upset that your fiancé wouldn't celebrate with you, so you decided to go out night with the pretense of grocery shopping, hoping you'd run into a man? That's when you spotted my client, Mr. Owens, at the supermarket, flirted with him, and took him for a fling in the woods?"

Sweeney couldn't have cared less what was on Olivia's mind. His goal was to plant the seed in the minds of the jurors that she was out looking for a good time and hoped at least one of them bought into the fable.

Blake knew he'd be overruled if he objected to the question. Sweeney would argue it was his client's defense. He'd already told the jury his client would testify to that untruth, and he knew that Olivia would deny the allegation. In fact, he'd anticipated Sweeney's tactic and was prepared for it. When Blake first interviewed Olivia, she'd told him about her state of mind the night of the attack and the adverse after-effects of the sexual assault. He planned to ask her about it on redirect, and whatever points Sweeney thought he'd gained by presenting this preposterous defense would be crushed. Blake also knew that Sweeney hoped Blake would object so he could insinuate that the prosecution was concealing the "other side of the story" he'd referred to in his opening statement. But when Blake didn't object, he left Sweeney out on a limb, and he couldn't wait to cut it off.

Olivia had been prepared for the question, but she was indignant, nevertheless. "No, that is not true, and you should be ashamed of yourself. Your client raped me, and he has destroyed my life!"

Sweeney didn't even pause. "Ms. Spencer, among the few grocery items you purchased that night was a six-pack of Guinness Irish beer. Isn't that true?"

"Yes, sir."

"Let's stop playing games with this jury. It was you who took my client for a ride in your vehicle to a secluded area in the woods to celebrate Saint Patrick's Day with a six-pack of Irish beer, hoping to engage in sex with him. Yes, or no?" Sweeney didn't care about her answer. Again, he was planting seeds of doubt.

"No, Mr. Sweeney, you're twisting everything around."

"Ms. Spencer, it doesn't take twisting to figure out what happened that night. As I told this jury in my opening statement, there are always two sides to a story."

He stepped from the witness stand. "I have no further need to question this witness, Your Honor."

Blake watched Sweeney peeking at the jurors' reaction as he returned to his seat. In the front row, juror number eight, an older woman, was taking notes on his cross-examination. He only needed one "not guilty" vote to hang the jury. He pulled up his chair at the defense table, looking pleased with himself.

Judge Croghan said. "Mr. Moretti, I suspect you have redirect examination of this witness. Would you like to take a break first?"

Blake appreciated the judge's suggestion, but he had only one simple question for Olivia, and no need to discuss it with her. He had asked her that question at their first meeting and she was certainly ready to answer it again now. If Sweeney's drivel created doubts in the minds of the jurors, the sooner he responded, the more likely he could put it to rest.

"Thank you, Your Honor. I have only one question for Ms. Spencer and would like to proceed without a break."

"Very well, please do."

Blake gazed at Olivia with sympathetic eyes. "Regarding Mr. Sweeney's claim that you invited the defendant to celebrate Saint Patrick's Day and engage in a tryst, I have one question. Before you respond, I ask you to reflect on your state of mind on the evening of March 17, 1987, as well as your current state. Please do your best to explain your state of mind then and how it has been affected since that nightmare."

Her response could sink his defense. Sweeney was on his feet. "Your Honor, I object. This question goes beyond my cross-examination of the witness."

Blake turned to the judge. "You're Honor, may I respond? I fully anticipated Mr. Sweeney would object to this question for the reason he stated. But he opened the door to this question during his cross-examination when he salaciously attempted to mislead this jury into believing she'd planned a one-time affair with the defendant. I am simply allowing Ms. Spencer to respond to Mr. Sweeney's unsubstantiated slander."

Sweeney shot out of his chair like a rocket. "Your Honor, if I may?"

"No, Mr. Sweeney, you may not. I heard your objection, and I am overruling it. Mr. Moretti is correct. You opened the door to his question during your cross-examination of the witness. What's good for the proverbial goose is good for the gander. Please sit down. I will not hear further arguments on this issue. Ms. Spencer, I am permitting you to answer Mr. Moretti's question. And Mr. Sweeney will not need to continue to object during your response. For the record, I take his objection as a continuing one. Do I make myself clear?"

Blake thought, *Sweeney get ready to hit the ground. I just sawed off that limb you climbed out on.*

"Olivia, do you recall my question?" he asked.

"Yes, I do." She took a moment to gather her thoughts. Blake didn't need to stand near the jury box to remind her to face them.

He returned to his table and waited for her response so that the stage belonged to her. It was her last opportunity to convince the jury she was telling the truth and nothing but the truth. She had waited months for this opportunity to have her voice heard. She was prepared to end this nightmare.

She turned to the jurors and spoke to them directly in a slow, deliberate tone. "Mr. Moretti, you ask what my state of mind was. I was terrified when that man," she pointed at Owens "attacked me from behind, stuck his gun in my back, and made me climb into my car and drive to some god-forsaken place to violate me. He said vile things and threatened to kill me if I didn't comply with his demands. He beat me with his hands and pistol whipped me to submit to his depraved desires. He stripped me of my clothes and my dignity. I kept thinking how repulsive he was as he lay on top of me, repeatedly violating my body. He smelled like he hadn't taken a bath in weeks. While he lay on top of me, breathing directly into my face, the stink of alcohol was overwhelming. I'll never forget that stench, not because I don't want to, but because I am unable to."

She took another sip of water. No way Blake would come to her rescue by asking some meaningless question. Too often, he'd witnessed prosecutors interrupt a witness overwhelmed with emotion just when the jurors had begun to sympathize. He glanced at the jurors and spectators and saw that Olivia's words were tugging at every heart. No one stirred or made a sound. Her emotions were real, and her words were heartfelt.

"I felt so helpless and sorry for myself," she continued. "I began to feel anger. I had so much physical pain, and when I begged him to stop, he just smiled, enjoying every second of agony he caused me.

"I asked him why he wanted to hurt someone he didn't even know. I thought of my mom and dad, my fiancé, my friends and associates, and the students at the school where I teach, and I believed I would never see them again, never have the chance to say goodbye and that I loved them so much. My entire life flashed before my eyes."

She paused again, holding back tears. Then she rhetorically asked everyone in the courtroom, "Do you know what it feels like to wish yourself dead? To think you'd be better off dead. I do."

Blake noticed that several of the jurors had tears in their eyes. None of them were taking notes. He knew they didn't need notes to remember Olivia's story. They wouldn't forget her ordeal any more than she would.

"I'm still physically and mentally traumatized by the Defendant's violent physical attack."

She felt as though she were waging an incessant war, perpetually standing on the battlefield, looking over her shoulder to see if anyone was advancing on her. She wanted to disappear, to hide from prying, judging eyes. Why was it so achingly difficult for a wound to heal? Aside from her parents, sister, and a few close friends, no one wanted to hear the story because they already knew it or thought they did. No one knew what to say, especially her fiancé. She didn't know whom to trust or where to turn for help. She was broken.

"I'm attending counseling sessions to address both the short- and long-term effects of the trauma. I'm plagued with fear and shame and feel very much alone. I'm tormented by nightmares, and no longer feel safe anywhere. The simple act of going to the neighborhood grocery store is impossible for me. I trust no one, including myself. Sometimes I even blame myself for what happened and feel like damaged goods.

I find myself questioning my judgment, self-worth, and sanity. My engagement broke off, mostly because I could no longer maintain a relationship with a man. That is the world I live in today. At night, when I'm alone, I often play over how this happened. I went to the supermarket that night because I was too busy teaching all day long to go earlier. At times, I wonder if this would have happened had I parked somewhere less isolated. Sometimes I blame myself for being raped, like somehow, I should have prevented it. Then my common sense screams, 'My goodness! He's not the victim; I am.'"

Olivia fell silent, and Blake said, "No further questions, Your Honor."

She turned to the defense. "Mr. Sweeney, do you care to ask anything further?"

As Sweeney began to reply, Owens tugged his arm and handed him a legal pad with questions he wanted the lawyer to ask on re-cross examination.

"Your Honor, please, with your indulgence, would you give me a moment to confer with my client?"

"Yes, be my guest."

Blake knew that Sweeney had just fallen on his sword. The defense had nothing to be gained by keeping Olivia on the stand, and Sweeney certainly wouldn't ask her to answer Owens's dumbass questions. He'd had enough.

After pretending to consider Owens's questions, Sweeney rose and said, "No, thank you. No further questions."

"Very well. The court stands in recess for fifteen minutes."

Blake called Zelene Elliot to corroborate Olivia's story. She'd been the first-person Olivia encountered after surviving the brutal attack. When she saw her standing naked on her front porch, she'd been shocked, and when Olivia begged for help, saying she'd been brutally assaulted, Zelene was devastated. She was ready and willing to testify.

Blake opened with, "Mrs. Elliot, would you kindly share with us how and under what circumstances you encountered Ms. Spencer on the evening of Saint Patrick's Day 1987?"

"I'll never forget it. Around midnight, I was awakened by my dog Rocco's incessant barking. Someone was pounding on my front door. I got up, found my twelve-gauge shotgun under the bed, then turned on the house lights as I proceeded downstairs to my front door.

"At night, I keep the front of my house and yard lit up like a ballpark to ward off trespassers. When I peeked out a window, I saw a young woman— you'll excuse me— 'buck naked' on my front porch, begging for help, repeatedly saying she'd been kidnapped, beaten, and raped. I told her I was coming, give me a second.

"I set my rifle down, grabbed a blanket, and unlocked the door. There stood the woman, whom I now know as Olivia Spencer, shivering in the cold night air. Her face, head, arms, and legs looked like she'd gotten run over by a Mack truck. I covered her with the blanket, called the sheriff and waited with her until they arrived. The entire time Ms. Spencer appeared numb. Who could blame her?

"I did what little I could to comfort her until the medics took her to the hospital. It was difficult for me to witness her in so much pain. I became sick to my stomach when she described the sexual degradation her assailant had put her through."

"Thank you, Mrs. Elliot. No further questions."

Blake couldn't wait for Sweeney to challenge Zelene's testimony. She was not the sort of woman who would buy his consensual sex story.

As Sweeney approached the lectern, she gave Blake a look that said, "I got this."

Blake whispered to Detective Barnes, "Watch this."

Sweeney approached the witness with a brash attitude. "Isn't it true, Mrs. Elliot, that you were not with Ms. Spencer and my client, Mr. Owens, when the two were engaged in consensual sex?"

"Well, Mr... What did you say your name was?"

"Sweeney."

"Well, Mr. Sweeney, that's two questions. I'll try my best to answer them both. First, you're right; I was not in the woods with your client and Ms. Spencer the night this happened. Second, I would not call putting a gun to a woman's head and forcing her to engage in sex consensual."

Sweeney appealed to the bench. "Your Honor, I object and move to strike the witness's wisecrack. Non-responsive answer."

"You asked the question, Mr. Sweeney. You didn't like the answer. Overruled. Ask your next question."

"Mrs. Elliot, since you were not present in the woods with my client and Ms. Spencer, you don't know what happened, isn't that true?"

"No, that's not true. When I discovered Ms. Spencer standing naked on my front porch, covered in mud with fresh swelling on her face and head, sobbing and pleading with me to call the sheriff because a man beat and raped her, it didn't take Sherlock Holmes to figure out what happened, and that the sex hadn't been consensual."

"Come now, Mrs. Elliot, you can't know that Ms. Spencer wasn't acting and making up the story. Isn't that true?"

"Mr. Sweeney, in my humble opinion, if Ms. Spencer had been play-acting, she would have to be a better actress than Audrey Hepburn. Lord knows that isn't the case. I've been around long enough to know when someone's trying to hoodwink me, and all I can say to this jury is that given her appearance and demeanor, poor Ms. Spencer wasn't faking."

Blake loved watching Sweeney get sucker punched and sensed that the jurors enjoyed it even more.

Sweeney returned to the defense table, set his notepad down, and retired to his seat.

"Any further questions, Mr. Sweeney?' Judge Croghan asked.

"No, Your Honor."

On her way out of the courtroom, as she passed his table, Zelene winked at Blake who nodded his thanks.

"Very well, Mr. Moretti, you may call your next witness," said the judge.

"Thank you, Your Honor. The state calls Dr. Jeff Price."

A thin man with sparse gray hair and wire-rimmed spectacles was ushered to the witness stand.

"Doctor Price, please share with the members of the jury your observations of Ms. Spencer's demeanor and injuries when you met her in the hospital emergency room on the night of March 17, 1987."

"Yes, certainly. When I first observed Ms. Spencer, she was dressed in misfitted clothes provided by Mrs. Elliot. She'd told our trauma team that she had been pistol-whipped, slapped, and punched, forced to remove her own clothing, and sexually assaulted. She was extremely distraught and in a great deal of pain, having suffered severe blunt-force trauma to her head and face, consistent with the information she provided. My physical examination revealed tearing and contusions in her genital and anal areas."

"Thank you, Doctor. Your witness, Mr. Sweeney."

Blake knew that Sweeney would ask the doctor a question to bolster his consensual encounter defense. He'd prepared his witness for that question and wasn't worried about the doctor's response.

As he suspected, Sweeney asked, "Isn't it true that Ms. Spencer's injuries could also be consistent with consensual rough sex?"

"Yes, that is possible as it relates to the tearing and contusions I described, but only if one looks at those injuries in a vacuum. Before I render a medical opinion, I look at all the injuries the patient sustained, then compare that with the patient's report of the events that led to the injuries, as well as all other relevant accounts, such as reports from Mrs. Elliot and the initial responding officer, both of whom provided consistent corroborative information.

"I learned that the victim escaped her assailant and ran naked for approximately a mile, searching for comfort and medical and law enforcement assistance. Therefore, counselor, it is possible that her sexually-related injuries could have been caused during consensual sex, but given the history I collected, my expert opinion remains that the injuries Ms. Spencer sustained are consistent with a forced violent attack."

The doctor's testimony had damaged Sweeney's assertion of consensual sex. He'd stood poker-faced as the witness's response hit him in the head.

Blake wasn't surprised that Sweeney overtried his case. He was banking on it. Most defense attorneys overtry their cases.

"Your Honor, that concludes my cross-examination of this witness."

Judge Croghan refrained from making a derogatory statement. "Great," she said. "The State may call its next witness."

"The people call Valerie Fleming to the stand."

Valerie Fleming had dressed for the occasion. Her conservative blue dress and heels could not have been staples of her regular wardrobe. She testified that she'd been the defendant's on and off girlfriend for the past six years.

Blake asked, "Directing your attention to March 17, 1987, going into the early morning hours of March 18, 1987, tell us where you were when you came in contact with the defendant."

"Billy and I were back together, living at my place. When I got home from work around six p.m., he wasn't there, and I didn't know where he was. It wasn't like he was working. He didn't have a job. So, I made supper for the both of us, but when he still didn't come home, I suspected he was out carousing."

Sweeney stood to object that Blake was asking the witness to speculate.

"Let me do this," the judge said. "Ms. Fleming, do you know firsthand that the defendant was not at home for supper because he was out carousing?"

"Hell, yeah. I know he was out drinking. Bill's a drunk. When he's not home drinking beer, he's at some funky neighborhood bar mooching off the regulars. He has no money unless I give him some or he steals it from my purse."

Blake wondered how long it would take for Sweeney to object.

Right on script, he rocketed out of his chair. "Your Honor, I vehemently object and move for a mistrial."

The judge was becoming impatient. "Ms. Fleming has testified that in her experience, as a matter of routine, when the defendant is at home, he is drinking, and when he is not at home, he is drinking elsewhere. She provides first-hand knowledge of the defendant's behavior, so your objection is overruled.

"In addition, her comment that the defendant does not have any money of his own because he is not employed, will remain in evidence. The jury may assign any weight they choose to that remark. I will also note that the victim testified that the defendant smelled of alcohol when she was in contact with him. Mr. Sweeney, during your cross-examination, you attacked Ms. Spencer's credibility, which has been bolstered by Ms. Fleming's comment concerning the defendant's drinking habits.

"For the record, as it relates to the witness's testimony concerning the defendant stealing money from her purse, I will sustain your objection, and I advise the jury to disregard that comment and not to consider it during their deliberations."

Blake was nonplussed. Any trial lawyer knows that even if the judge instructs jurors to disregard evidence, it remains in their minds.

"Mr. Sweeney, your motion for a mistrial is overruled. Finally, Ms. Fleming, I would caution you to answer only the question put to you by the lawyers. You may continue."

Valerie thought for a moment. "As I was saying, I was at home asleep in bed. Sometime after midnight, I woke up because I heard Billy—the defendant, I should say—come in the front door.

"I hadn't seen him all day, so I got up and went into the living room. His clothes were filthy and disheveled. He was sweating and out of breath. When I asked him where he'd been, he didn't respond. Instead, he tried to divert my attention. He reached into one of the front pockets of his jeans, pulled out an expensive-looking engagement ring, and said he wanted to marry me.

"I knew he didn't have the money to purchase that ring and figured he'd been up to no good, so I asked him where he got it. When he didn't answer my question, I let it go and went back to bed.

"The next day, he turned on the TV news, which was odd because he'd never been interested in it. That's when I learned that a woman had been sexually assaulted the night before. I couldn't believe my eyes when they put up the sheriff's sketch of the assailant. I thought, *My god, that's Buck.*"

Blake nodded. "Ms. Fleming, is it true that later that day, you called the sheriff and told Detective Barnes what you just told us?" He carefully framed his question so that the jury wouldn't learn about the defendant's involvement in the Amoia murder case, which would have resulted in a mistrial.

"Yes, I certainly did."

"Thank you. No further questions."

Sweeney approached the witness stand with less swagger, and Blake thought he must have realized that he couldn't ask open-ended questions without getting shot down on redirect.

"Ms. Fleming, isn't it true you had no firsthand knowledge of how Mr. Owens obtained the ring? Yes or no?"

"Yes, I would have to say that is true."

"I have no further questions."

"Mr. Moretti, please call your next witness," Judge Croghan instructed.

"Your Honor, the State calls Deputy John Otto. Deputy Otto has been a member of the Leigh County Sheriff's Office for ten years, serving as an evidence collection technician. He was dispatched to the scene of a reported rape at approximately two in the morning on March 18, 1987."

Otto took the stand, and Blake said, "I will show you exhibits twenty and twenty and ask you if you recognize them. If so, please identify them."

"Certainly, Mr. Moretti, I recognize exhibit bags twenty and twenty-one. Both exhibit bags bear my initials and the handwritten date. State's exhibit twenty contains the bag containing groceries and the grocery receipt that I found in the grocery bag, proving that the items were purchased at Hangers the night Ms. Spencer reported being raped. State's exhibit twenty-one contains clothing belonging to the victim, which I recovered at the scene of the rape."

"Deputy Otto, were their perishable grocery items in State's exhibit twenty?"

"Yes, sir. I recovered a one-pound package of ground hamburg and a two-pound package of chicken."

"Deputy Otto, please display the victim's clothing in State's exhibit twenty-one, recovered from the scene of the rape."

Deputy Otto displayed the victim's blue sweater, bra, panties, sneakers, and blue jeans, for the jurors. As you can see, each of the items is stained with red clay soil, which matches the soil where I found them. The items were found close to each other."

"What happened to the mini skirt, Deputy Otto?"

"Mr. Moretti there wasn't any mini skirt to collect at the scene of the rape."

"Are you sure about that?"

"If there had been a mini skirt at the crime scene, I would have recovered it."

Moretti intentionally didn't ask Deputy Otto about lighting when he looked for evidence at the crime scene. He gambled Sweeney would. To set Sweeney up, he said, "Thank you, Deputy Otto. Mr. Sweeney may have a question for you about the mysterious mini skirt."

"I object, Your Honor …"

Sweeney had barely finished his sentence when Blake said, "Strike that. Nothing further."

"Mr. Sweeney, do you have any questions?"

"Yes, Your Honor."

"Deputy, do you agree it was pitch black when you arrived at the scene?"

"Yes, sir, that would be accurate."

"And do you agree that you overlooked Ms. Spencer's mini skirt because it was pitch black?"

"No, I do not."

The predictable gotcha question amused Blake, who knew Sweeney was about to violate the golden rule of never asking a question without knowing the answer.

"Deputy, do you think this jury will believe you didn't miss Ms. Spencer's mini skirt, even though you just admitted it was pitch black at the scene when you searched for evidence?"

"Yes, Mr. Sweeney, that's an easy one for me to explain. It was so dark that I plugged my portable utility pole lights into my evidence truck generator. I lit the woods up like a football field during a night game. I didn't have any difficulty looking for evidence. I don't know who told you there was a mini skirt, but I am saying unequivocally there was no such garment at the crime scene. If there had been, I would have seen it and collected it. The victim appeared to have been wearing jeans, not a mini skirt."

"No more questions, Your Honor." As Sweeney returned to counsel's table, he looked harshly at Owens, who was pretending to write in his trial notebook.

Blake called his last witness, Detective John Barnes. He always saved the case detective for last so he could discuss what the investigation had revealed and address any issues raised by the defense during cross-examination.

Then it was time to play the recorded statement Owens had insisted on making during the interview. Blake was sure that when the jury heard him boasting that women couldn't resist him, they would loathe him. Especially the nine female jurors.

"Detective Barnes, having identified the audio recording of my interview of the defendant, in the presence of his lawyer, Mr. Sweeney, as fair and accurate, I have placed it in evidence subject to the redactions stipulated by Mr. Sweeney and myself and approved by Judge Croghan. Please play it for the ladies and gentlemen of the jury."

Blake returned to his seat at the counsel's table, and waited as the recording was played in open court. He knew that Sweeney could not object but would be forced to pretend that his case hadn't been demolished, so he sat back and relaxed, sure that Owens would pay dearly for disregarding the advice of both his lawyer and the judge to keep his mouth shut. No juror with a modicum of common sense would buy Owens' fanciful tale.

Early on, Blake's mother had taught him that he would learn more from listening to others than listening to himself talk drivel.

"Son, let me give you some free advice. You can learn things the easy way or the hard way. It's your choice. But remember, words have meaning. You can open your mouth and stick your foot in it as much as your little heart desires. You may have the right to speak but be careful that your words don't result in undesirable consequences." *Jesus, she was always right.*

Owens was about to learn the price of requesting a meeting and lying to Blake and his investigator. His own words would trap him.

The jurors listened intensely to every word of the recording. Blake watched their reactions as Owens bragged about his alleged sexual conquests.

Several of them looked puzzled or disbelieving as he attempted to picture himself as the victim of Olivia's advances.

"I didn't rape that woman. I was going to the grocery store to buy a six-pack of beer, and she approached me and started flirting with me. Before I knew it, she asked me if I wanted to fuck her. So, I thought, what the hell?"

Blake saw that the jurors had stopped taking notes, as their looks of bewilderment had turned to disgust. Every word that left Owens's lips was a lie.

Blake's question about possessing a firearm forced him to admit he'd had a gun the day Olivia was raped. And when asked about stealing the ring, he'd said, "She gave me her engagement ring because she enjoyed the sex so much."

Blake was confident the jury would vote to convict when the recorded interview finished. Still, before he rested his case, he had two final questions for Detective Barnes.

"Detective Barnes, did Olivia Spencer provide a detailed and consistent rape account to the deputy sheriffs and Mrs. Elliot?"

"Yes, absolutely one hundred percent consistent."

According to Doctor Price, Ms. Spencer suffered blunt force trauma to her face, head, arms, and legs, as well as contusions and tears to her vagina and anus. Did those medical findings match the injuries Olivia described she sustained during the sexual assault? "

"Yes, absolutely one hundred percent."

"Thank you, Detective. No further questions."

Sweeney attempted to save his case on cross-examination. "Detective, isn't it true that Billy Owens cooperated with law enforcement and offered to speak to Prosecutor Moretti so he could clarify the events of March 17, 1987?"

"No, it is not."

Blake knew Sweeney would ask that question. Most defense attorneys do. They think a defendant who agrees to speak to the sheriff, forgoing the right to remain silent, appears to have nothing to hide, so they must be innocent.

Seasoned detectives like Barnes don't fall for that. At the pretrial interview, Blake discussed the question with him. Barnes intentionally didn't attempt to explain his "no" response, because Sweeney, like every other defense attorney, couldn't help but ask a follow-up.

"Detective Barnes, how can you say my client didn't cooperate with your investigation? He gave Mr. Moretti a recorded verbal statement."

"Thank you for asking that question. Yes, your client did request to speak with the prosecutor. However, his purpose was to tell him a far-fetched story that the events of March 17, 1987, took place at the request and with the full consent of the victim, Ms. Spencer, which is inconsistent with her statement to the sheriff, the prosecutor, and the testimonies of Mrs. Elliot, Valerie Fleming, and Dr. Price regarding the physical injuries she sustained.

"Hiding and telling fictitious stories to law enforcement officials are not signs of cooperation. Bottom line: your client's actions and words hindered our investigation."

Barnes glanced at Blake, looking for his approval. Like a third-base coach giving signals to the batter, Blake touched his right ear with his right hand.

It seemed to Blake that Sweeney had no more questions for the detective. He couldn't have felt good about his last mistake. But the defense attorney couldn't help himself.

"Are you suggesting that my client's recorded statement to this jury is inconsistent with the evidence?"

"No, counselor, I am not suggesting it, I am telling you it is a fact. Your client's story regarding his encounter with Ms. Spencer is undoubtedly one hundred percent inconsistent with the evidence presented at trial."

Sweeney walked back to the counsel's table and spoke quietly to Owens, who pointed to his notepad. Sweeney shook his head no, and announced he had no further questions for the detective.

"Does the state have any redirect?" Judge Croghan asked.

"No, Your Honor, it isn't necessary."

"Very well, Detective Barnes, you are excused. Let's take a fifteen-minute recess. I ask that the lawyers meet me in chambers."

Judge Croghan poured herself a cup of coffee and invited the lawyers to do the same. Sweeney demurred.

"Rough morning, Sweeney?" Blake asked. "Perhaps you could use something a little stronger than coffee."

"Moretti, you're killing me. At least throw me a couple of bones now and then."

Blake never lets up with an opponent. Not when he played chess, not when he played a playground game of one-on-one basketball. During a trial, he never took his foot off the gas pedal.

"Sweeney, that's not going to happen. You and your client made it impossible to resolve this case. You requested a speedy trial, and I granted your wish." In Blake's mind, it was time for retribution.

"Well, gentlemen," Judge Croghan said, "I want to get a handle on where we are. Moretti, do you have any more witnesses?"

"No, Your Honor, the State is ready to rest its case."

"Good. I'll have you do that on the record when we return to the courtroom. Sweeney, do you intend to put on any evidence?"

"Yes, ignoring my advice, my client has elected to testify."

"Okay, gentlemen, let's get the show on the road."

CHAPTER 24

The Defendant's Side Of The Story

The Rape Trial continues

"Ladies and gentlemen of the jury, the State has rested its case. Accordingly, the defendant may call his first witness."

"The defense calls Billy Owens."

For the best part of an hour, Owens answered Sweeney's questions regarding his dysfunctional upbringing. He told the jury that his ex-girlfriend, Valerie Fleming, had lied because he'd broken up with her after she'd fabricated the story, she told the sheriff. He testified that Olivia Spencer lied about the kidnapping, robbery, and rape so her boyfriend wouldn't know that she'd initiated sex. He insinuated that she had mental problems. He testified that Mrs. Elliot had misconstrued her observations, that Olivia had pulled the wool over her eyes, acting as though she'd been raped to cover her tracks.

"I have one more question," Sweeney asked at last. "Did you kidnap, rob and rape Olivia Spencer on the night of March 17, 1987?"

Owens turned to look at the jurors. "No, sir. Everyone lied. I've been framed. I did my best to tell the prosecutor what happened, but he didn't care about the truth."

"Thank you, Billy. I am sorry you had to endure this nightmare."

"Mr. Moretti, any cross of the defendant?" Judge Croghan asked.

"Yes, Your Honor."

Blake was more than ready. "So, Mr. Owens, how often do you shop at the local grocery store?"

"I don't know. Why do you care?"

"Mr. Owens, according to you, you're quite the ladies' man. I was attempting to determine how often you get lucky and run into a woman at the local grocery store who falls in love with you at first sight and tells you she wants to have sex with you?"

"More than you think. You know how soccer moms are. They can't get enough sex at home, so they go out looking for it."

Blake could tell from Owens's body language and the tone of his voice that he'd gotten under his skin, as he had during the jail interview. The guy was an easy target, so he fired more questions.

"Do you get lucky with these soccer moms once a week or more often?"

"Look, Moretti, women like me. I can't help that. It's not unusual for a woman to approach me for sex. Maybe twice a week sometimes. I don't keep track."

"Mr. Owens, do you have to go to the same grocery store to get lucky, or since you don't have a vehicle, do you walk to more than one grocery store to give women an equal opportunity to have sex with you?"

Owens gripped the arms of the witness chair. "I'm getting tired of your mocking me. I'm done answering your questions."

Blake smiled. "Your Honor, please direct the witness to answer my question."

"Mr. Owens, you may not pick and choose the questions you wish to answer. You made a conscious decision to testify after being fully appraised of your right not to talk. Answer Mr. Moretti's question."

"The same one!" shouted Owens, digging himself into a deeper hole. Blake needed only two more questions to finish him off.

"Mr. Owens, I would imagine if you enjoyed your sexual liaisons with these women, you must have obtained their names and contact information if you wished to see them again."

"What if I did?"

"Unfortunately, Mr. Owens, I get to ask the questions, not you. So, please answer my question, or the judge will order you to answer it. Your choice."

Owens couldn't stop himself from lying every time he opened his mouth. He had no clue where Blake was going with his line of questioning.

"Yeah, I did that on a few occasions."

Blake was playing with the defendant now. Catching him in lies was like shooting fish in a barrel. He picked up his legal pad and tore off a blank page, approached the court reporter and asked her to provide him with a state exhibit sticker. He wrote the number thirty-five on the sticker representing the following sequence exhibit number, placing it on the blank page's top right-hand corner.

Then he turned to the judge. "Your Honor, may I approach the witness?"

"Yes, you may."

"Mr. Owens, I am handing you State's exhibit thirty-five and a pen. Please write the names and contact information of the women with whom you wished to continue a sexual relationship."

Blake knew the defense would challenge his pretense on the grounds that it would potentially damage the reputation of the women Owens identified. But he was ready to defuse that argument. He also knew it wouldn't matter because Owens always lied and wouldn't list one real name.

Sure enough, Sweeney was on his feet. "Your Honor, for the protection of the women with whom my client engaged in a relationship, I voice an objection."

"Mr. Moretti, help the court out here. I share Mr. Sweeney's concerns. Unless you can provide a solution to this dilemma, I will sustain the motion."

"Yes, Your Honor. The remedy is to seal the exhibit from the public and allow only the jury to view it with an instruction that they may not divulge the names to anyone."

"Right. That will work. Mr. Owens, please comply with Mr. Moretti's request."

Owens sat staring at blank exhibit number thirty-five, then picked up the pen as though he were ready to provide the information. "I can't remember any of their names or personal information."

Standing within arm's length, Blake asked, "Mr. Owens, that's because it was all a lie. Despite your testimony to the contrary, there were no other women. Isn't that true?"

Owens was trapped. If he didn't provide the women's names, the jury would know he'd been lying. But if he listed fake names, Moretti would investigate and catch him. Either way, he was screwed.

Sweeney knew what Blake was doing. "Your Honor, Mr. Moretti is confusing my client. I ask that you order him to stop."

Blake turned to face Sweeney. "Your client and I are fine, thank you. We don't need your help."

"That's enough, gentlemen," the judge admonished. "Mr. Sweeney, your objection is overruled. Mr. Owens, answer the question."

"I prefer not to because it may incriminate me."

The courtroom erupted in laughter. The judge banged her gavel several times. "Order in the court, or I will have you removed."

Blake didn't care. The damage had been done. Everyone within earshot knew that Owens was a liar. "Mr. Owens," he said. "I will accept your silence as an admission that no such women exist. I now present you with State's exhibit twenty-one. For the record, what is State's exhibit twenty-one?"

"You know what it is," Owens said, "It's just a pair of blue jeans."

"That is correct. But it isn't 'just' a pair of blue jeans, is it?"

"What do you mean?"

"Here is what I mean." Blake walked towards the jury box, raised the blue jeans, and asked, "Isn't it true, Mr. Owens, that the blue jeans I now hold in my hands were worn by Olivia Spencer the night you kidnapped her at gunpoint, and forced her to remove all her clothing?"

Owens's temper was boiling over. If looks could kill, Blake would be dead. He stood up in the witness box and yelled, "How the hell would I know, Moretti? You're trying to frame me to make a reputation for yourself. Who the hell knows where you got those clothes from? For all I know, you could have bought them from Goodwill."

Judge Croghan leaned toward the witness box. "Mr. Owens, calm yourself and sit down, or I'll have the deputy assist you," she ordered.

Blake wasn't finished. "Mr. Owens, you were sitting beside Mr. Sweeney when the evidence technician, Deputy John Otto, identified for this jury all the clothing he recovered from the scene of the rape. These blue jeans, Ms. Spencer's blue sweater, sneakers, bra, and panties were found in the same pile. Isn't that true, or do you want to call the evidence technician a liar?"

"Yeah, he's a liar, too!"

"Answer this last question, Mr. Owens. You testified under oath that when you first observed Ms. Spencer in the grocery parking lot, she was wearing a mini skirt that caught your attention.

"In fact, during your recorded interview, you said she was wearing a 'tight skirt'. I commented that it must have been a short, tight mini skirt. And you asked, 'Is there any other kind of mini skirt?' You don't deny that do you? I can play the recording again or ask the court reporter to read your testimony if you like."

"That won't be necessary. I know what I said."

"Then answer my question, Mr. Owens. If Ms. Spencer wore blue jeans the night you met her, and, as she testified, she took them off along with the other clothing that the evidence technician recovered in the woods, then tell us, Mr. Owens, how is it that no mini skirt, tight or otherwise, was found at the crime scene?"

Owens glanced at his lawyer, looking for help to no avail. He sat for a moment, looking around the courtroom, then said, "How the hell do I know? They're all liars."

"Thank goodness, Mr. Owens, the jury will determine who is telling the truth, not you. Your Honor, that concludes my examination of the defendant."

"Mr. Sweeney, any recross of the defendant?" the judge inquired.

"No, Your Honor."

"Call your next witness."

"Your Honor, the defense rests."

"Very good. Ladies and gentlemen of the jury, we will take a thirty-minute recess. When we return, you will hear the closing arguments of the parties."

CHAPTER 25

He Said-She Said

The Rape Trial

"Ladies and gentlemen of the jury. During jury selection, you all agreed that my client, Billy Owens, was presumed innocent. I submit to you that the government has failed to prove any of the criminal charges pinned on my client, and therefore has done nothing to change his status as an innocent man. There are more holes in the government's case than Swiss cheese.

"As I told you folks, a story has two sides. My client has cooperated with the government since day one. At his own request, Mr. Owens met with the prosecutor and provided his story. But Mr. Moretti didn't listen to a single word my client said. Mr. Owens explained that his encounter with Ms. Spencer was consensual, and that it was she who instigated the event. Ladies and gentlemen, my client is the victim, not Ms. Spencer. This case is nothing more than 'he said, she said'. You have not been presented with anything close to proof beyond a reasonable doubt, the highest burden of proof in our judicial system.

"Can you imagine if someone made up a false accusation against you, and all you had to disprove the lie was your word against the accuser's? My goodness, without the burden of proving the accusation 'beyond a reasonable doubt', innocent people would be convicted daily and spend the rest of their lives in prison.

"Before I review the government's poor excuse for proof, allow me to digress and discuss two matters.

"First, I will not defend my client's comments that women are attracted to him, because he is not charged with being a braggart.

"Second, we all saw Mr. Owens lose his temper with Mr. Moretti. However, please remember that he has cooperated with law enforcement since the inception of this case. Unfortunately, every word has fallen on deaf ears. Yes, he is frustrated by this legal process, but ask yourself if this nightmare was happening to you or your loved one, wouldn't you be upset, as well?

"I beg you not to hold any of that against him. Instead, judge this case on the evidence or, should I say, the lack of evidence.

"So, what evidence does the government want you folks to rely on to convict an innocent man? Think about it. They brought in Ms. Spencer, who wants you to believe she is in love and engaged to be married. In reality, nothing could be further from the truth. Ms. Spencer and her so-called fiancé fought constantly. The very same day she cried rape, the so-called love birds engaged in a significant fight. And she never got married. That's because she was already done with that relationship and was out on Saint Patrick's Day night looking to hook up with a man to party with. So, please, don't fall for her 'poor me' act. Mrs. Elliot did. She meant well, but Ms. Spencer pulled the wool over her eyes.

"Then there was Dr. Price who examined Ms. Spencer. Remember what he said when I asked him if bruises and contusions could result from rough sex? The doctor agreed that indeed, they could have been.

"Then there was Ms. Fleming. When you think about it, she didn't tell law enforcement anything my client didn't tell them, and he reiterated that on the witness stand.

"Finally, I would be remiss if I didn't remind you about the shoddy rush to judgment on the part of the sheriff's investigation. Their sole purpose was to clear paper, so they ran with Ms. Spencer's fable and arrested, charged, and indicted my client without obtaining his side of the story.

"Ask yourselves, what kind of government locks up their citizens without obtaining their side of the story? It certainly isn't the America we grew up in. Sinful!

"Now you know why Billy Owens told you he was framed.

"Find him not guilty."

"Mr. Moretti, are you ready to proceed with the closing argument for the state?" asked Judge Croghan

Of course, Blake was ready. He'd been either working on the case or thinking about it every waking moment since Hardy assigned it to him.

The closing argument was his favorite part of the trial. He was a natural storyteller. In his speeches, he gave voice to victims and survivors whom he firmly believed had a right to be heard and remembered.

Blake recognized the importance of delivering the closing in a way that commanded the listeners' attention and tugged at their hearts. To persuade the jury that their cause should prevail, he chose a suitable theme and words that would empower the jury to decide in his favor on the grounds that it was the just and right thing to do.

A lot depended on how he was perceived in the courtroom, where he stood, the tone of his voice, the cadence of his words, and the way he looked the jurors in the eye and let them know he was being truthful.

The closing argument was the last leg of his Rule of Three storytelling. It began with the opening statement, continued during the State's case, and finally, the closing argument when the jury heard it again. If he was consistent from start to finish, why wouldn't they believe it?

He walked to the middle of the courtroom, set his legal notepad down on the lectern, and then slowly approached the jury box, being careful not to invade their space. He took a moment and glanced at each juror, so no one would feel left out. In a soft tone of voice, he slowly began.

"May it please the court, ladies and gentlemen of the jury, Detective Barnes, and Mr. Sweeney."

As he delivered the closing, he moved slowly from one side of the jury box to the other, watching their eyes to be sure they were listening.

"Where were you when …? You can fill in the blank. Maybe it was a big moment in history. Perhaps it was a small moment when you were on the playground or in a bar. A time when someone needed your help. Did you do something? Did you say something? Did you help?

"Where were you on March 17, 1987, when the defendant kidnapped Olivia Spencer at gunpoint in Hanger's supermarket parking lot and forced her to drive her vehicle to a secluded, dark place in the woods along the Misty River?

"Where were you when the defendant chased Olivia Spencer down like an animal as she attempted to escape?

"Where were you when the defendant pointed a gun at Olivia Spencer's head and ordered her to remove her clothing, her blue cotton sweater, her sneakers, and not a tight mini skirt, by the way, but her blue jeans, her bra, and finally, her panties?

"Where were you when the defendant pistol-whipped Olivia Spencer's face, knocking her to the cold, wet, muddy ground?

"Where were you when the defendant removed his own clothes, laid his foul-smelling body on hers, and still holding a gun to her head, exhaled his alcohol-laden breath in her face, screaming that if she didn't stop fighting him off, he would kill her and then fuck her?

"Where were you when Olivia Spencer was being raped by the defendant, over and over? When she cried out for help and begged him to stop?

"I suspect most of you were at home. Maybe some of you were working. Perhaps you were out with friends. You didn't know. You couldn't see her. You couldn't hear her. You couldn't help her."

Blake raised his voice and said, "But you can now. You are here now. Olivia needs you. She needs you to do the right thing. Olivia Spencer is not asking for a lot. She only asks you to hold this defendant accountable for his brutal and heinous crimes against her.

"In the opening statement, I told you I would return to this story and explain why the State has met its burden of proof and why you must hold this defendant accountable for his actions. Everything I told you we would present in the trial, we did. The evidence we presented has been consistent throughout. The witnesses all corroborated Olivia's testimony. The physical evidence confirmed it. That's because it is the truth. The truth is consistent, like the needle on a compass, which always points north.

"Mr. Sweeney was correct when he said you would hear two stories. Unfortunately, that was the only accurate statement he made.

"You see, Mr. Sweeney is a lawyer and is just doing his job. Like all lawyers, he wants to win. The law and facts were not in his client's favor, so he disparaged the victim. It was clear from the evidence that the defendant's entire defense was based on a fairytale intended to obscure the truth.

"The defendant's fairytale goes like this: on Saint Patrick's Day evening, Ms. Spencer dressed provocatively for a night out on the town and seduced the defendant into having consensual sex. She took him to a secluded wooded area along the Misty River, where she voluntarily had sex with him, gave him her engagement ring as a gift, and allowed him to drive off in her car. The story was intended to cast the victim in a negative light and to make you ignore the truth.

"So, here's the deal. It doesn't matter what he thinks or what I think. At the end of the day, finding the truth is all that matters.

"The law gives you the power to decide the facts for yourselves. Each of you is like a judge, except you don't have a robe like Judge Croghan. As jury members, it's your responsibility to determine the truth by evaluating the witnesses' testimony and the physical evidence admitted as evidence, applying Judge Croghan's instructions, and your everyday common sense.

"Here's what I have: I have a victim who lives a nightmare every waking and sleeping hour of the day. A woman who made an ordinary late-evening grocery run and wasn't looking for sexual encounters. She wore jeans, not a seductive tight mini skirt. The evidence technician recovered her blue jeans, not a mini skirt, with the other clothing she was forced to remove. A bag of groceries containing perishable grocery items she purchased was recovered in her stolen vehicle and found only two houses from where the defendant was arrested. You also learned that at the scene of the rape, Before she could enter her car and return home with her groceries, this defendant stuck a firearm in her back and directed her to drive to a secluded wooded end of town along the Misty River where he humiliated her, forced her to remove her clothes with a gun pointing at her head, brutally beat and raped her repeatedly.

"She didn't take the defendant to her place or a rented motel room. She was forced to drive to a secluded wooded area where no one could see her being beaten and raped, nor hear her cries for help."

With an unforgiving face and a grave voice Blake pointed at the jury and said, "The defense put one witness on the stand. That witness stunk up this courtroom with his lies and inconsistent demeaning accusations of consensual sex."

Blake turned and pointed at Owens, who had nowhere to hide. "That witness was this defendant.

"Ladies and gentlemen, think about this: to believe the defendant, you would have to believe he's God's gift to women, and the sex was so good the victim handed over her engagement ring and the keys

213

to her car as a reward for giving her the most sexually satisfying night of her life.

"To believe the defendant's lies you would have to disbelieve not only the victim, but also Zelene Elliot, Doctor Jeff Price, and the first responding deputies who confirmed that Olivia Spencer's injuries and appearance were consistent with her story that she was beaten and raped.

"To believe the defendant's fable, you would have to disbelieve the testimony of his girlfriend, Valerie Fleming, who testified to his disheveled appearance when he returned home after raping Ms. Spencer. You would have to disbelieve her testimony that he tried to give her an expensive engagement ring he didn't have the money to buy, which, coincidentally, belonged to Ms. Spencer.

"Finally, ask yourselves why Olivia left the scene of the attack naked if the encounter was consensual.

"The truth is that the defendant is not the victim here. Olivia Spencer is the victim.

"Ladies and gentlemen of the jury, Olivia Spencer had the courage to walk into this courtroom, swear to tell the truth, and endure ridicule from the defense. She had to relive the nightmare that began on March 17, 1987, which started in the supermarket parking lot when she was kidnapped at gunpoint and forced to drive to the secluded banks of the Misty River, where she was repeatedly raped. Nevertheless, she took the stand and shared her story with you in hopes that you'd hold her assailant accountable.

"The defendant wants you all to believe that he did nothing wrong. He wants you to believe Olivia Spencer's actions are why we're here today. The truth is that's not true."

Blake turned his attention to Owens, raised his voice, pointed at him, and said, "It's that man's fault, right there. He is the reason we are all here today. On Saint Patrick's Day night of 1985, Billy "Buck" Owens kidnapped, raped, and robbed Ms. Spencer. He wrote this script. He picked the judge, the lawyers, the witnesses, and you, the jury. He did all that right here, in the town of Misty River, in your backyard, the night he raped Olivia.

"Folks, those are the facts. You know Ms. Spencer spoke the truth because her story is consistent with the testimony of all the other State's witnesses. Furthermore, you know it's the truth because her story is consistent with all the physical evidence. Finally, you know it's the truth because her injuries were consistent with rape and assault as depicted in the photographs you observed during trial."

Blake walked closer to the jury box, looked the jurors in the eye and softly said, "Today you can use your voice to say Billy Owens is responsible for the crimes he committed against Olivia Spencer. Today, you can use your voice and tell the defendant he is guilty and should be held accountable for his actions.

"Ladies and gentlemen of the jury, on March 17, 1987, this defendant kidnapped, robbed, and raped Olivia Spencer. I respectfully ask you to find him guilty. It's time he is held accountable for his actions."

While the jury deliberated, Blake told Jennifer he was going for a walk to get fresh air, which wasn't true. He had to get out of the courthouse because every five minutes someone asked him if the jury had reached a verdict yet. Not that he was concerned about the outcome, but he wanted to be alone to review the trial presentation and make mental notes of what he should have done differently for future reference.

Jennifer knew that during jury deliberations, he hung out on a quiet park bench a couple of blocks from the courthouse. Two hours had passed when she received a call that the jury had reached a verdict.

Blake found himself lost in thought, perched upon the unforgiving surface of the cement park bench. He nibbled on a *Snickers Bar*, its caramel sweetness mingling with the weight of his ruminations. Suddenly, piercing through the haze of his introspection, Jennifer's voice rang out like a clarion call, shattering the silence that enveloped him. "Blake," she declared with a sense of urgency, "we have reached a verdict."

Blake and Barnes took their places at the prosecutor's table in the packed courtroom. Jennifer and Ralph sat with Olivia directly behind them.

Tension was high when the bailiff called, "ALL RISE."

Judge Croghan took the bench and announced, "Please, everyone be seated. I do not want to hear a peep from anyone when the verdict is announced. Bailiff, bring in the jury."

When they had all filed into the jury box, she swiveled in her chair to address them. "Who is the foreperson?"

"I am Your Honor," said woman juror number eight.

"Have you reached a verdict on all counts?"

"Yes, Your Honor, we have."

"Very good. Please pass it to the bailiff."

The judge retrieved the documents from the bailiff, looked them over, and returned them. "Will the bailiff read the verdicts?"

He began, "On count one of the indictment, kidnapping, we, the jury, find the defendant, Billy Owens, guilty as charged.

"On count two of the indictment, aggravated robbery, we, the jury, find the defendant, Billy Owens, guilty as charged.

"On count two of the indictment, rape (vaginal), we, the jury, find the defendant, Billy Owens, guilty as charged.

"On count four of the indictment, rape (anal), we, the jury, find the defendant, Billy Owens, guilty as charged.

"On count five of the indictment, motor vehicle theft, we, the jury, find the defendant, Billy Owens, guilty as charged."

Judge Croghan asked, "Ladies and gentlemen of the jury, are these your verdicts?" Each of the jurors verbally acknowledged the verdicts.

"Very well. Mr. Moretti, do you have any requests?"

"Yes, Your Honor, I respectfully request that the defendant's bond be revoked, and that he be remanded into the sheriff's custody."

"Granted. Sheriff, take the defendant away. Sentencing will take place after Mr. Owens's murder case is completed. That matter is scheduled for trial in December."

That night, Blake invited Barnes, Ralph, and Jennifer to celebrate at The Exchange, his favorite neighborhood watering hole. As much as he loved his solitude, he knew this had been a team effort, and that he needed to show his appreciation. They all deserved to celebrate the day's victory.

"Andrea, grappa shots for everyone on me!" Blake called out as he came through the door. They huddled around a table, shoulder to shoulder, buzzing.

Andrea had seen the news and congratulated them as she set down four glasses and the grappa bottle. She'd been watching Blake and Ralph hash out the case over drinks for weeks. They raised their glasses, and Blake stood up.

"Great effort, everyone. *Salute!*"

As the celebrations for the successful prosecution of Billy Owens for rape ended, prosecutor Blake Moretti and his trial team faced an even more daunting challenge. The upcoming trial for the cold case murder of small-town baker Frank Amoia loomed over them like a dark cloud, casting a shadow of uncertainty and intrigue.

As the trial date approached, whispers of a mysterious figure lurking in the shadows began to circulate among the townspeople. Rumors spread like wildfire, painting a picture of a cunning killer who had managed to evade justice for years. The small community was gripped with fear and anticipation, wondering if justice would finally be served or if the murderer would slip through their fingers once again.

The trial would push Blake's skills and determination to the limit, unraveling a web of secrets and lies that would leave them questioning everything they thought they knew.

Will Moretti be able to overcome the mounting challenges and secure a conviction? Or will the truth remain elusive, leaving Frank Amoia's murder unsolved? The answers lie within the courtroom walls, where justice will ultimately be served.

CHAPTER 26

The Murder Trial

December 7, 1987, Monday morning

Since 1980, more than 250,000 complex crimes have gone cold in the United States alone. In instances where there are no witnesses or confessions, the case quickly grows cold.

However, every wrongdoer inevitably leaves behind a trail of clues. It is crucial for the investigator to possess the knowledge and expertise required to identify these clues and discern their significance.

The investigative work often involves piecing together fragments of evidence, unraveling complex webs of deceit, and delving into the depths of human psychology. Crime scenes must be constantly reexamined for any overlooked clues or traces of evidence. Months or even years later, just one new clue may finger the person responsible for the crime. Frank Amoia's murder was one of those cases.

Based solely on the information he obtained from Owens's girlfriend, Detective Massey believed Billy Owens murdered Frank Amoia. Massey worked diligently to solve the case, but there were no eyewitnesses to the murder, no fingerprints of value, no trace evidence or tests that would reveal who the killer was. Owens's girlfriend made a statement, which was the sole piece of evidence they had. The initial statement by Owens's girlfriend appeared to be the breakthrough they sought. It could shed light on the circumstances surrounding the crime and the perpetrator's identity. The statement provided critical details such as motive, opportunity, and even direct involvement in the murder. With this evidence in hand, Massey was hopeful they were one step closer to solving the case and bringing justice to the victim.

However, just as things seemed to fall into place, she recanted and they were left with nothing. This sudden turn of events left investigators stunned. They now found themselves back at square one, grappling with the absence of substantial evidence to proceed with their investigation. It undermined their progress and raised doubts about the credibility and reliability of their primary witness. The sudden change of heart from Owens's girlfriend left investigators questioning her motives and integrity, further complicating an intricate case.

Detective Massey made three attempts to convince the Leigh County Prosecutor's Office to accept charges on Owens for the murder and was rejected all three times. The Amoia murder became one of America's 250,000 cold cases.

Fortunately, in January 1985, the Leigh County Sheriff's Office had received a grant to purchase its first camcorder and started videotaping crime scenes, beginning with the Amoia murder.

It never hurts to have a new set of eyes look at a cold case. That may be all it takes to uncover the evidence. Blake Moretti was the fresh eyes the murder case needed. Blake spent countless hours studying that video. He knew from experience that crime scene photos could explain not only what, how, and when a crime occurred, but the identity of the perpetrator, as well. There was no reason to believe a crime scene video couldn't do the same. Sure enough, Blake found the clue.

But just as it seemed like victory was within reach, cracks appeared in the seemingly airtight case. Defense attorney Sweeney skillfully exploited these weaknesses, casting doubt on key pieces of evidence and raising questions about alternative suspects. The jury hung on every word, torn between their desire for justice and their duty to consider all possibilities.

As each day of the trial unfolded, the tension grew thicker, leaving everyone on edge. The courtroom became a battleground, with Moretti and Sweeney locked in a fierce legal duel. Every witness, every piece of evidence, and every argument held the power to sway the outcome of the trial. The fate of Frank Amoia's murderer hung in the balance, and with it, the reputation and legacy of Blake Moretti.

Mary Amoia had lived in Leigh County for thirty-five years. After her husband's murder, she was too devastated to do anything for a while, but within a few months, she re-opened the bakery and hired staff to run the daily operations.

Mary had a sister in Fort Meyers she was visiting when she got the call from Blake Moretti's office. She was horrified at the thought of having to testify, but she wanted her husband's death avenged, and at least the prosecutor was Italian American. Jennifer made all the travel arrangements, told her what to wear and what to expect, and Blake sounded very reassuring when he interviewed her over the phone.

On the morning the trial began, he was waiting to greet her at the courthouse when she arrived with Jennifer.

"Mrs. Amoia, I'm pleased you could make it here for the trial. I hope you had a pleasant flight," she said.

She was wearing the gray linen suit she had saved for Sunday mass and had spent extra time with her hair. Looking nice gave her confidence, and she needed all the reinforcements she could find to withstand the pain of facing the man who'd killed her husband.

"The flight was fine," she said, "but you know, I have mixed emotions about testifying."

"I understand. We'll do our best to assist you through the criminal process. We all understand how disturbing it is as a survivor to relive the tragic event. Thank you for agreeing to testify. You can help me put a human face on Frank, who can't be with us to speak for himself, by telling the jurors who he was and that his life mattered."

"Don't worry about me, Mr. Moretti. You're right; I'm a survivor. I can get through this."

Blake Moretti, known for his relentless pursuit of truth and justice, couldn't shake off the feeling that there was more to this case than met the eye. Late nights were spent pouring over evidence connecting dots. The more he dug, the deeper he found himself entangled in a complex web of motives and alibis.

As the trial began, tensions ran high in the courtroom. The prosecution presented a compelling case, meticulously piecing together evidence pointing to Billy Owens as the prime suspect in Frank Amoia's murder. Witnesses took the stand one by one, recounting chilling encounters and suspicious behavior that painted a damning portrait of Owens.

Blake opened by putting the young man who had first discovered evidence of the murder on the stand.

"Mr. Benton, you've told us you arrived at Mr. Amoia's Italian bakery on March 2, 1985, at 7:35 a.m. Can you tell us what caused you to contact the Leigh County sheriff soon after you entered the premises?"

"Yes, Mr. Moretti. I customarily stop by the bakery to get my espresso and cannoli fix. I was concerned that although the front door was unlocked, the "Closed" sign was displayed. Mr. Amoia never did that, so I entered the shop. No one was there, not even Mr. Amoia, so I walked to the back and saw blood seeping under the closed door to the public restroom. I called Mr. Amoia's name several times, and not hearing a response, I ran out and called for help."

"Did you attempt to open the restroom door?"

"No sir, I did not."

"Thank you, Mr. Benton. Mr. Sweeney, your witness."

Sweeney pointed to his client. "Mr. Benton … am I correct, sir? Is it true that you didn't see my client in or around the bakery that morning?"

"You are correct. I didn't see your client that morning. I've never seen him before in my life."

"No further questions."

$$Q$$

Next, Blake called the homeless man, Chris Stewart. He looked far from wealthy, but Jennifer had helped him clean up to give him credibility.

Chris entered the courtroom through the double doors wearing a stylish scissor haircut and razor shave, a starched white shirt, a black necktie, dress slacks, and a red knit cardigan. As he marched confidently past the jury box, he nodded to the jurors.

While he was being sworn in, Detective Massey jotted something on his notepad and nudged it toward Blake. "I love the Mr. Rodgers look."

Blake grinned, then approached the witness stand. "Mr. Stewart, tell us where you were and what you saw the morning of March 2, 1985."

"I was homeless at the time and still am today. I sleep and hang out wherever I can without having someone complain to the sheriff, who usually shows up and arrests me for trespassing. Early that morning, I was sitting on the bus stop bench across the street from the bakery when I observed a man standing behind the lamppost on the other side of the street. He looked like he was trying to stay out of view of anyone in the bakery. I remember what he looked like because he seemed out of place on that street. His hair was dark, long, and greasy, and he was wearing a leather jacket, dirty jeans, and worn-out cowboy boots. He was around six foot two with a husky build. I kept eyeing the man because he acted like he was up to no good. I watched him enter the shop and flip over the sign from "Open" to "Closed". Within about ten minutes, he rushed out of the bakery and took off running down the street."

"Did you get a look at the man's face?"

"No, because when he left the store, he turned so fast all I could see was a mark or scar of some sort over one eye."

"Would you recognize the man if you saw him in court?"

"No sir, but I could recognize the mark over the man's eye if I saw it again."

"Chris, look around the courtroom and tell the jury if you see anyone with a mark or scar over their eye that resembles the one you observed the morning Mr. Amoia was murdered."

Owens slumped in his chair and rested his head on his hand to cover the scar.

Blake grinned. "Your Honor, would you kindly order the defendant to remove his hand from his head?"

"Mr. Owens, please sit up and remove your hand from your face and head. Mr. Stewart, continue your observation and answer Mr. Moretti's question."

Stewart locked eyes on Owens. "The scar over that man's eye resembles the mark I saw on the man I just described."

"Thank you, Mr. Stewart. Your witness, Mr. Sweeney."

Sweeney came out swinging. "Mr. Stewart, you manufactured this story to get your greedy hands on the twenty-five-thousand dollar reward, isn't that true?"

"No, that's a lie. I don't know anything about a reward. When do I get the money?"

Laughter erupted in the courtroom, and Judge Croghan. reminded everyone to remain silent.

Sweeney asked, "Mr. Stewart, isn't it true that you remained on the scene when the Sheriff arrived, yet never told them this con-trived story?"

"It's true I hadn't left the bus stop when the sheriff arrived. But I didn't speak to them because they didn't ask me, either. Besides, the sheriff would have most likely cited me for trespassing. And there were outstanding warrants for my arrest for failing to appear in court. I'm not a fan of being arrested. I know they're just doing their job, and perception is everything. I suspect they think I'm dangerous because I'm grungy. looking, unshaven, and I probably don't smell particularly good. I can't help it. Ever since I got back from Vietnam, my mind's been pretty messed up."

"That's interesting, Mr. Stewart, because you don't appear any-thing like what you just described, with your stylish haircut and clean-shaven face, dressed like a liberal arts college professor. Do you work every day like these ladies and gentlemen of the jury?"

"No, sir."

"I see. Who paid for your stylish cut and shave and the clothes your wearing?"

"Sir, no one."

"Did you just find your Tommy Hilfiger outfit in the trash dumpster and cut your own hair and beard?"

"No."

"Mr. Stewart, please tell us who paid to clean you up so you could deceive this jury."

"I didn't come here to deceive anyone. You can shoot arrows at me all day long, and you're not going to intimidate me by making fun of me and accusing me of being deceitful.

"It's true that I have mental problems and have trouble integrating back into society. But here's the thing. I was sent to Vietnam to fight a war I didn't start, to protect your liberty, while you were in law school learning how to make witnesses like me look bad in court. I witnessed atrocities you might have read about in a newspaper or seen on the nightly news. I served two tours of duty and was seriously wounded both times. As a result of my service, I received the Purple Heart and was honorably discharged. I make no excuses for who or what I am. The truth is that I may be a lot of things, but deceptive is not one of them.

"To answer your question about my appearance in court, Vinnie, the barber, cut my hair and shaved my beard for free since I am a veteran.

"I borrowed a shirt, pants, and tie from Mr. Moretti, and I must return them at the end of the trial. Mr. Moretti felt sorry for me because I told him court is a place of respect like church. In court, I didn't want to look like I always do since that would have been disrespectful.

"I borrowed the sweater from my sister's husband. Their home is located just outside Misty River in Troy. My sister's husband is a professor at Misty River Community College. I moved to Misty River two weeks before Mr. Amoia was murdered and was invited to live with my sister. I appreciated the invitation but declined because I didn't want to be a burden. To clean up for court, my sister let me shower at her house … and she didn't charge me.

"Mr. Moretti's assistant washed, starched, and ironed the white shirt I'm wearing free of charge. The bloodstain could not be removed despite her efforts. The pocket also had a bullet hole. So, I borrowed my brother-in-law's red sweater to cover it."

"Why, Mr. Stewart, does the shirt you're wearing have a bullet hole? It makes no sense at all. Could this be a delusion caused by your mental illness?"

Blake stood and addressed the court, "Your Honor, may I explain?"

The judge nodded. "Go ahead."

"All Mr. Stewart's clothes except the sweater are from the district attorney's property room. The shirt with the bullet hole, blood-stained pants, and necktie belonged to a murder victim who went by the name John Allen. Mr. Allen was murdered in a carry-out stop and rob ten years ago. Since the killer pled guilty, the shirt was never introduced as evidence and because the surviving family didn't want the shirt back, it was kept in our property room. From time to time, we lend shirts and other clothes items to defense attorneys for impoverished clients to wear in court."

Judge Croghan responded, "Thank you Mr. Moretti. I am fully aware of your office's assistance when defense attorneys face such a similar challenge. Mr. Sweeney, I hope you are satisfied with Mr. Moretti's explanation. The implication that something sinister—or to use your word, deceitful is going on, is misleading at the very least. Don't you agree?"

"Your Honor, I certainly didn't mean to imply any such thing. I am satisfied with the explanation."

"Very well. Do you have any other questions of this witness?"

"Yes, Your Honor"

"Proceed."

"Mr. Stewart, isn't it true that you were seen outside the bakery the morning Mr. Amoia was murdered, and that you fled the scene when the police arrived?"

"You can say that."

"I did say that. Isn't it also true that you are the only person who could be positively identified as having been outside the bakery within seconds of the Amoia murder? You may answer that question with a yes or a no."

"Yes."

"Last question Mr. Stewart. Have you ever killed anyone?"

"Yes. Of course, I have."

"No further questions."

"Anything more from the state?" the Judge asked.

"Yes, Your Honor."

"Chris, Mr. Sweeney has explicitly called you deceitful and implicitly attempted to label you as a murderer when he asked you if you'd ever killed anyone. Mr. Sweeney didn't allow you to explain your answer. So, I will ask you to explain. Who have you killed and under what circumstances?"

"Mr. Moretti, the only people I had to kill were enemy soldiers in Vietnam during war."

"I noticed that Mr. Sweeney never asked you if you murdered Frank Amoia, or for that matter, anyone else? Have you ever murdered anyone?"

"No sir, I didn't murder Frank Amoia or anyone else.

Chris continued, "Mr. Sweeney is a lawyer and knows the distinction. That's why he asked the question the way he did. Mr. Sweeney has an obligation to zealously defend his client, which I guess includes attempting to distort the character of a witness in a court of law. I fought for his right to do that. What I didn't fight for is his right to distort the truth."

Blake paused for a moment. "Mr. Stewart, thank you for your service to our country and for performing your public duty today by coming forward to testify."

A sense of sympathy spread in the courtroom, and Blake could see Sweeney stepping back.

Sweeney said, "No further questions."

Blake continued to present his case in chief methodically. Trial lawyers often second-guess their strategies and alter their presentations during the proceedings. Sometimes plans go awry, and they must adjust on the fly. But everything was going as he expected.

"Ms. Fleming, tell us what happened on March 2, 1985, when your boyfriend, Billy "Buck" Owens, arrived home after Mr. Amoia was murdered."

"It was about ten a.m. I woke up when I heard sirens coming from the direction of Mr. Amoia's bakery a couple of blocks away. Then I heard a noise in my bathroom. I went to check and saw Buck removing his clothes. I noticed fresh blood all over him. Before he took off his bloody jeans, he reached into one of the front pockets and pulled out a wad of blood-stained cash.

"When I asked him where he got the money, he said he'd gotten it from a guy who tried to rob him at knifepoint. He said he got the drop on the guy, grabbed the knife, and wrestled it out of his hand, and that he was so pissed off, he stabbed the guy with his own knife and took his money."

"Did you believe him?"

"Hell no. Buck tells more lies than the devil."

Sweeney was on his feet.

The judge raised a hand in his direction. "I know, Mr. Sweeney, you object. Objection sustained. The jury is instructed to disregard the witness's last comment that the defendant 'lies more than the devil.'"

"What happened next?" Blake asked.

"The next morning, Buck turned on the local TV news, which I thought was strange because he never showed any interest in watching the news. That's when I learned Amoia had been found dead the day before. They didn't say how he died, but they said the sheriff's office was investigating a homicide, and I realized that Buck didn't stab some stranger. He killed Mr. Amoia."

Sweeney jumped out of his chair like a ground-to-air missile. "Objection! And I move for a mistrial."

Blake could see that Judge Croghan was becoming concerned with Valerie's off-the-cuff responses and asked for a sidebar.

"Permission to approach the bench?"

Blake asked her to overrule Sweeney's objection and motion for a mistrial. "This witness is prepared to testify that not only does she think Owens murdered Amoia, but he admitted to her that he killed him and forced her to help him dispose of the bloody clothing and the murder weapon."

Sweeney argued, "Your Honor, this witness told the sheriff that story, then recanted and said it was a lie."

The Judge fingered her pearls for a moment, considering. "Mr. Sweeney, you may cross-examine the witness regarding her recantation. Mr. Owens's alleged statements to this witness are incriminating and may be admitted. The fact that she concluded he was the murderer caused her to question him, and he admitted as much. Therefore, I will allow her testimony. In addition, your motion for a mistrial is overruled. Let's keep going here. I want this jury to get the case sometime this year."

"Ms. Fleming, what happened next?" Blake asked.

"He wrapped the blood-stained Buck knife and sheath in his bloody clothes and coerced me to go with him to bury them in a secluded area near the Misty River. He told me that if I didn't do what he said, he'd tell the sheriff my eighteen-year-old son killed Amoia for his money and that I assisted my son in concealing the evidence. I didn't have a choice. I took his threats seriously, so I did what he said. After we buried the evidence, he told me to stop at a local carryout where he purchased soda pop, cigarettes, and gas. When he returned to the car, he poured soda pop on the blood-stained money.

"When I asked him what he was doing, he said, 'What's it look like I am doing? The acid in the soda pop will wash away the blood.'"

"Ms. Fleming, why do you call the defendant "Buck?""

"Because he always carries a knife."

"The knife you referred to with the blood on it, what kind of knife was it?"

"It was a large Buck hunting knife. The same one Buck always carried."

"One last question: did you provide Detective Massey with this information?"

"Yes. Shortly after the murder, I told him."

Blake didn't ask Valerie why she recanted. He knew Sweeney wouldn't be able to stop himself from asking the "why" question, and her answer would be more devastating when he asked it.

"Isn't it true you lied to Detective Massey when you told him Mr. Owens killed Mr. Amoia so you could get your greedy hands on the twenty-five-thousand-dollar reward for information leading to the arrest of Mr. Amoia's killer?"

"No sir, that's not true. I inquired about the reward, but I never pursued it. I have not received any reward money.

"I lied to Detective Massey when I recanted Buck killed Mr. Amoia because I was frightened that Buck would kill me. I was also concerned Buck would frame my son Joey for the murder.

"I am here to tell this jury that your client killed Mr. Amoia with his Buck hunting knife, stole his money, buried the murder weapon with his bloody clothes, and purchased cocaine with the stolen money. That's the truth. It's time for Buck to be punished. I know that coming here and finally telling the truth won't fix what I did, but it's the right thing to do. What I have to say today may not be what you want to hear, but it's the gospel truth. That's why I initially told Massey Buck killed Mr. Amoia."

"Ms. Fleming, isn't it true you lied to Detective Massey when you told him Billy murdered Mr. Amoia in order to protect the real murderer, your son, Joey Fleming?"

It pissed Valerie off that Owens told Sweeney that bullshit story as he threatened to do. She bit her tongue, sipped water, and took a deep breath before responding.

"No, sir, that is a lie. If you didn't hear anything I said today, hear me now. Had my son butchered Mr. Amoia in cold blood, I would have no use for him and would have turned him in to the sheriff myself. I have known Mr. Amoia for my entire life. When I was a kid, I often stopped by the bakery after school because he knew I didn't have money and let me choose whatever cookie I wanted for free. Then he'd say, 'We'll just put it on the tab.' I'm sure he did the same for other kids. He was a great guy. When Buck admitted what he did to Mr. Amoia, I threw up. I'm ashamed to say he bought cocaine with the blood money. Buck Owens killed Mr. Amoia."

"That's a heartwarming story, but the fact remains your son worked for Mr. Amoia, and you didn't tell Detective Massey about that until after he confronted you, having learned from Mr. Owens that was indeed the case. Isn't that true?"

"Yes."

"Isn't it also true that you told Detective Massey your son saw Mr. Amoia hide thousands of dollars in the bakery?"

"Yes."

"Isn't it also true your son was addicted to painkillers and spent his earnings purchasing painkillers on the black market to feed his addiction?"

"Yes."

"Isn't it true Mr. Owens sought counseling for your son's addiction to painkillers, but your son refused to go?"

"Yes, sir."

"Mrs. Fleming, your son stole the money hidden in the bakery to feed his drug habit. Isn't that true?"

"I don't believe that."

"Of course not. You're Joey's mother."

"Ms. Fleming, what we do know is when you took Detective Massey to the alleged burial spot, you say Mr. Owens buried his blood-covered clothes and murder weapon; none of those items were recovered, despite a massive effort by the sheriff. Isn't that true?"

"Yes"

"Ms. Fleming, that is because your son, with your assistance, buried the murder weapon and clothes; God only knows where to protect him from being apprehended and punished for killing Mr. Amoia. Isn't that true?"

"No. That's a lie."

"Finally, Ms. Fleming, did you know that two hundred thousand dollars was laundered by mobster Sonny Calo, who, with the help of Frank Amoia, hid the dirty money in a ventilation duct?"

"I don't know anything about that."

"Isn't it true your son observed Mr. Amoia hide the money in the ductwork, which the sheriff's investigators never found?"

"I don't know anything about that."

"Would you be surprised to learn your son told Mr. Moretti about the money hidden in the vent ducts?"

'I am not surprised about anything in this case. Why don't you ask Joey?"

"I plan to."

"Your Honor, I don't have any other questions of this witness."

"Very well, Mr. Moretti, do you have any more questions of this witness?" Asked Judge Croghan.

"No, Your Honor."

At the counsel table, Detective Massey whispered to Blake, "Blake, why didn't you clean that up? "

There was no reaction from Blake.

"Your Honor, the state calls Mary Amoia," Blake announced.

The nightmare of her husband's murder had never left her. How could it? She'd told Blake that wherever she went around town, she could hear people whisper, "Is that her? Is that the baker's wife?" She'd felt as though she were trapped in a revolving door, and her sorrow never lessened.

She was sworn in, and Blake asked if she was ready to proceed.

"Yes, Mr. Moretti, as much as I ever will be."

"Tell the jury your name and how you know Frank Amoia."

"My name is Mary Amoia. Frank Amoia was my husband. We were married for thirty-five years before he was murdered on March 2, 1985. Frank and I moved here from Brooklyn, New York in 1950 to open Amoia's Italian bakery. We were so proud of the shop."

"Mrs. Amoia, please tell the jury about the last day you saw Mr. Amoia alive."

She sat still for a moment, clutching her hands in her lap, collecting herself. "The bakery business is tough. The shop was open six days a week between the hours of seven a.m. and four p.m. So, Frank had to be at the shop by five a.m. to get ready for business.

"That morning started like it always did. We were up by two. I put on the coffee and made Frank breakfast. We talked about everything from family to national politics. Every morning, Frank kissed me on the way out of the house. He never said goodbye. He felt that was too permanent. He'd say see you later, love you and off he went. Funny. That morning, he didn't say see you later. He said goodbye. I thought it was odd at the time, but I never saw him alive again. When I tell people that story, some respond that maybe it was a premonition. I don't know. Perhaps God works in mysterious ways."

Blake had grown up a devoted Catholic, but in high school, an event caused him to question whether there was a God. Some of his friends thought he was an atheist, but he wasn't. As far as he was concerned, the verdict was still out. It wasn't that he didn't believe in God, but that he didn't need to rely on a priest to make that determination.

"Mrs. Amoia, would you share with us when you were first notified of your husband's murder?"

"Yes, I'll never forget that morning. The doorbell rang at ten, and when I opened the front door, Detectives Massey and Wilson were standing on my front porch. After they identified themselves, Detective Massey asked me if we could go inside. I could tell from the looks on their faces and the sadness in Detective Massey's voice that something terrible had happened to Frank. I had no idea it was more horrible than I could have ever imagined.

"Detective Wilson suggested I sit down, so I sat beside her on the sofa, waiting for them to tell me the news.

"Detective Massey told me he'd received a call to report to the bakery. He had been murdered that morning. His body was found in the restroom.

"I fell to my knees. Those words wouldn't stop ringing in my head. I felt like I'd been struck by a freight train. I was paralyzed with emptiness and pain. That's what I can recall. It's more than I care to remember."

"Mrs. Amoia, I'm so sorry to ask you to relive this tragic event. If you don't mind, I have only two more questions."

"It's okay."

"Can you tell us whether you or Frank were aware of anyone who wanted to cause him harm?"

"No, sir. Frank didn't have an enemy in the world. Everyone in the community who knew him, loved him. He would give you the shirt off his back. If the defendant had just asked Frank for the money, he would have given it to him."

Sweeney jumped up. "Your Honor, I object to this line of questioning regarding Mr. Amoia's character. It's irrelevant. The only purpose it serves is to invoke the jury's sympathy."

Blake began to counter Sweeney's masquerade objection, but Judge Croghan raised her hand like a traffic officer. "Overruled. Mrs. Amoia, you may finish your answer."

"Thank you, Your Honor. I was about to say Frank was a good and generous man. There was no need to kill him for his money. Frank worked hard all his life. He tried his best to talk me into retiring and selling the business. Maybe if I had listened to him, he'd still be alive today."

Blake had the last photograph of Frank Amoia, a thumbnail shot enlarged to eight by ten inches and mounted in an acrylate standing frame. He marked it as State's exhibit thirty-nine. He intended to ask Mrs. Amoia to identify it and introduce it into evidence to publish to the jury. The rules of procedure required him first to show it to Sweeney. When Sweeney saw it, he objected and asked the court for a sidebar conference.

"Your Honor," Sweeney said, "I object to Moretti parading around the photo of Mr. Amoia. His only purpose is to arouse the sympathy of the jury. This bush league move is uncalled for."

"Mr. Moretti, may I see the exhibit?" asked the Judge.

"Your Honor," Blake countered, "first, everything is admissible at trial unless a rule precludes the use of the offered evidence. No evidence rule prevents me from introducing the victim's identification photograph, and who better than Mrs. Amoia to attest to its veracity?

"Secondly, since you asked, Sweeney, everyone in this courtroom, including myself and this jury, has had to look at your client's mug every day for the past week. So, since we've been forced to see the defendant daily, at the very least, let the jury see that Mr. Amoia was a real person, not some TV character. With the court's permission, I will introduce Mr. Amoia's photograph and stand it on my table for the remainder of this trial, so you and your cold-hearted client will have to look at the victim every day."

"Well, Robert, I believe Blake is right," the Judge said. "The photo is admissible. Therefore, your objection is overruled."

Blake resumed his questioning. "Mrs. Amoia, do you recognize State's exhibit thirty-nine?"

"Yes, that is a photo of my husband, Frank. It was taken one week before he was murdered, on our thirty-fifth wedding anniversary."

She stared at the photograph for what felt like an eternity. No one in the courtroom moved a muscle. No one made a sound.

Blake stepped closer to her, as if that would somehow give her the strength to continue.

"You know, Mr. Moretti," she said softly, "it used to be that a photograph of Frank like this one would bring back so many memories. I haven't browsed through our old photos since he was murdered. Now, as I sit here looking at this photograph, I know why. It used to be that as I flipped from one photo to another, each one recalled a favorable memory and made me smile. I realize now that ended the morning Frank was murdered. There will be no more happy memories for me. Old photographs don't make me feel good anymore. They remind me that my best friend and lover was stolen from me."

Sweeney began to stand to object, but the Judge gave him a warning glare and he sat back in his chair.

"I can't stop thinking about how he died. You know, Mr. Moretti, taking a person's life is one thing. But the way Frank's murderer savagely killed him makes me wonder if in some twisted-minded way, he enjoyed it.

"To this day, it still makes me sick to my stomach. I asked Dr. Smith how much he suffered, and he told me the sharp-force trauma was so deep and severe, Frank would have died before he hit the floor. I don't know if that's true or if he told me that to make me think Frank didn't suffer long. Either way, it doesn't relieve how empty I feel inside.

"It used to be that I could forgive anyone who hurt me. But I don't have it in my heart to forgive Frank's killer, and I don't apologize."

It was a gut-wrenching moment for everyone in the room. Everyone but Billy "Buck" Owens.

Blake respected survivors. They had to deal with their loss and move on with their lives as though everything would be okay. Back to normal. Whatever that was. They were blind-sided and damaged by evil people who couldn't care less about the devastation, pain, and suffering they inflicted on others. He'd seen survivors who had it in their hearts to forgive, and others whose hearts were filled with hate. He believed they had that right.

There was nothing more he needed to ask Frank Amoia's widow and nothing more she needed to say. She was Frank's voice. She'd told his story.

He had no further questions for the witness, and neither did Sweeney.

In trials like this, Blake's last witness was always the medical examiner. He wanted to leave a present tense impression in the juror's minds of the brutal death by displaying autopsy photographs, both external and internal. The defense always objected and begged the judge not to allow the jury to see the photographs because of their prejudicial nature.

"Dr. Smith," he said, "we have autopsy slides depicting the injuries inflicted on the victim, Mr. Amoia, taken under your direction and supervision. Will presenting those to the jury aid you in explaining the manner and cause of his death?"

"Yes, sir."

"Doctor, have you reviewed State's exhibits one through ten to determine whether they are fair and accurate."

"Yes, I recognize them. I directed pictures taken during the autopsy of Mr. Amoia. Exhibits one through ten are slides you requested we prepare for presentation in court today. I've placed them in the carousel tray in order, and they are ready to be displayed. They are all fair and accurate."

"Thank you, Doctor. Your Honor, the state moves to admit exhibits one through ten into evidence and I request I be allowed to show them to the jury."

The familiar objection rang out. "I object, Your Honor. The jury was already told what caused his death. I will stipulate the manner and cause of death. The autopsy slides are prejudicial."

"Let's hear what Mr. Moretti has to say," Judge Croghan replied.

Blake knew his response would get under Sweeney's skin, and he could hardly wait for him to shoot out of his chair again. "Your

Honor, first, I'll address the offer of a stipulation by Mr. Sweeney. If Mr. Sweeney stipulates that his client killed Mr. Amoia in cold blood when he slit his throat from ear to ear, I will stipulate to the cause and manner of death."

Again, Sweeney shot out of his chair. "Your Honor, that comment was uncalled for. That is not a stipulation I can agree to."

The judge said, "Your choice not to agree is of no concern to the Court. Mr. Moretti's comment was a counteroffer. Accordingly, objection overruled. Mr. Moretti, you may continue."

"Thank you, Your Honor. Regarding Mr. Sweeney's argument that the autopsy slides are prejudicial, I submit to the Court that they portray a bloody, brutal, and heinous murder. Nonetheless, their probative value outweighs the prejudicial effects of displaying them. The defendant is charged with aggravated murder. The photos depict the assailant's intentional, willful, and malicious acts. Perhaps the defendant should have poisoned the victim instead of butchering him.

"Furthermore, Your Honor, the slides are part of the forensic imaging and essential to the doctor's autopsy findings. The doctor has testified that the autopsy slides will assist him in presenting and explaining his expert opinions regarding the cause and manner of death and will therefore assist the jurors in determining the truth. I worry more that given all the true crime content shown to viewers depicted in movies and on the national and local news, the public has become desensitized to real-life tragedies."

"Your point is well taken, Mr. Moretti. Mr. Sweeney, I overrule your objection. The autopsy slides are admitted and may be shown to the jurors."

"Your Honor ..."

"Mr. Sweeney, I know you object. Overruled."

"Thank you, Your Honor. Doctor, I direct your attention to State's exhibit one. Please describe the injuries and their significance as depicted in this slide taken during your autopsy of the victim."

Using a wooden teacher's pointer with a rubber tip, the doctor methodically pointed out Amoia's injuries projected on a large screen.

"As you can see, Mr. Amoia was stabbed once in the heart. Here, you can see the victim was stabbed once in the right side of his chest. Here, he was stabbed two times in the neck.

"All five wounds were at least two inches deep and approximately one to two inches wide. The skin is elastic, so the width is not exact. It could be wider. The significance of those sharp-force trauma injuries is that the assailant plunged the blade into the victim using great force with the intent to kill.

"In addition, you can see that the victim's throat was sliced or cut in one continuous motion because there are no hesitation marks. The significance of this is that the assailant intended to kill his victim in one motion, cutting from ear to ear."

"Doctor, do you have an opinion regarding the manner and cause of Mr. Amoia's death?"

"Yes, sir, I do. Homicidal throat cuts are produced in one of two ways, depending on whether they are made from the front or behind.

"Cutting the victim's throat from behind is the most common method. When the assailant is positioned behind the victim, the head is pulled back, and the knife is drawn across the victim's neck from left to right if the assailant is right-handed, and right to left if the assailant is left-handed.

"The wound inflicted is most profound in the beginning and tails off on the opposite side of the neck. Therefore, the gradually deepening left end would be the beginning of the cutthroat, and the tail end is indicated by the tail abrasion on the opposite end of the neck.

"From the sharp-force trauma I observed, in my opinion, Mr. Amoia's assailant was standing behind him. With his right hand, the assailant reached around the victim, pulled back his head, and slit his throat from left to right, from one ear to the other. The sharp-force trauma I observed deepened at the beginning on the left side of the throat and tapered off at the right side.

"Again, because no hesitation marks were observed, the assailant must have attacked his victim from behind. If the assailant had attacked the victim from the front, there would have been short, angled cuts to his throat, which I did not observe.

"So, to answer your question simply, the cause of death was sharp-force trauma to the throat, resulting in a complete transection of the left and right carotid arteries as well as the jugular vein. In addition, he suffered a significant loss of blood resulting in a lack of oxygen flowing to the brain. He would have died within five to 15 seconds."

"Doctor, would you expect to see a great amount of blood at the crime scene where Mr. Amoia was murdered?"

"Yes. Imagine hooking up a rubber hose to a faucet and turning the water to full pressure. Then imagine completely severing that same hose. The water would gush out of the severed end. Slicing Mr. Amoia's carotid arteries had the same effect. Blood would have gushed out, possibly striking the walls and ceiling and anyone near the victim. There is no question that the victim would have been lying in a pool of blood."

Blake returned to the prosecutor's table. These moments always left the jury shaken, and his point had been made. He'd done nothing to further prove Owens's guilt, as Sweeney would be quick to point out. But the Doctor's testimony would have surely made the jury loathe the murderer.

"Thank you, Doctor. No further questions."

"Mr. Sweeney, any cross of the Doctor?"

"Yes, Your Honor." Sweeney had only one question. "Doctor, would you agree that your autopsy of the victim did not reveal who killed Mr. Amoia? Isn't that correct?"

"That's correct. But whoever did, had access to a large knife such as a Buck hunting knife."

Sweeney glanced at Blake in disbelief. He'd been played like a violin.

Blake smiled. He was ready to rest his case. "Your Honor," he said, "perhaps this is an appropriate time for a break."

"Very well. Let me see counsel in chambers. We are in recess for fifteen minutes."

"Blake, I take it you're resting your case?"

"Correct, Your Honor."

"Very good. Robert, I'm afraid to ask. Please tell me your client isn't taking the stand."

Sweeney declared the defendant's intention to testify in the morning. "Yes, my client informed me he wants to testify."

"You're kidding, right?"

"Wish I was. Why stop talking now."

Blake's eyes gleamed with a mix of determination and satisfaction, eager to dismantle the defendant's defense and expose his lies.

"Very well, gentlemen. Blake, you can rest your case in the presence of the jury in the morning. Mr. Sweeney, aside from your client, do you have any other witnesses?"

"Yes, Your Honor. Joey Fleming,"

"That should prove interesting. We will recess and resume the trial in the morning."

The following morning, the courtroom buzzed with anticipation that the defendant would take the stand. Little did they know, however, that the defendant had a secret weapon, Joey Fleming, up his sleeve, a piece of evidence that would turn the entire case on its head. So, Owens thought.

The truth was about to be unveiled, leaving everyone in the courtroom stunned and questioning everything they thought they knew.

CHAPTER 27

Two Sides To A Story

The Next Morning

Judge Croghan asked, "Does the State rest?"

Blake responded, "Yes, Your Honor."

"Is the defense ready to proceed?" Judge Croghan asked.

"Yes, Your Honor. The defense calls Joey Fleming." Sweeney stared at Fleming with piercing eyes, then asked with a low and even voice, "Mr. Fleming, isn't it true you worked for Frank Amoia?"

"Yes."

"Isn't it true you told Detective Massey you observed Mr. Amoia hiding money in a crockpot in the pantry?"

"Yes."

Showing the witness the crockpot and the money, Sweeney asked, "Is this the crockpot and the fifty thousand dollars recovered by the sheriff?"

"Sure if you say so."

"I say so."

"Ok, So what is your point?"

"Here's my point: you also told Mr. Moretti you saw Mr. Amoia hide thousands of dollars in a duct vent. The deputy sheriff never recovered any money from the bakery except for the fifty thousand dollars in the crockpot. Mr. Moretti informed me, in writing, that Sonny Calo inquired about two hundred thousand dollars given to Amoia to hold for a "friend" of Calo's."

"Sir, is there a question?"

"Yes. Isn't it true the two hundred thousand dollars is what you observed Amoia hide in the duct vent?"

"I don't know how much money there was, but I saw Mr. Amoia hide money in the vent two days before he was murdered."

"Isn't it true, aside from Mr. Amoia, that you are the only person who knew about the money hidden in the duct vent?"

"I don't know what other people knew."

"Isn't it true you told Mr. Owens that Mr. Amoia hid money in the pantry?"

"Yes. In fact, your client tried to get me to tell him exactly where it was hidden, but I refused."

"Mr. Fleming, isn't it true you murdered Mr. Amoia and stole two hundred thousand dollars from the heating and cooling vent, and that is why that money was not recovered?"

"No, that's a lie."

"In fact, you killed Mr. Amoia with the hunting knife you stole from Mr. Owens?"

"No, that's also a lie."

"Isn't it true you and your mother buried the murder weapon and your bloody clothes?"

"No. That's not true."

"You hate Mr. Owens, don't you?"

"Sir, that's an understatement. Sure I hate Owens. He's a drunk, and he beat my mother."

"Isn't it a fact the only money Mr. Owens knew about is the money in the pantry, which was seized? Isn't it true you ransacked the pantry to make it look like Mr. Owens was searching for money so you could frame my client?"

"No, sir."

"Isn't it true you were willing to give up the cash in the crock-pot for a more significant treasure, the two hundred thousand dollars stashed in the duct vent?"

"Sir, you have an incredible imagination. I didn't kill Frank with your client's missing hunting knife. I didn't steal Mr. Amoia's money. I didn't bury any bloody clothing or murder weapon with my mother's help. Owens is the one who expressed interest in stealing Mr. Amoia's money in the pantry, not me. Your client killed Frank."

In a dramatic turn of events, Sweeney skillfully presented Joey Fleming with a question that left the witness speechless and unable to respond satisfactorily.

"Mr. Fleming, the fact remains: two hundred thousand dollars is missing, and you're the only person alive who knew where it was hidden."

"Sir, is that a question?"

"No. Here is my question. How pray tell, did the two hundred thousand dollars disappear if you didn't steal it after you killed Frank? Tell this jury."

Joey Fleming sat silently for what felt like an eternity, trying to come up with a satisfactory answer. Finally, he sheepishly answered, "I can't."

Sweeney grinned, faced the jury, and said," that's because you're the person responsible for murdering Mr. Amoia and stealing the two hundred thousand dollars!"

The courtroom erupted in a cacophony of shocked gasps and murmurs as spectators were taken aback by the unexpected revelation. Joey's eyes widened in horror. He knew he was in deep trouble now.

"No more questions, Your Honor."

"Very well. Mr. Moretti, any questions?"

"No, Your Honor."

"Mr. Sweeney, call your next witness."

Sweeney responded, "The defense calls Billy Owens."

"Last question, Billy. Did you kill Mr. Amoia?" Sweeney asked.

"Absolutely not. Moretti has nothing on me. Joey Fleming stole my knife and killed Mr. Amoia so he could steal his money to buy drugs and alcohol.

"His mother, Valerie Fleming lied and framed me to protect her son and claim the reward money. She lied to the homicide Detective when she told him I buried the bloody knife and clothes. She is the one, along with Joey, who got rid of the murder weapon and clothes. She's the one who took the Detectives to a phony burial site. Now you know why. I've been framed.

"The homeless bum can't identify me. He said he saw a man with a scar. Lots of people have scars. That doesn't prove a thing. I wouldn't be surprised if Joey Fleming gave him money to tell the Detective he saw a man with a scar. Think about it: they go to the same sleaze bar. That's how they met. Valerie and Joey Fleming, along with that drunk, framed me for the money. All I know is I didn't kill anyone. If the damn Detective did his job, the real killer would be sitting in this chair, and I wouldn't be here today. How's that justice?

"The first statement that drunk gave the Detective was after my arrest six months ago. Why didn't he tell the police the morning of the murder what he allegedly saw?

"Then there is the Medical Examiner. He can't identify the killer. He could only testify that Amoia was stabbed to death and show the jury gory pictures.

"There is no evidence I killed anyone. No eyewitnesses, no confession, no fingerprints. The prosecutor doesn't even have circumstantial evidence I killed Amoia. And then there was Joey Fleming, who pretended not to know why the two hundred thousand dollars was missing. That's because Joey stole the money after he butchered Amoia with my knife.

"They got nothing. Nothing, except that liar, Valerie Fleming, who is covering up for the real killer, her drug addict son.

"Yeah, I found Amoia dead in the restroom, but the only thing I did was commit a misdemeanor theft when I took cash out of his pants pocket. That doesn't prove I killed anyone."

"Thank you, Billy. I know how frustrating this ordeal has been. No more questions."

Judge Croghan, directing her attention to the jury, said, "Since it is after five, we stand in recess. The trial will commence in the morning at 8:30 sharp. Please keep in mind all my admonishments and get some sleep. I expect the parties will wrap this case up tomorrow. Let your families know it may be a long evening. I would like to see the lawyers in chambers."

"Gentleman, have a seat. Mr. Sweeney, good job this afternoon."

"Thank you, Your Honor. The truth finally came out."

Blake responded, "Tomorrow is another day. Fortunately, the jury will decide the truth, not you."

Judge Croghan asked, "Blake, do you expect to have any rebuttal evidence?"

"I suspect we will."

"That's fine. I will see you both bright and early in the morning."

Exhausted, Blake returned to his office with his trial team after a grueling day in court. Despite Sweeney's skillful manipulation of the last witness, Joey Fleming, making it appear as though he was the actual murderer and his client was framed, Moretti remained calm and collected.

Unbeknownst to Massey, who was disappointed by Moretti's lack of questioning to rehabilitate the witness, Blake had strategically set up Sweeney. With unwavering confidence, Moretti knew that in the morning, he would unveil evidence that would shatter Sweeney's theory and expose Owens as the true killer. Moretti set down his trial notebook and broke open a Snickers bar.

Detective Massey said, "Sweeney did a number on Joey. I expected you to rehabilitate him."

"Yeah. Me too," said Ralph.

"What do you think, Jennifer?"

"I think the letter you requested I deliver to Sweeney was a deliberate trap, and he fell for it hook, line, and sinker."

"Why Jennifer, how astute."

Blake told Massey, "I need you to go to the bakery and search the return duct vent for the missing two hundred thousand dollars. Mrs. Amoia will be expecting you. I'll see you in court in the morning. I suspect you will have something to bring me."

As the night settled in and Moretti prepared for the next day's proceedings, a sense of anticipation filled his office. The weight of the case rested heavily on his shoulders, but he was determined to prove who murdered Frank Amoia.

And so, with a renewed sense of purpose and determination burning within him, Moretti prepared himself for the battle that awaited him in the courtroom. The stage was set for an epic showdown between truth and deception. Tomorrow promised to unveil a truth that clever tactics and manipulation had obscured. As Moretti closed his eyes for a brief moment of respite, he couldn't help but feel a surge of excitement coursing through his veins.

At that moment, The narrator's voice from an old Batman TV series seemed to whisper: "Tune in tomorrow, as Blake Moretti unveils the truth and delivers justice with unwavering resolve."

It was Blake's turn. As he approached Owens, he observed the Judge sit back in her chair, ready to be amused. Whenever Owens opened his mouth, he dug himself a deeper hole, and Blake was prepared to bury him in it.

"Mr. Owens, tell this jury, isn't it true that you have been charged and convicted for committing the violent crimes of kidnapping, aggravated robbery, and two counts of forcible rape committed on March 17, 1987? Yes or no?"

"I was framed."

"Mr. Owens, what is it about the words yes and no that you don't understand? Please answer the question. A jury of twelve people, just like this jury, unanimously found you guilty of those crimes after listening to the evidence, and they didn't buy your fairytale-framed story then, any more than this jury is today. If you like, I am prepared to ask the court reporter to read back my question as often as necessary until you answer it."

Sweeney's objection was inevitable. "Your Honor, I object. He is badgering my client."

"Overruled. Mr. Owens, answer the question yes or no"

Owens began to answer, "Well—" but the Judge cut him off.

"Mr. Owens, did you not listen to me? Only the words 'yes' or 'no' should leave your lips."

"Yes!" he shouted.

"Let me guess," Blake said. "You got your nickname "Buck" because you're known for carrying a Buck hunting knife. Again, yes or no."

"I suppose so."

"There you go again. Don't suppose anything. The question called for a yes or no answer."

"Yes, but I didn't kill anyone."

Blake had reached his breaking point. "Mr. Owens, the good news is you're not the one who will determine who butchered Mr. Amoia. This jury will make that determination. After all, we wouldn't want a guilty man getting away with murder, would we?"

Owens turned to the Judge. "Do I have to answer that question?"

"No, I believe it was rhetorical."

"What?"

"No, you don't have to answer it."

Blake asked, "Isn't it true the knife you were known to carry was a 124 Frontiersman, 11 ¾ inches overall with a 6 ¾ inch satin finish 422HC stainless steel straight back bowie blade and a black micarta handle, made right here in the good old USA. It came with a leather sheath and a forever warranty?"

Blake obtained a description of the knife and the sheath from Valerie and Joey Fleming. Then he conferred with the manufacturer's representative and concluded it must have been a 124 Frontiersman. The bluff paid off.

Owens' puzzled look on his face told Blake that he'd nailed him. Ownes began to wonder if the sheriff had found the buried knife. He didn't want to get caught lying, so he admitted it was the model he carried. Owens didn't know that Blake hadn't found the murder weapon.

For the first time, Owens told the truth, at least partially.

"Yes, I owned a knife like that at one time, but Joey Fleming stole it."

Moretti asked, "So, you want to play *Let's Make a Deal*. Where could that knife possibly be? Door number one, stolen and buried by the Flemings somewhere. Door number two, the one-hundred-and-eighty-dollar knife that you always carry in a leather sheath hanging from your belt, is just misplaced. How about door number three, you buried it after you used it to kill Mr. Amoia. Go ahead, pick a door."

"Objection, Your Honor," Sweeney yelled. This time he didn't bother to stand up. Blake had worn him out.

"Overruled. But Mr. Moretti please, just one question at a time. Mr. Owens, do you understand Mr. Moretti's question?"

Blake knew Owens was becoming annoyed with his sarcastic questions and the judge's "do-what-I-tell-you" attitude.

"Yes, I understand the question. Of course, I didn't misplace an expensive knife. Like I said, it was stolen from my house. Valerie took it and buried it to cover for her deadbeat son. I keep telling you the truth, and you blow me off. This is my life we're talking about."

"Once again, Mr. Owens, this jury will determine who is telling the truth. By the way, I'm guessing you never reported that your expensive knife was stolen."

"What good would that have done?"

"I want you to be clear. When Valerie Fleming testified that the two of you ditched your bloody clothes and murder weapon, she was lying. Is that correct?"

"Yeah."

"Is it your testimony that Ms. Fleming lied when she testified that you told her you killed Mr. Amoia?"

"You got that right."

"And is it your testimony that Ms. Fleming pinned the murder on you to protect her son and collect the reward money?"

"That's right."

"Isn't it a fact that Ms. Fleming did not receive a reward?"

"How would I know?"

"Sir, you told this jury that she framed you for the reward money. If that is true, tell this jury the name of a witness with firsthand knowledge of that accusation. The jury is anxiously waiting for your answer. Or was that another one of your lies?"

"I don't know. Ask my lawyer."

"I'm asking you. You made that false claim, not Mr. Sweeney."

Owens turned to Sweeney, his expression asking for help.

Blake said, "Mr. Owens, look at me. Your lawyer can't save you."

Owens sat silently. Blake knew this was his chance to really get under the man's skin. He casually walked back to the counsel table, but before he sat down, he said, "That's okay, Mr. Owens. I'll give you all the time you need to make up a name."

Owens was screwed, and it was evident that he knew it. The jurors stared at him for several minutes, waiting for an answer.

Finally, the judge said, "Mr. Moretti, it does not appear that Mr. Owens can give you an answer."

That was precisely what Blake hoped she'd say. He got up and returned to the lectern. "Mr. Owens, I accept your inability to answer my question. There is no evidence that Ms. Fleming identified you as Mr. Amoia's killer for the reward money, so your claim is unfounded."

"Okay, fine. Are you done?" Owens stood up to leave the witness stand.

"No, sir, I am just getting started. Sit down. Chris Stewart told this jury that the morning Mr. Amoia was murdered, he observed a man with a scar on his face matching your physical description, wearing the same items of clothing that matched the description given by Valerie Fleming to Detective Massey. Is it your testimony that Mr. Stewart is a liar? That Chris made up his testimony to collect a reward. Did I get that right?"

"Yeah."

"Well, Mr. Owens, we can go through another dog and pony show when I'll ask you to provide to this jury the name of a witness who will corroborate your testimony that Mr. Stewart is a liar and that his motive for lying was to get the reward money. Or you can admit the truth, that there is no witness who will corroborate your assertion, and that your testimony was false."

"I don't have any corroborating witnesses."

"Mr. Owens isn't it true that during my recorded interview, when I asked you if you had been at the bakery the morning Mr. Amoia was murdered, you replied that you were not there?"

"Maybe I had my days mixed up. Which day was that?"

"Look, Mr. Owens, I will not play *Name That Tune* with you. Your game-playing days are over. Answer my question. I can play the recording again if you don't remember."

"No, I don't need you to play the recording again. Yeah, that's what I said."

"Isn't it true that when I confronted you with the testimony of Chris Stewert, who provided an account of observing a man matching your physical description and clothing you wore that morning, you admitted you lied and told us you were there?"

"Yeah, right."

"Mr. Owens, isn't it true you were the man seen hiding behind a lamppost outside the bakery, watching every move Mr. Amoia made? And that when you saw Frank leave the front of the store, you entered the bakery, followed him into the restroom, slit his throat with your Buck hunting knife, and robbed him?"

Owens, agitated, said. "I didn't kill anyone! You're framing me! You don't care who murdered that man. All you care about is closing a cold case. You haven't heard a single word I said!"

The trap was set. Blake was ready to prove that Owens murdered Amoia. He was banking on the assumption that Owens considered himself more intelligent than everyone else and was convinced he could lie his way out of a conviction. He'd always known he could trap the man with his own words. It was time to present Owens with the damning evidence he had carefully uncovered while observing the crime scene video, the single piece of the puzzle that would seal his fate.

Owens wanted to play games. Blake was ready to play "Who Killed Mr. Amoia?"

"You admitted on tape that you went to Amoia's bakery the morning he was murdered. Did I get that right?"

"Yeah, I said that already."

"Right. I heard you. You also said that when you entered the bakery, the door to the restroom was open, and you observed Mr. Amoia lying dead in a pool of blood. Did I get that right?"

"Yes. That is what I said."

"Good, I got that right. You then said that while Mr. Amoia lay in a pool of blood, you bent over his body, put your hand on him, and allegedly called out his name, 'Mr. Amoia.' Did I get that right?"

"Yeah, right."

"But calling out his name when he was dead as a doornail doesn't make sense unless that story is also a lie. You agree with me, don't you, Mr. Owens?"

Blake didn't care how Owens answered that question. Either way, he was screwed.

Owens paused, searching for some incredulous story to spin but came up blank. "How the hell would I know?"

"You were there, that's why you should know! You slit Frank's throat with the Buck hunting knife that is mysteriously missing."

Sweeney began to object, but the Judge signaled him to sit down.

"You gotta be kidding me," Owens responded.

"No, Mr. Owens, I wish I was.

"You also said there was so much blood in the bathroom that you were scared and decided to leave. However, you returned to the restroom because you needed money, reached into Frank's pants pocket, and stole two hundred and sixty dollars. Did I get that right?"

"Yeah, right."

"Next, you admitted, closing the bathroom door before you ran home. Did I hear you correctly?"

"Yeah. So, what the hell is the point?"

"Tell you what, I'll get back to your question. Mr. Owens, when I asked you during the recorded interview if blood was flowing into the hallway outside the restroom door, you answered no. Did I get that right?"

"Yeah. I didn't see any blood in the hallway."

"When I asked if you were wearing cowboy boots that morning, you told me you always wear cowboy boots. Correct?"

"That's true."

"Mr. Owens, after finding you hiding in the attic, the deputy sheriff searched the house, and your cowboy boots were not there. Neither was the black leather jacket nor your expensive Buck hunting knife with the leather sheath. So, tell us, Mr. Owens, were those items also coincidently stolen simultaneously, or could you have buried them, as Ms. Fleming described?"

Owens turned his eyes to Sweeney again. He knew the missing clothes, jacket, boots, knife, and sheath were a problem.

"Mr. Owens, as I said before, Mr. Sweeney can't help you now. So, look at me and answer my question."

"Look, Moretti, I don't know. They must have been stolen along with my knife."

"Mr. Owens, that makes no sense. You want the jury to believe that Ms. Fleming's son stole your knife to kill Mr. Amoia, and that Ms. Fleming or her son stole your boots and clothes to set you up. Why would they do that? If she was framing you to save her son, why not turn your boots, jacket, and clothes over to the sheriff? Since you admitted to stealing Mr. Amoia's money from his pants pocket, your clothes and boots would undoubtedly have had his blood on them. The fact is that Frank Amoia was lying in a pool of blood, and his clothing was soaked with blood. The restroom and hallway floors were covered in a river of blood. When you returned, you would have had to tread through the blood to steal Frank's money. Explain how you managed not to get blood on your boots and clothes."

"I don't know, Moretti. I guess I was just careful."

"My goodness, Mr. Owens, you're a regular Harry Houdini."

"Look, I don't know. Why don't you ask her?"

"I already did. It appears to me that you're the one who's not listening. Ms. Fleming testified that she was forced to go with you to bury your bloody clothing and the murder weapon, your Buck hunting knife."

"She's a liar."

"The truth is, Mr. Owens, you took the stand and swore before God to tell the truth, then stank up this courtroom with one lie after another, trying to deceive this jury to avoid punishment for the heinous murder of Frank Amoia. Getting back to your question, I asked you whether the restroom door was open when you found Mr. Amoia lying in a pool of blood, because you testified that you closed the door on your way out."

Blake had been pacing in front of the witness stand. Now, he stopped and addressed the bench. "Your Honor, after Detective Massey's direct testimony, I reserved the right to recall him. The defense agreed to my request, and Your Honor granted it. Now would be the time to recall the detective so I can answer Mr. Owens's question. With your permission, I would ask Mr. Owens to step down and reserve the right to continue my cross after Detective Massey testifies."

"Any objection, Mr. Sweeney?"

"No, Your Honor."

"Very well. Mr. Owens, step down. Mr. Moretti will have the right to further cross-examine Mr. Owens after Detective Massey completes his testimony."

Blake nodded and moved away from Owens who was returning to the defense table. "Thank you, Your Honor. I now ask that the crime scene tape be played one last time. I would ask the jury members to pay particular attention to the restroom door and the hallway flooring in front of that door and the one set of bloody boot prints leading from the restroom into the pantry and fading as the killer exited the bakery."

The jurors put their notepads and pens in their laps as Massey took the stand and turned their attention to the screen. The images were gory, but the detective was an old hand at this. He sat comfortably with his elbows on his knees, his clasped hands between them.

Blake stood at an angle, so he could keep his eyes on the jury. "Detective, for the record, please describe what is depicted in the video."

"As you can see, the video shows that when the first responding officers arrived at the crime scene, the restroom door was closed. Here, you can see a stream of blood flowing from the closed restroom door. Next, we see technician Murray attempting to push the bathroom door open, but something is blocking it. Now Murray is checking the door to determine if it is locked. You can see him easily turn the doorknob, indicating that the door is not locked.

"Here I'm ordering the evidence technicians to remove the door and frame so we can get inside the bathroom …

"Okay, you can see that the door is removed now, and the men are standing in the hallway looking into the restroom.

"You can now see the large pool of blood in the room, which explains why we saw so much blood on the floor flowing into the hall-way from under the closed door.

"And here you can see why we couldn't get the door to open. You see Mr. Amoia's body lying against the door in a pool of blood. His body acted like a barricade, preventing us from pushing the door open.

"Finally, follow the cameraman as he records one set of vibrant bloody boot prints that obviously began as the killer exited the restroom and began to fade by the time the killer exited the bakery."

Blake tapped the witness stand, as though bringing the show to a close. "Your Honor, that concludes my examination of Detective Massey. Unless Mr. Sweeney has questions, Mr. Owens can return to the stand."

Sweeney stopped whispering in Owens's ear to respond. "No questions."

The Judge looked at him for a moment, then swiveled her gaze to the suspect. "Very well, Mr. Owens, please return to the stand."

Blake looked at the jurors and caught a glimpse of one of them giving another a "gotcha" look and receiving an affirmative nod.

He turned to face the witness, his gaze piercing and determined. "Mr. Owens," he began, his voice steady and commanding. "You seem to have missed the significance of my inquiries regarding the state of the restroom door. Let me make clear its importance."

"Sure, it's your show."

The room fell into a hushed silence as all eyes turned towards Mr. Owens, who shifted uncomfortably in his seat. The weight of the moment seemed to settle upon him as if he could sense the impending revelation that would forever alter the course of his life.

A collective gasp rippled through the room, mingling with a mix of shock and anticipation. The truth hung heavy in the air, waiting to be unveiled like a hidden secret long kept in darkness.

"Pay close attention because now you will be held accountable for your actions." As the words settled upon Mr. Owens, a wave of realization washed over him. The gravity of his deeds began to sink in, and he could no longer evade the consequences that had long eluded him.

The room remained still; each person present was acutely aware of the pivotal moment unfolding before them. The truth was about to be laid bare, exposing the dark underbelly of a crime that had haunted them for decades.

With a final glance at Mr. Owens, Blake took a deep breath and prepared to reveal the damning evidence that would seal his fate once and for all.

"You were the man in the black leather jacket, blue jeans, and cowboy boots with a scar over your eye, hiding behind the lamppost, watching Mr. Amoia open the bakery, just as Mr. Stewart described. When you saw Mr. Amoia walk to the back of the store, you went inside and flipped the "Open" sign to "Closed", so no one else could enter the shop. Then, you went down the hallway where the public restroom was located."

Owens looked at Sweeney, as though he were asking where all this was going.

"Mr. Owens, do you know what the one set of bloody boot-prints proves?"

"No idea."

"You watched Mr. Amoia go into the restroom. The door was open, not closed. It had to be, or you couldn't have opened the door any more than evidence technician Murray could. You looked in and saw that Mr. Amoia's back was to you. In our interview, you told me you were right-handed. With your right hand, you drew your Buck hunting knife and attacked him from behind, pulled his head back with your left hand, and slit his throat ear to ear, left to right, as Doctor Smith described. You stabbed him in the heart as he lay on the floor for good measure. As Dr. Smith testified, blood spewed all over, covering your jacket, jeans, hands, knife, and boots.

"You proceeded to exit the bakery leaving one, not two, trails of bloody bootprints.

"Do you know what that proves, Mr. Owens?"

"No."

"It proves you lied to the jury when you said you went into the restroom, came out, and returned. We would have seen two sets of bloody bootprints if that were true. It's clear that stealing money wasn't just an afterthought. You entered with one purpose. When you rolled out of bed and strolled to the bakery that morning, you intended to steal Mr. Amoia's money and not leave any witnesses to avoid detection."

Mr. Owens listened intently, trying to grasp the implications being presented to him.

As the explanation unfolded, Mr. Owens remained silent, absorbing each detail being presented to him.

"Finally, Mr. Owens, everyone who commits a violent crime leaves a clue that will eventually identify the perpetrator. You are no exception. So, to answer your question: what was the big deal about whether the door was open or closed? The answer was in the videotape all along. Your testimony and the tape prove that you murdered Frank Amoia for money."

"I didn't kill that man."

"But you did. Here's why we know you killed Mr. Amoia. The murderer had to have been the last man in the restroom. Anyone who came along after the murder wouldn't have been able to open the door. We know that after Mr. Amoia was murdered, he collapsed to the floor on his back. The murderer had to roll him onto his side, leaning his body against the door to riffle through his front pants pocket and steal his money. The room was tiny, and as the murderer exited the room, pulling the door shut to hide the body, Mr. Amoia's body rolled over, blocking the door. That's why the deputies had to remove the door.

"With that said, tell me I didn't listen to every word you uttered during your interview. Tell us, sir, why you are not the murderer! Tell us, sir, why the murder weapon and your bloody clothes and boots are missing. Look this jury in their faces and tell them why I am wrong. I dare you!"

Owens was screwed no matter how he answered that question. He had no moves left. Lying wouldn't save him. It was checkmate. Game, set, match. That's what's meant by "It's all over but the shouting."

Owens looked at Sweeney, but his head was in his hands. Owens looked at the jurors, anxiously leaning forward, waiting for a response. Perhaps for the first time in his life, he realized he couldn't talk his way out of this mess. The expression on his face said all that needed to be said. Billy "Buck" Owens looked like a murderer. "Mr. Moretti," he said. "I'm done talkin'."

Blake could feel the adrenaline leave his body. He'd done it. Owens was guilty beyond any fucking doubt.

He scanned the gallery, looking for Mrs. Amoia who was sitting with Jennifer and Ralph. He winked at her, and she nodded her appreciation. As Blake turned his attention back to the judge, from the corner of his eye, he spotted Sonny Calo in the last row of the galley. The stoned face Calo smiled.

Judge Crogan asked, "Mr. Sweeny, do you have a redirect examination of this witness?"

"No, Your Honor. The defense rests."

"Mr. Moretti, do you have any rebuttal evidence?"

"Yes, Your Honor. The people call Detective Massey."

In the courtroom, the tension was palpable. as the defense attorney, Mr. Sweeney, had confidently presented his case to the jury yesterday. He had skillfully planted doubt in their minds by suggesting that the witness, Joey Fleming, was the true culprit behind the murder of Frank Amoia and the theft of two hundred thousand dollars. Sweeney argued that Joey knew about the money because he had seen Frank hide it in a duct vent at the bakery where they both worked.

Rising from his seat, prosecutor Moretti approached Detective Massey with a confident stride. "Detective Massey," he began, "were you tasked with searching for the missing money in the duct vent alluded to by Mr. Sweeney?"

Massey nodded and replied, "Yes, sir. After trial yesterday, you directed me to the Amoia bakery shop to search the return duct vent for what Mr. Sweeney called the missing two hundred thousand dollars he alleged Mr. Fleming stole."

"What did you find?" Blake asked with a glimmer of triumph in his eyes.

"I found the money, all two hundred thousand dollars," Massey stated matter-of-factly.

"While examining the duct vent, I noticed some loose screws. Upon further inspection, I discovered a hidden compartment in it. That's where I found the money. I must admit, on the day of the murder, we didn't look in the duct vents for money."

Gasps filled the courtroom as everyone turned to look at Billy "Buck" Owens, whose face had paled considerably. Sweeney had believed this revelation would seal his client's innocence, but now it seemed that his theory had crumbled before his eyes.

Moretti turned to face the jury and continued, "Detective Massey, do you agree this discovery not only proves that Joey Fleming did not steal the money, but it also raises questions about the credibility of Mr. Sweeney's entire argument?"

Massey answered, "Absolutely. Why would Joey Fleming go to the bakery, with the intent to kill Frank Amoia, set up Owens by not stealing the fifty thousand dollars in the crockpot, and leave the two hundred thousand dollars behind, which was in a readily accessible hiding spot?" Sweeney's face fell as he realized the flaw in his reasoning. He had assumed that the missing money was evidence of Joey's guilt, but now it seemed that there was a different explanation altogether. In this unexpected turn of events, Moretti had effectively dismantled what Sweeney believed to be a winning point.

"Detective, are you saying that when Mr. Sweeney accused Joey Fleming of murdering Mr. Amoia and stealing the two hundred thousand dollars, he misled the jury?"

"Well, I don't know that I would say misled, but it certainly was not true."

Sweeney's face fell as he realized the flaw in his reasoning. He had assumed that the missing money was evidence of Joey's guilt, but now it seemed that there was a different explanation altogether.

In this unexpected turn of events, Moretti had effectively dismantled what Sweeney believed to be a winning point.

"No further questions."

Judge Croghan asked, "Mr. Sweeney, any questions?"

As Sweeney stood, Owens tugged his suit sleeve.

Sweeney brushed his hand away and said, "No, Your Honor."

After the attorneys made their closing arguments and the judge instructed the jury, deliberations began.

The jury returned their verdict after deliberating for only thirty minutes.

"What is your verdict on count one, the charge of aggravated murder?" Judge Croghan asked.

The foreperson announced, "Guilty as charged."

"What is the verdict on count two, aggravated robbery?"

"Guilty as charged."

"Very good. The jury is discharged with our thanks. The court will stand in recess for thirty minutes, and I will see counsel in chambers."

CHAPTER 28

The Reckoning

December 18, 1987, Friday Morning

"Blake, is Ms. Spencer present?"

"She is, Your Honor."

"Good. Robert, I am prepared to sentence your client on both cases unless you have some objection."

"No objection. I anticipated that and informed my client he would be sentenced and given the notice to appeal."

"Alright, gentlemen, let's do it."

"The defendant shall rise."

Owens shuffled to his feet beside Sweeney.

"Mr. Owens, do you have anything to say before I pronounce sentence?"

"Yeah. As I said, I was framed."

"Well, Mr. Owens, a jury of twelve disagreed with you. Therefore, I am prepared to sentence you in both the rape and murder cases. I hereby sentence you to the maximum of twenty-five years in prison on each count of rape.

"I sentence you to the maximum sentence of twenty-five years in prison on the count of kidnapping. In addition, I sentence you on the count of aggravated robbery to a maximum sentence of twenty-five years.

"On the charge of grand theft auto, I sentence you to an additional two years.

"Finally, I sentence you to three years for the illegal possession of a firearm during the commission of those offenses.

"These sentences are to be served consecutively for a total of one hundred and five years.

"In addition, on the count of aggravated murder, I sentence you to life in prison with parole eligibility after thirty years.

"On the count of aggravated robbery, I sentence you to twenty-five years in prison.

"All sentences are to be served consecutively at a facility to be determined by the Department of Corrections."

"Judge, what kind of a sentence is that?" Owens asked.

"I'd call that a just sentence. Some people may call it a death sentence. You have the right to appeal."

Owens turned to Blake. "I am appealing my cases. I'll see you again."

"Don't kid yourself, Owens. Charlie Manson had a right to appeal, but we know how that turned out."

"Deputies, Mr. Owens's bond is revoked, and he is remanded to the custody of the sheriff. Please remove Mr. Owens from the courtroom. He apparently has never learned to keep his mouth shut."

Escorted by sheriff's deputies, restrained in handcuffs and leg irons, Billy "Buck" Owens waddled out of court.

EPILOGUE

December 18, 1987, Friday night

Blake's team celebrated at The Exchange again, drinking and sharing war stories. The stunts Ralph pulled off got the most laughs.

"Hey, guess who just walked in the door?" Jennifer announced.

"Well, I'll be!" Ralph said. "It's our prosecutor, Graham Hardy. To what do we owe the pleasure?"

"I love you, too, Ralph. I knew you guys would be here, and I wanted to stop by before I head over to the sheriff's boring fundraiser to tell you all that you did a great job, Moretti, it appears you had that case in the bag the entire time. I don't understand why this wasn't a death penalty case."

"Hey, Andrea," Ralph called to the waitress, "Prosecutor Hardy said to put our drinks on his tab. He'd love to stay but he's late for a fundraiser. Thanks, boss. We won't overcharge your credit limit. Bye."

Hardy took his cue to leave.

"Do you believe that guy's office turned down murder charges on Owens three times over the past two years and threatened to fire Moretti if he lost the case?"

"Heck yeah, Ralph," Jennifer said, "I believe it. If it weren't for Blake, Owens would be out raping and killing more people."

"This was a team effort," Blake said. "The clue to solving the murder was at the crime scene. We just had to keep looking until we found it. And it didn't hurt that Owens loved to talk and talk and talk."

"I noticed Calo and his son were in the courtroom." Ralph said. "What was that all about?"

"Frank Amoia was godfather to Calo's son. I suppose they came to support Mary."

"I thought you told me Mrs. Amoia didn't care for Calo. By the way, whatever happened to the two hundred thousand dollars stashed away in the bakery vent?"

"All I know is Sonny and Mary mended their relationship and the money situation. After the trial, Mary told me she finally sold the bakery. Apparently, Sonny Calo is now in the bakery business."

"No kidding," Ralph said. "It's funny how life turns out sometimes. One minute, you're down, and the next minute, things turn around, and you're back on top of the world."

"You know," Ralph said. "I always liked Frank Amoia. He was a good guy. It is a shame people will forget about him now that he's gone forever."

Blake responded, "Ralph, don't you know we're all going to die one day? But always remember no one is dead and forgotten if someone is around to say their name, give them a voice, and tell their story."

UP NEXT FOR BLAKE MORETTI

WHISPERS FROM DARK WATERS
A BLAKE MORETTI THRILLER

December 24, 1987, Christmas Eve

The small town of Misty River, located in the heart of New York's snow belt, was blanketed in a thick layer of snow as if nature had painted the landscape with a brush dipped in icy hues. The air was crisp and piercing, with each breath visible as it escaped the lips like a puff of smoke from a steam engine. The trees stood tall and unyielding, and branches etched against the sky like a pen and ink drawing. At the same time, the snow-covered roofs of the houses glistened like a sea of white crystal under the flickering porch lights.

On a biting cold Thursday evening, December 24, 1987, the stage was set at Blake Moretti's residence, a remarkable two-story Tudor-style house, exuding an air of authenticity that surpassed the modern replicas, nestled deep within Misty River's Noda neighborhood.

Blake had extended a personal invitation to a carefully chosen circle of intimate friends to partake in the joyous festivities of Christmas Eve, among them being Jennifer and Ralph.

Brimming with curiosity, Jennifer was eager to explore Blake's home, but he seemed uninterested in showing it off. Undeterred by his lack of enthusiasm, Jennifer took it upon herself to explore. She ventured through each room, taking in the unique decor and design choices.

His living room served as a testament to his passions and interests. Upon entering the living room, Jennifer was greeted by a captivating sight. The eclectic mix of vintage items created an atmosphere hinting at his character's hidden depths.

The room's centerpiece was a pool table, its rich history evident in every scratch and worn edge. In one corner of the room, a Wurlitzer 800 jukebox emanated a nostalgic aura, ready to serenade anyone who dared to select a tune. An ebony Steinway grand piano stood proudly in an opposite corner, its polished surface reflecting the warm glow of the room's lighting. Its keys beckoned to be played, promising melodies that could transport listeners to another world. Adding to the ambiance were a 1980 Black Knight pinball machine and a Project Debut Carbon turntable. Wooden crates held a treasure trove of alphabetized musical delights, primarily blues and jazz vinyl records. Each record carried with it a story, waiting to be told through the crackling sound of a needle meeting vinyl.

Eventually, Jennifer found herself back in the great room where everyone had gathered for cocktails. Blake greeted her with a glass of chilled Prosecco, which she graciously accepted. As her eyes scanned the room, she joked, "I love what you've done with this place. What do you call it, early eclectic?"

"That's cute, Jennifer. You're a regular Martha Stewart."

In the dimly lit room, Ralph's voice echoed through the air, breaking the silence. "Where's Roxanne?" he asked, his tone filled with curiosity and concern.

Sitting on the worn-out couch, Blake glanced at Ralph with a hint of amusement. "Most likely hiding in the closet," he replied nonchalantly. "She does that when I have friends over."

Ralph's eyebrows furrowed in confusion as he tried to comprehend Blake's choice of companionship. "Blake, what's up with your choice of women? You've got everything going for you. You're better than picking up with some woman who hides in closets when your friends stop over."

Blake let out a chuckle, shaking his head at Ralph's misunderstanding. "What are you talking about?" he asked, his voice tinged with amusement.

"Remember the time when we went out drinking, and you announced that you had to leave early to take care of Roxanne?"

"Ralph, that's not my girlfriend. Roxanne is my Maine Coon cat."

"Thank God. You were beginning to worry me."

Blake shook his head in disbelief at the comical turn of events while Jennifer, who had been quietly observing the exchange from the corner of the room, burst into laughter. "Ralph, what in the world are you smoking these days?" she teased playfully. "Cut this guy off."

As the room filled with laughter and lighthearted banter, the mystery of Roxanne's whereabouts was solved, leaving behind a tale to be retold in the annals of their friendship.

Ten o'clock rolled around when the phone abruptly rang, "Moretti here." Who is this?"

"This is Detective Gleason. I apologize for interrupting your evening."

"No problem. How can I help you?"

"You'll never believe this, but I'm actually standing right next to Officer Fanon and Malvina Breckenridge, knee-deep in a murky swamp in the Misty Moon Wildlife Reserve," Detective Gleason exclaimed.

Perplexed by the circumstances and unfamiliar with Malvina Breckenridge, Blake sought clarification. "Why are you standing in a swamp and who the hell is Malvina Brecken ... whatever?"

Detective Gleason proceeded to shed light on the situation. Gleason revealed that "Ms. Breckenridge is a nationally known psychic who has helped law enforcement agencies solve several murder cases in the past."

"You still haven't answered my question. Why are you standing in a swamp?"

Gleason replied, "Are you familiar with the case of Sandy Blevins, the eighteen-year-old woman who was reported missing in the fall of 1984?"

"Yeah, I remember. She left a bar at two in the morning, and her car was parked on the side of the road a few miles away. It was like she vanished into thin air."

"Right. Sandy's uncle hired Ms. Breckenridge to find her as a last resort. At Miss Malvina's request, Officer Fanon escorted her to Sandy's bedroom, where she touched Sandy's personal effects and did some hocus pocus stuff. Then, he took her to where Sandy's car had been found. She told Fanon she heard a disturbing voice telling her the missing woman's body had been buried in swampy water, so we ended up here."

"You've got to be kidding."

"You can't make this stuff up."

"That's absolutely crazy."

"Honestly, I thought so, too, until I found a decomposed female body with missing limbs lying in a swamp."

"My investigator, Ralph Morgan happens to be with me. We can be there in twenty minutes. Don't touch anything and call the medical examiner."

"I can do that, but Blake, please don't say anything to Hardy until you give me a chance to talk to you. There is more to this mystery than meets the eye. Things are not what they appear to be. You're in grave danger."

"What are you talking about? You're not making any sense."

"Ever since this girl went missing, three people involved in this case died, or should I say they were murdered."

As Blake stood silently in the dimly lit study, Detective Gleason's words echoed in his mind. The weight of the conversation settled heavily on his shoulders, and he couldn't shake off the feeling of impending danger. The swamp, the dead body, and the mention of Sandy Blevins all intertwined in a web of mystery that seemed to be closing in on him.

"Blake, what's wrong? You appear as pale as a ghost," Ralph observed.

"Nothing. Just grab your coat. That was homicide Detective Gleason. He's located a dead body and needs assistance. I'll explain everything in the car. You won't believe what Gleason told me."

Moretti's heart raced as he tried to process Gleason's words. Trusting someone he barely knew went against his instincts as a prosecutor, but something about Gleason's tone made him pause.

The case of Sandy Blevins was just the tip of the iceberg. With each passing moment, the walls seemed to close in on Blake, and he couldn't help but wonder who he could trust. The lines between right and wrong blurred as he delved deeper into the darkness surrounding him. The fate of his own life and those around him hung in the balance.

He did not realize that his journey into the depths of this mystery was far from over, and that he would eventually become entangled in a dangerous game of cat and mouse.

As Ralph grabbed his topcoat, he complained, "What's up with these criminals? Why are they always committing crimes when I'm off duty?"

"Very funny, Ralph," Blake, pulling on his coat, said, "Let's go!"

Don't miss:

Whispers From Dark Waters

A Blake Moretti Thriller

Click here to find out more ==>

https://www.davidfranceschelli.com

ACKNOWLEDGEMENTS

My deepest gratitude to everyone who helped me bring my idea for *Misty River*, the first book in the Blake Moretti Thriller Series, to life.

My heartfelt thanks go out to my editor, Joie Davidow, for her invaluable guidance and insight in helping me understand "less is more" when writing a compelling story. Additionally, I am deeply appreciative of Paula Marais, my diligent line editor, whose meticulous attention to detail greatly enhanced the overall quality of my novel. I am immensely grateful to Rachel Kelli, the exceptionally talented cover design artist, whose creative vision brought my book's visual representation to life. I also want to acknowledge Tessa Elwood, my web design artist, responsible for crafting my novel's engaging and user-friendly online presence. Their contributions have been instrumental in shaping and refining my work.

Special thanks go to my beta readers, Rob Modic, George Katchmer, Tom Schiff, Meghanne Franceschelli, and Valerie Cannon, whose invaluable commentary helped shape the story.

I wish to thank my daughter Andrea for always believing in me and encouraging me to write this book. Last but not least, a special thanks to my wife, Debbie, for her guidance and patience while I authored this story. Once again, I am indebted to you.